JUMPER III

JUMPER III

KENN AMDAHL

Jumper III

Clearwater Publishing
845 Dorris St.
Eugene, OR 97404

Table of Contents

Thanks

First, thanks to my family, not only for their kindness and patience, but also for reading early drafts of this book and making excellent suggestions. These saintly people include my wife Cheryl, and our sons Paul, Scott, and Joey.

Also thanks to Liz Hill for her ongoing friendship and support as we whined at each other and commiserated about the travails and trammels of our respective writing paths. She made several helpful suggestions and gently pointed out several typos.

Thanks to the many thousands of people who have bought, borrowed, or stolen my previous books, especially those teachers who have sweet-talked and coerced their students into reading them. Special heartfelt thanks to people who have written kind reviews, whether in publications or on websites.

I also thank you, the person reading these words right now. Because of the self-publishing boom, as of July, 2025 experts estimate that over 10,000 new books are published every single day. You could choose to be reading any of those other books, but here you are, so thanks. I hope you decide you made the right choice.

—Kenn Amdahl

Introduction

Welcome to the third book featuring John Cable, also known as "Jumper." If you've read either of the first two, you know what to expect. But if you haven't met Jumper before, or if it's been a while since you visited, let me help get you up to speed.

Jumper is a gentle, big-hearted guy in his mid 20s who lives in a tiny apartment near Colfax Avenue in Denver, Colorado. He was orphaned as a kid but slipped through the social services cracks and wound up living alone, raising himself. He'd already learned to read by then, but it didn't interest him much. He's not stupid or mentally challenged but his grammar and vocabulary remain stunted. These books are written in his simple, uneducated voice. As with Huck Finn, sometimes that's funny.

A kindly (or opportunistic?) landlord, Mr. Levy, lets him live in a tiny apartment in his building in exchange for cleaning apartments and minor handyman duties. Jumper also collects aluminum cans for their cash bounty and sometimes supplements his income with various entrepreneurial adventures.

Ever since he was a toddler, Jumper loved to jump off things and that's how he got the nickname. He practiced jumping daily and it became his "sport." Now, as a man, he still "trains" every day. Jumping out of trees and off garage roofs, then climbing back up over and over is great exercise. His bones and muscles are now remarkably strong; his physique might intimidate if his disposition were not so mild.

His friends include: Officer Mike, the policeman who patrolled Jumper's neighborhood until his recent retirement; Holly a pretty nurse who lives in his building; Jim who works at the local thrift store; and Linda, a little girl to whom he gave "art therapy" lessons while she was in the hospital for cancer treatments.

In Jumper and the Bones, our hero gets cross-wise with a dangerous gang of drug dealers. This conflict accelerates after Jumper witnesses a murder and the gang threatens Holly and Linda.

In Jumper and the Apple Crate, burglars terrorize Jumper's neighbors and steal his beloved apple crate. Bringing the crooks to justice involves sneaking into the Denver Zoo at night and infiltrating a traveling circus.

Now in Jumper III, he's thrust into the completely alien world of professors of English Literature and their feud about the authorship of Shakespeare's plays. While navigating those dark waters, Jumper tries to find a stray dog's home and solve a murder.

Reading the first two books, a literate reader could feel smugly superior because of Jumper's linguistic limitations. In this book, that smugness might be tempered by a few unfamiliar literary references, some big words, and a few very old passages sporting archaic language. Some readers (but obviously not you or me) might question their own literary limitations. Don't panic; these passages are brief. If you feel a little confused a couple of times, just remember: that's how Jumper feels every day.

—Kenn Amdahl, 2025

A very old letter:

Kindest Kit,

Forgive me if caution prevents a plain response. Your proposal surges with the danger of a storm-clouded sea, yet calls like the lissom siren to a sailor land-locked by his worldly position. To leave the stage—to step into the crowd—to feel the jostle and hot breath inflamed by words that dripped from your own quill and yet be invisible to friend and foe alike— surely that is the appeal of heaven itself. To then reappear in new disguise, with freshen'd dialog—resurrected as if touched by Saint Thomas's bloody tunic— i'faith 'tis the actor's fondest dream. When fates converge as they do upon you, the angel Raphael surely beckons. The bare-fanged hounds of our former benefactor already taste the blood of your ankles. Make haste! Perchance I hear Raphael's whispers and soft steps behind my own dark curtain...

(To be continued...)

Chapter One

Sometimes when you walk down Colfax Street in Denver you meet someone who ain't that ordinary and you think they might make an interesting friend. That happened to me real early on a Sunday morning when it was mostly still dark and there wasn't any cars driving. The guy I met was a dog.

Pretty much every dog is interesting, but this Golden Retriever just sat there looking sad even when I said, "Hey, buddy, did you get lost?" He didn't even wag his tail, which is about the favorite hobby of Golden Retriever dogs. So I went over and sat next to him on the sidewalk.

"My name is Jumper," I told him. "Well, it's really John Cable but everybody calls me Jumper. What's your name?"

Obviously, he didn't say nothing. Dog words and people words ain't mostly the same. But he let me pet him so I felt his neck for a collar but there wasn't one.

"Nobody likes to be sad," I told him. "But it's worse if you're sad and alone. The best thing to do is tell somebody. Friends will sit there with you and let you be sad til you feel better, instead of giving advice on how to be happy, or saying it's all in your own brain or snap out of it.

"You probably got great reasons to be sad, but it won't do no good for you to explain it, since I don't talk dog. Best I can do is sit here with you while you think about it. It ain't a perfect solution. But at least you ain't alone."

We sat there like old buddies watching the sky get lighter. A few cars started to drive on Colfax.

"Denver cops is strict about loitering," I said. "They explained that to me about a hundred times. You probably ought to go home if you don't want to get thrown in the pokey."

11

He looked at me with his sad brown eyes and I rubbed the fur behind his ears.

"Yeah, I ain't real strict about rules either," I said. "But I might get arrested as an alleged accomplice on a loitering charge. You don't want to get me in trouble do you?"

He lifted his head a little and you could tell he was thinking about wagging his tail, but then he didn't.

"I'm sorry you're sad," I said. "But Colfax gets busy when the sun comes up. It ain't a safe place for resting. You should go on home."

He laid down with his front paws stretched forward on the sidewalk and his head on top of his front elbows. I stood up.

"Yeah, that's a good argument," I said. "Just take a nap and maybe it'll all work out. I use that argument myself. But maybe you ain't from around here so you got the wrong idea about how safe it is. I seen dogs get hurt by cars all the time."

He sort of sniffled.

"I ain't gonna force you," I said. "If you want to stay here, it's a free country." I turned and started walking away toward my apartment. I could hear dog toenails clicking on the sidewalk behind me. I turned around.

"Hey! I never said you could follow me! My apartment has rules that you can't have dogs. Anyway, you got your own home. Go on, scoot!" I started walking away again. In a minute I heard him following me again. I turned around. He was staying far behind me and when I stopped he stopped. "You probably think if you stay back a little I won't figure out you're following me. It was a good plan, but I figure out plans all the time. Listen…" I stopped. A big black four-wheel-drive pickup truck was coming down the street toward us. It had its bright headlights on, which didn't make much sense since the sky was already starting to get light. It was going way too fast for a Sunday morning. If that dog decided to take a step or two onto the pavement it would get flattened like a mosquito under a slap. I didn't want to say something that sounded like, "Why don't you wander into the street?" in dog words. So I didn't say nothing and the dog stood there watching me.

Then that pickup truck did the dumbest thing I ever seen a truck do. When it was about a block away, it swerved onto the sidewalk and kept coming about as fast as a space ship. The dog didn't notice.

"Don't just sit there!" I shouted. "Move out of the way!"

Well, the dog wasn't sitting, it was standing. But "sit" must have been a word he knew and he plopped himself down on the sidewalk.

"Oh, crackers!" I said and started to run back to him. "Move out of the way!" I shouted. "Move!" The dog did not move. I'm a fast runner but that truck was also going fast. My odds wasn't great that I could get to the dog and pull him off the sidewalk in time, plus I'd probably get squashed too. But I couldn't just watch. And it was sort of my fault he was in trouble, since I accidentally told him to sit. When I got almost to the dog, and there wasn't time for thinking, I did the thing I'm best at.

I jumped.

Now mostly I jump off of stuff, like garage roofs and tree branches. My legs got strong from that hobby, so I can jump farther than most guys. I ain't a comic book hero or something, but I'm a good jumper. I didn't think about it, I stretched my arms out in front of me like Superman and jumped as hard as I could toward the dog. I sort of tackled him when I hit. I flung both arms around his stomach, hung on tight, and rolled hard onto the grass. The truck whizzed by us about a half second later.

I sat up to get its license plate number but it was all covered with mud. The truck drove off as fast as it come. It was lucky that both me and the dog was safe. I whispered, "Thanks, Mortimer" real quiet so the dog wouldn't hear me and ask questions with his eyes. Mortimer is my black cat, whose eyes is a bright yellow-green color like celery. Mortimer's imaginary so I don't talk about him much, since people might think he was weird and hurt his feelings.

The dog sat up beside me. He didn't seem much bothered by getting rolled onto the grass.

"I told you it ain't safe out here," I said. None of them was words he understood and he just sat there.

"OK, OK," I said. "You win. You can come to my apartment but only as a visitor. If you're real good, maybe we can promote you to a sidekick. Mr. Levi's got strict no-pet rules which he says is both hard and fast. But there ain't a rule that a guy can't have a visitor, especially if he's a sidekick. But only until I find your real home. Come on."

I stood up and slapped my leg but he didn't do nothing.

"One minute ago you wouldn't leave me alone and now you're all stuck-up! You ain't much of a sidekick if you don't even come when that's the plan. Come on boy. We can be Starsky and Hutch, or maybe the Lone Ranger and Tonto."

I slapped my leg again while I said it. His head come up sudden and he gave two wags of his tail. It was like I figured out some dog word that he knew.

"Is that your name, boy? Sidekick? Is that it? Come here, Sidekick."

He didn't move. "OK, are you the Lone Ranger?"

He didn't wag at that or anything. So I said, "Starsky? Hutch? Tonto?"

When I said Tonto, he jumped up and come over to me. "Come on boy," I said. "I mean Tonto. I got frozen liver in my freezer which I bet you'd think was as good as ice cream." At the idea of liver, Tonto wagged his tail three times before he remembered he was sad and stopped wagging. I started walking and he followed me down the sidewalk.

I tried telling him some other names to make sure, but Tonto was the only one he wagged at. It was lucky I guessed his name so easy. But then, I'm a pretty lucky guy. While we was walking we had a nice conversation where I talked and he didn't say nothing.

"Tonto was about my favorite TV guy in them old western shows. He was smart, he was a good friend to Mr. Ranger and he knew lots of tricks, like walking real quiet and following tracks. My dad said Tonto got his name from being in the Tonto Apache tribe. In that language, Tonto means a guy who ain't been tamed. Like a wild horse who ain't ever been rode. But not so many people speak Apache today, but lots of people speak Spanish. In Spanish, Tonto means silly and people who ain't seen the show thinks silly is about the same as stupid. To them, calling somebody Tonto is an insult."

He listened real polite but he didn't wag.

"I'm just saying, you'd have an easier life if you changed your name. Elway would be a good name for one example, especially here in Denver. Let's try it. OK, Elway, come here buddy. Elway! Come here!"

He didn't move. I could have just as easy been speaking Canadian.

"OK, OK, you win. I gotta admit, you got a pretty cool name. My dad watched The Lone Ranger on TV when he was a kid, and his dad listened to it on the radio before that, and then I watched reruns. I only met my grandpa a couple of times when he come to visit, but he'd sit me on his knee and call me Kemo Sabe, like we was both secret Apache scouts. Back when the show started, most of the other shows had cowboys as good guys and Indians as bad guys. Cowboys and Indians was enemies with each other. But in this show, Tonto and the Lone Ranger was friends and partners. They was both good guys, fighting bad guys, which could be anybody. My dad said it goes to show, you can't tell about somebody by how they look, or what their name is, or if somebody tells you they're supposed to be your enemy. They might really be your best friend. So I ain't gonna hold your name against you."

He looked up at me and gave a quiet little woof.

"Thanks," I said. "But Elway would be a pretty good name if you change your mind. I'm just saying."

We walked over to the thrift store where my friend Jim works.

"Hey Jumper," Jim said as soon as he seen me. "You got yourself a new accomplice?" He pointed at Tonto.

"He's more an associate," I said. "Or maybe a Deputy Sidekick."

"Yeah, that sounds right," Jim said. Jim is a good guy who's older than me and skinny as the scarecrow in Wizard of Oz. He don't talk much, but when he does he loves to talk about cars. He used to race them until he went in the army and lost one of his legs from shrapnel which is something you get in the army. I never asked him much about it. He still drives cars about as fast as anybody I ever seen.

"The boss might not like your deputy sidekick wandering around the store, though," he said.

"I know. That's why I come in here. Tonto would do about anything a guy asked, only he talks dog and I talk people and we ain't figure out a good way to have a conversation. I'll show you."

I turned to Tonto and talked to him in a soft friendly voice.

"Hey Tonto," I said. "Would you be willing to please sit down for a while? Thanks."

Tonto sat down about as quick as I said it.

"Looks like you guys communicate all right to me."

"Thanks," I said. "We're starting to." I spelled out S-I-T so Tonto didn't get confused. "That's about the only word we both know. I met him this morning on Colfax and he looked lost and sad. But then a truck tried to run him over and I took him into protective custody."

Jim stared at the dog.

"You know, I think I've seen that dog before." He thought for a minute. "It was on the Internet this morning." He stopped to think again. He didn't like to say stuff until he knew it was right, which is one reason I like him. Finally he nodded his head.

"Might not be the same dog," he said. He was still thinking hard. "But a guy was murdered... poisoned I think... and they were looking for a dog. They showed a picture of the dog and it looked a lot like Tonto here."

"Wow," I said. "Do they think he was a witness or an accomplice?"

"I don't know. They caught a suspect. But that guy got some poison too, so he's in the hospital."

"OK, Tonto," I said. "Looks like you're wanted by the police as an alleged witness to a murder suspect. And maybe also a so-called sidekick. You're kind of in a pickle and if I don't turn you in I'm going to be in a pickle too."

Tonto wagged his tail, but in a sad way and looked up at me with his big brown eyes. "It ain't funny," I told him.

"Maybe Tonto is the brains behind the crime," Jim said.

"Yeah," I said. "He looks like a top dog."

"Maybe you could turn him over to Officer Mike."

"That's the first thing I would of done only he's on a fishing vacation to some island by Mexico. He won't be back for two weeks."

"You could give it to one of the guys they hired when Mike retired."

"I ain't had much luck with the young cops. If you ain't got the right paper form they think you're a idiot."

"Well, the victim won't get any deader and the suspect won't be waltzing out of the hospital very soon. It's probably OK if you wait."

"Which gets us back to why I come here today. Tonto needs a collar and leash so he don't get in trouble if he don't understand some human words. Nothing fancy, not gold or dilithium for one example."

"I got a box of collars and leashes back here behind the counter." He pulled it out. "You take your pick." "This leather one looks good," I said

He nodded. "That's probably the best one. On sale today for one dollar."

Jim likes to bargain and wishes he was a mean business guy, but he's about as mean as my imaginary cat Mortimer, who mostly just purrs when I'm trying to go to sleep. But when a guy likes to pretend he's mean and wants to bargain with you, it ain't fair if you don't play the game back.

"I don't know," I said. "Maybe I'd pay you a dollar for it if you throw in that clipboard back there." Jim wrinkled his forehead, going back and forth on my offer in his brain.

"Tell you what," he said. "You can have the collar plus the leash and the clipboard for one dollar if you take this envelope of health department forms too. I don't want to throw them out and the back sides are blank. You can draw on them if you want." Jim tries to be a tough negotiator, only he keeps walking his deals backward. If I would of kept talking he probably would have thrown in the cash register and a set of steak knives for free.

I pretended to think hard if I'd take his deal or not, but inside I felt like I was rolling around in fresh-mowed grass. I would of paid a buck for the collar all by itself, without the leash or clipboard. I didn't want to wait too long, though, since I ain't got room in my apartment for a cash register. Finally I said, "OK, Jim, you win. You got a deal."

Tonto followed me home pretty easy since he was on his new leash and didn't have much choices. But when it was time for us to go up the stairs, I could tell he had his doubts.

I live on the third floor of an old brick apartment building two blocks from Colfax street. The third floor is cheapest since there ain't a elevator and some people think steps is a downside. Going up steps don't bother me and if I'm alone I usually run up them about as fast as I can. But when we got to the steps, Tonto just sat down on the floor.

"Yeah," I told him. "Steps can be confusing if you ain't done 'em before. Let's just go slow. Did I tell you there might be doggy snacks like frozen liver in my apartment? Come on, boy, you can do it."

After a while I convinced him and we started walking up the steps real slow. Pretty soon, he got the hang of it but we still walked slow. Maybe he knows how to do stairs, only something happened when he was a puppy that made him scared of them. You can't blame a guy for having something stamped on his brain when he was a puppy and you can't erase it either. If you like a guy, you don't say nothing about it or joke on it. You like a friend the way he is including the stuff he's got stamped on his brain.

"Hey Tonto, this is a lot of steps for an old guy, too. I bet when I'm thirty I might have to take rest stops on the landing." I laughed a little at that joke, since I couldn't picture myself being that old. I was proud of how fast Tonto learned about stairs. If he was still scared, he didn't show it.

"What do you think you're doing?" A voice ahead of us said. Holly was standing on the next landing with her hands on her hips. Her voice was stern. Holly's a pretty nurse who lives in my building and has a brown ponytail. I like her a lot when she's in a happy mood. Like if she sees me in the hall and says, "that was a good Denver Broncos game wasn't it?" But when she sounds like she's about to send me to the Principal's office I get confused and my best words go out the window.

"It ain't what it looks like," I said while I tried to figure out what it looks like. She stood there waiting for a better answer. She's a fast thinker, which could be an advantage lots of times, like if she was a lawyer asking a guy for the truth, the whole truth, and nothing but the truth. But she was also fast at not saying anything. Sometimes lawyers wait for the alleged perp to say something dumb and get in even more of a pickle. Which is what she was

19

doing now. Holly could have been a TV lawyer. She was standing there looking at me and saying nothing at light speed. I had a good idea what she was thinking.

"Tonto ain't a pet," I said. "That would be against the rules. He's a visitor."

"He's a dog," Holly said.

"The rules don't say a visitor's got to be a human. I bet Mr. Spock could be a visitor and he's a Vulcan which ain't exactly human either."

"I think humanity is implied."

"You can't blame a guy for breaking a rule that ain't even a rule. I'm gonna have to throw it out on appeal."

"On appeal?"

"Yeah. I think I got grounds."

"You got coffee grounds and banana peels. You also got a dog."

"That's just circumstantial…"

"Jumper! Why do you have a dog?"

Well, she had me there so I decided to come clean.

"I found him on Colfax and it seemed dangerous to leave him there alone. So I bought this leash at the thrift store. I'll find him a better place tomorrow."

"Why didn't you just say that? He probably won't destroy the building in one night. He seems gentle." She stared at Tonto. "He looks sort of familiar."

"Golden retriever dogs all got a family resemblance. You probably seen his cousin or something."

"Why don't you take him to the shelter? I bet they could find his owner."

"That was my first idea, too. Only it's a longer story."

"All your stories are longer. What, is he wanted by the police or something?" She said it like a joke only it was maybe true.

If you ever seen the old Perry Mason TV show you know sometimes lawyers say jokes when they're really trying to get the perp to incarcerate themselves. Holly was a lot prettier than Perry Mason but she was about as smart. Anyway, she's a nurse not a lawyer but the jobs ain't all that different.

"They don't think he was the perp," I said. "Just an interesting person."

"A person of interest?" She looked at Tonto a lot harder. "What was the crime."

"It was a murder crime," I said. I don't even try to lie to Holly. She can see through me like I was a broken window. But sometimes I skip the "whole truth" part. "Only they used poison which don't seem like a dog method."

"I think I saw something about that on the news. You should turn him over to the police."

"That was my second idea. I was going to give him to Officer Mike, only he's gone for a couple of weeks. Them new cops is more interested in investigating old loitering tickets than solving murders."

"Mike retired, remember?"

"Yeah. But even if a guy ain't getting a paycheck, that don't mean he ain't still a cop."

"I don't think a dog would be much of a witness," she said.

"Well, somebody tried to run him over with a pickup truck this morning. So somebody thinks he seen something." OK, now I was getting too close to the whole truth except the whole truth was I didn't know what was going on better than she did.

She smiled a little.

"OK, I won't turn you in for having a non-human visitor. Unless there's a reward out for you. I could use some reward money."

I relaxed. She was joking on me now which is always a good sign.

"If there was reward money I'd turn myself in to get it. This ain't been a good month for cleaning apartments and collecting cans."

"Well, Jumper, you let me know if you need anything."

"Thanks, Holly. See you tomorrow."

Tonto and me walked up to the third floor and went into my apartment. Right away Mr. Silver, the parrot who lives in my apartment but who also ain't a pet, started flapping his wings and squawking at us. He could say lots of real words and sounded just like a guy. Mostly he said curse words.

"Take it easy, buddy," I said. "This is Tonto and he's a dog. He'll only be staying here one night."

Mr. Silver is a special case of visitor. I cleaned an apartment when some tenant moved out, which is my main job, and the tenant left his bird behind. Mr. Silver was probably that guy's pet and he broke the rule by having him. But I didn't bring him into the building first, and I ain't never adopted him, so I don't see how it would count against me. I told a pet store guy about him but that guy shook his head and said no. Nobody's gonna buy a bird that shrieks and cusses all the time and kicks his bird food seeds out of the cage every night. It would be like trying to sell a dog with rabies. I told the pet store guy he could have the bird for free but he shook his head real strong and said no way. So Mr. Silver stays here and neither of us is all that happy about it but there wasn't much alternatives.

That was one time where telling "the whole truth" about the bird didn't do me no favors.

I took a baggie out of the freezer with three slices of liver froze together. After a minute in the microwave they was thawed and I pulled them apart. The middle slice had a little part carved out where I had hid some emergency cash I accidentally got from a gang called The Bones. I probably already told you about that. I gave Tonto two slices and fried the other one for me. He ate his pretty quick and so did I. Liver ain't bad if you got enough ketchup. I put an extra blanket down on the floor for my new friend.

"OK, Tonto," I said as I lay down on the couch, which is where I always sleep since I ain't got a separate bed and there wouldn't be a place for it in my apartment anyway. "Tomorrow we solve the mystery of what to do with you."

xxxxx

If you're going to solve a question, first thing is to know what the question is.

In the morning I made a cup of coffee and put a pan of water down next to the apple crate on my little balcony. Then I sat down on the apple crate to drink the coffee. My balcony is only about three feet wide and six feet long and you get to it by opening the window and stepping out there. Tonto didn't have no trouble following me. The balcony has a good view of the roof of the garage and an alley with some dumpsters and trash cans. You can't see the mountains in the west because of other buildings, but sometimes at sunset the sky makes cool colors on the clouds. Sometimes in the morning the whole sky goes pink. Obviously, my balcony is a good place to drink coffee and think stuff up.

The first question to solve was who is Tonto? If he really was the dog of interest to the cops, then Holly or Jim could maybe use their computers to answer that question.

The second question is why was the cops looking for him? What secret was hid in his dog-brain?

And the third question was why was a guy in a pickup truck trying to kill him? Or did we just have bad luck and run into a guy who hates dogs?

The bonus question is where could Tonto stay safe while I was answering them other questions?

Then I thought, hey, what if he ain't the dog the cops is looking for? If they could tell me that, my list of questions got shorter in about ten seconds. Maybe I should take him to the cop station and ask them. Sure, the new cops might get interested in my old loitering tickets and want me to pay a fine or something. But maybe I should be a grown-up and do the honorable thing. Even better, I could always say I was somebody else, which James Bond done all the time.

So I put the collar on Tonto and hooked up the leash and started walking toward the precinct, which is what cops call their office. Tonto still wasn't all that cheerful, but he followed along and didn't complain.

We passed by a little park close to where I found Tonto in the first place, and suddenly he got all excited and pulled at the leash. There was a squirrel on the grass sitting up and chewing on a nut. That squirrel was about the most interesting thing Tonto ever seen. He barked but the squirrel didn't pay no attention, which made Tonto even more excited. He barked and pulled at his leash. He put his head down real low so his jaw was almost touching the grass, then he rolled over real hard and gave a big push and he slipped right out of his collar and ran at light speed toward that squirrel.

That got the squirrel's attention and he ran as quick as his furry little legs could carry him toward a big tree. It wasn't the very closest tree, but it must of been his favorite. I was a little ways away but I wasn't too worried. The squirrel was far enough ahead I could see he'd make it safe. And Tonto wasn't going to wander off when there was a squirrel in a tree that needed barking at. Plus, Tonto probably needed the exercise of running and barking, so I just casually walked toward him. Next time I'd put that collar on a little tighter.

On the other side of the tree was a little road that run through the park. A black pickup truck zoomed over the road and screeched to a stop right by the tree. A guy dressed all in black jumped out and ran over to Tonto. Tonto was still busy explaining stuff to the squirrel and didn't pay much attention. I was so surprised I done about the dumbest thing I could of, which is that I stopped and watched. The guy in black grabbed Tonto around his waist and picked him up. Carrying the dog, the guy ran back to the truck. He wrapped some kind of belt around Tonto's belly and threw him in the back of the truck.

"You're a idiot," I said to myself and ran toward them. The truck spun its wheels for a second. Smoke came off its tires and then it raced off.

OK, I'm a fast runner, but there's no way I could catch a pickup truck in a straight-line race. But I been in that park about a hundred times and I knew the little road curved and wandered around before it come to a regular street. I started running and made a bee-line across the grass. I got to the city street before the truck did. Another big tree grew right next to the road. I quick climbed that tree and got out to a limb that hung over the road.

I don't think the truck driver seen me since they probably wasn't looking up in the trees. They had to go right under me and slow down to turn onto the street.

So that's when I jumped.

I ain't gonna get no style points on that jump, since I only had about one second to get ready. But I stuck my landing in the truck-bed. It was easy to get that belt thing off Tonto, which I had to since it was hooked to a rope that was tied down. Tonto seemed glad to see me even if he'd got interrupted in his squirrel business. I grabbed him around the middle and picked him up. Then I did a little standing jump to the edge of the truck bed. Tonto licked my face and we jumped from the truck to the grass.

The driver must of seen me do that since he slammed on the brakes and put it into reverse. Before he caught up to me, I started running across the grass. The truck started chasing us, but the ground was wet and he got bogged down enough we got a good head start.

When something weird happens a few times it's just a coincidence. You'd be dumb if you think every weird thing is magic or the government playing tricks on you. But you get enough coincidences in a row and before you know it, you got probably causes.

When I was sure we outran them, I put Tonto down and put his collar and leash back on.

"No more squirrels today, buddy," I told him as stern as I could. "We gotta go report to the cops even if they dig out all my old tickets and throw a book at me. And I don't want no arguments from you."

Tonto looked up at me smiling, with his tongue dangling out. I think the squirrel chase put him in a good mood.

We walked up to the police station, which was an old brick building. The bricks looked extra clean and red like somebody hosed off the wall. I stared at the bricks for a minute while Tonto sniffed at stuff on the ground. I pictured some guy laying them bricks one on top of the other a long time ago, before there was even black and white movies or electric guitars. The guy I pictured was wearing old coverall pants and a flannel shirt. He put each brick down careful as if it was a robin egg that was about to hatch. Each one had to go in the exact correct spot, so he moved slow. After he laid down a brick and scraped off the extra cement, he wiped the sweat off his forehead with the back of his hand before he picked up the next brick.

Tonto and me walked to the front of the building. There was a patch of grass next to it, and concrete steps up to the front door. There wasn't no weeds in the grass and the steps was real clean. The brick guy I'd been thinking about would have liked that they kept the place neat, even if he'd been dead for a long time. A sign on the door said, "No pets" so I held Tonto's leash extra hard when we went in.

It looked more like an office than the precincts you see on TV. A young skinny cop sat behind a big shiny wood desk. A young woman in tight clothes was talking to him. When he seen me walk in you could tell he'd rather keep talking to her than me. He looked up for a second, pointed at Tonto and said, "No pets. Read the sign."

"He ain't a pet," I explained as polite as I could. "He might be an alleged perp or a witness or even a dog of interest but he ain't a pet. At least he ain't my pet which is all I know for sure."

"Let me make myself clear," he said, a lot louder than he needed to so he'd look tough to the woman. "Get your dog out of here!"

"OK, OK," I said "We're going. But he might have been involved in a killing…"

"Animal Control handles dog killings. Take him down there. It's on Colorado Boulevard."

"Thank you, sir" I said. "You been very helpful and extra good at your job so I hope you get bonus points. But don't he look at all familiar to you?"

"No," he said without even looking. He'd already turned back to the woman.

So the good news was the young cop didn't even think about checking for old loitering tickets. Maybe I got my own limitation statue on them. The other good news is, if they was looking for Tonto, they wasn't looking all that hard. Maybe he was a dog of interest or maybe not. Either way, somebody with a pickup truck was interested in hurting him or swiping him. He already felt like my buddy so I wanted to help him, but I'd get kicked out of my apartment if I let him stay.

As we was going down the steps to the parking lot I had an idea.

I knew this little girl named Linda who had a back yard. Her house was about as big as my whole apartment building and her parents liked me since I helped her when she had issues with a gang called The Bones. They had me come over for lunch once and give me a ham sandwich with mayonnaise and a slice of tomato and which Linda knew I liked. Obviously, that made me like them even better and they said if I ever needed anything to let them know. If their neighborhood ain't got rules about dogs, that seemed like my best shot of getting a vacation spot for Tonto.

So we walked over to her house. It took a while since our neighborhoods ain't real close to each other, but it was a nice day for a long walk.

Linda's house has a long black driveway that curves a little before it gets up to the house. By the street, there was two brick columns standing like guards with a black metal gate between them. Linda told me it was wrought iron and they locked it at night. It was open now, so Tonto and me walked up toward the house. Even if Linda's mom and dad told me I was always welcome, I was nervous. It felt like a place I'd be in trouble for going, which every nice place feels like.

I didn't have to be nervous for very long. A little girl's voice hollered out, "Jumper! Mommy it's Mr. Jumper!" and Linda come running down the driveway about full speed, her pigtails flapping around her head like cocker spaniel dog ears. She was wearing jeans and a Denver Broncos T-shirt. When she got to me, instead of slowing down she launched herself at me like a bullfrog. She grabbed me around the neck with both arms and wrapped her skinny little legs around my waist. I was so surprised she about knocked me over but I wasn't gonna let myself get tackled by a girl, and I sure wasn't gonna fall down while I was holding my little buddy. I took a couple of steps backward to get my balance.

"I was looking for a little girl named Linda," I said in my most serious voice. "Do you know where I could find her?"

She giggled. "Mr. Jumper, you're about the silliest grown up I ever met."

I shook my head like I didn't believe her. "She looks a lot like you," I said. "Only the little girl I know ain't got no hair from her medical treatments."

"It's science," she said back in her own most serious voice. "They discovered that hair can grow back. You haven't been keeping up with your science studies."

"You got me there," I said.

Tonto barked a friendly little bark, wagged his tail and then sat down. He looked up at us like he thought we had snacks for him.

"Who's your friend?" Linda said. She climbed down to pet him.

"I ain't sure what name's on his birth certificate," I said. "I was saying some names and he liked Tonto about the best so that's what I call him."

She looked up at me with that same stern look Holly uses sometimes..

"Mr. Jumper!" she said and pointed a finger at me. "Are you supposed to have this dog?"

I looked down at my shoes.

"It's kind of complicated," I said. "Nobody told me I couldn't have him…"

"You got a story, don't you? Probably a mystery."

"Well, yeah, I guess you could say that. I don't think I done anything wrong…"

She grabbed my left hand and pulled me along behind her. I held Tonto's leash in my right hand.

"Let's go up to the house and you can tell me the whole thing," she said. "Maybe Mommy will make us lunch. It'll be like a date."

"I got a rule about dating women who ain't even eleven-years-old," I said.

"Poo on that," she said, pulling me toward the house. "In lots of ways we're the same age."

I smiled at her joke and let her drag me along with Tonto trotting beside us.

Linda's mom met us inside the front door, in a little room that didn't have much purpose I could see except to be the first room. It had some pairs of shoes lined up against one wall so maybe it was the shoe room.

"Mr. Jumper," Linda's mom said, as friendly as if I was President of the United States. She reached out and shook my hand. "How lovely to see you again."

"Yes, ma'am." She was about thirty years old with brown hair and a big smile. She looked like an older version of Linda and her smile reminded me of Holly, my nurse friend. I could feel my face getting hot for no good reason.

"It's about lunch time," she said. "I'm sure you guys have a lot to catch up on. Linda, would you like me to bring you something in the dining room?"

Linda started to say yes and then she stopped herself.

"It's such a nice day," she said. "And Jumper brought his dog Tonto. Could we have a picnic on the back porch?"

"Of course." She turned to me. "Tonto isn't a very politically correct name these days. Some people think it plays into racial stereotypes."

"Yeah, I ain't positive it's correct either. But it's the name he liked so I ain't arguing with him. You mostly don't win when you argue with a dog. Or a parrot. I only argue with Mortimer since he don't care."

She nodded and smiled. "Honey, why don't you walk around the house and I'll bring sandwiches in a few minutes."

"Thanks!" Linda said and started pulling me back out the door.

"Thank you, ma'am," I shouted before the door closed.

The grass by the side of their house could could have been a park with a museum on it. The grass was all cut the same length, there were flat stepping stones to walk on and patches of flowers and bushes almost like somebody planned the whole thing before they planted anything.

The porch in the back was set off the ground about as high as my waist. There was a roof over it so you could sit out there even if it was raining. Linda sat in a big wooden chair with flat arm rests and a bright blue cushion. I sat in the one next to it which looked the same.

"OK, Mr. Jumper. What's the part of the story you didn't say yet? You didn't lose your apple crate again, did you?"

I smiled at that. I think every girl goes to the same Perry Mason school. They start asking questions and even an innocent guy like me thinks he's supposed to confess to something. A guy ain't got much choices except to stick to the truth, the whole truth and nothing but the truth. Even if you do, you're probably guilty of something. But courts got mercies and your best idea is to throw yourself at them and take your consequences.

"You know I never lost my apple crate. It got stole. Ever since I got it back, I bring it in from the balcony at night and put it next to the couch. It's handy for holding a glass of water in case you get thirsty in the night."

She looked at me using them big little-girl eyes with the same look Holly uses that means, "I'm waiting." I think they teach that the first day of Perry Mason school.

"Well, I was walking down Colfax street early in the morning. There wasn't much cars and it was still mostly dark. Then I seen this dog sitting on the sidewalk all alone. He seemed kind of sad so I sat down next to him."

"And you asked him what was wrong, didn't you?"

"Anybody would."

"Only he didn't answer, did he?

"Well, he's a dog. We got some communications issues. So now he's my friend. And that's the whole story."

She stared at me for a minute like she was about to cross-examine me. Then she shook her head.

"No it isn't. Maybe it's the truth, but it isn't the whole truth." Then she stopped and waited for me to talk some more. Sometimes it was hard to remember she was a ten year old kid and I wasn't under arrest.

"Well, there's some details. I didn't think you probably wanted details…"

She stared at me and kept waiting.

"Well, there was a pickup truck…" I stopped for a second. Sometimes if you say something the person you're talking to will jump right in and say something, like 'I had a pickup truck once' or 'my favorite pickup truck is made by this company.' And then you can say, why do you like those trucks? And in about ten seconds you're talking about a whole new thing and the other person don't even notice. But Linda wasn't falling for it.

"Well, OK," I said. "The detail about the truck that was interesting is that it swerved off the street, over the curb and come racing right at us."

Linda's eyes got big.

"Did the driver fall asleep or something?"

"I don't think so. It was coming our direction, and Tonto didn't notice, so I had to help him get off the sidewalk and onto the grass. He was real brave."

"Wow!" Linda said, then she smiled. "You had to jump didn't you? I miss seeing you jump." Then she thought some more. "Why would someone do that?"

I'd been hoping we'd already checked off the box of "the whole truth," so I tried not to answer.

Linda leaned forward and pointed her finger at me. "You know, don't you! There's more to the story."

"Well, I don't actually know. But I got suspicions."

She waited some more. I thought, boy, some people are really good at not saying anything. They must teach that in lawyer school too. She was backing me into a corner real good. I sighed.

"OK," I said. "Some people think he looks like a dog of interest in a murder case."

"Jumper! Really? You need to take him to the police!"

"That's a smart idea. Only I tried and today's cop wasn't interested. Plus the guy in the pickup truck tried to kidnap Tonto so I ain't sure what to do. I'm kind of in a pickle."

I decided to try not saying anything for a little bit, which is harder than it sounds. While I was busy saying nothing, Linda was thinking so fast I could almost hear her brain buzzing.

"You're going to solve the murder case, aren't you? And then you'll be able to get Tonto back to his home. That's your plan, isn't it?"

"It ain't so much a plan as a thing I'm thinking about."

She thought for a minute more. Ideas was flying around inside her head like bats by a street light and she was rocking back and forth in her chair. She looked up quick. I could tell an idea had landed inside her and grabbed hold with all its fingers.

"They don't allow dogs in your building, do they?"

"Well, the rule is no pets and he ain't exactly a pet since we just met. But they might get picky about it."

Linda's mom come out onto the porch. She had a tray with two plates and two glasses of milk. She handed me a plate with a ham and tomato sandwich on it. The sandwich was cut from corner to corner like they do in fancy grocery stores.

"Thank you, ma'am," I said. "This looks as good as a cafeteria sandwich."

Linda's mom smiled. Linda looked up at her and about as fast as snapping your fingers she changed from Attorney Linda to Sweet Little Girl Linda. It was like she took off a lawyer hat and put on some cute little girl cap. If I live to be fifty years old I'll never understand girls.

"Mommy, could Tonto stay with us for a while? Pretty please? Jumper's got some business he has to do and it would be better if he didn't have to worry."

Her mom frowned.

"There's a lot of work involved in caretaking a dog," she said. "Some of it's hard and not very pleasant. Plus, we don't really know anything about dogs."

"Carlos the lawn guy always talks about the dogs he had in his old country. I bet he'd show me how to do everything."

"We're really not set up…" her mom stopped. Linda stuck out her bottom lip and looked like she was about to cry. I reached over and touched her little elbow and she calmed down.

"It's OK," I said. "Your mom's right that it could be a lot of work. But it was a nice idea so thanks."

Linda wasn't paying attention. She crossed her arms in front of her chest and stuck out her chin.

"Mommy," she said, as firm as a judge on TV. "We owe Mr. Jumper. Don't you remember when he saved my life?"

There wasn't a good way for Linda's mom to answer that one. Maybe she wasn't crazy about dogs, but she knew she got trapped in Linda's cross-examination. She swallowed hard.

"Of course Tonto can stay with us for as long as he needs to. Your dad and I will help, too." She swallowed again. "It will be fun."

"Oh, thank you, Mommy!" Linda stood up grinning and gave her mom a big hug.

If I ever need a lawyer I hope I get one as good as a little girl who wants a dog.

A very old letter: (continued)

As to your inquiries: Indeed, I have space enough to accommodate an unknown guest, who mayhap resemble your own countenance but for hair grown long or colored with lye, and a beard cut in a fashion more suited to Venice than London. None would mark the visage of a departed poet in a new friend. Nor would any mark visitations by Verulamium who I have known since he was mewling and puking in the house of C, a house in which I also dwelt. In faith, Verulamium may direct the bloody scene from his lofty dark rafters and join our cheere cabal of ingenia universitatis anon. Mark his instructions with care.

(To be continued...)

Chapter Two

After I left Linda's house I walked straight to the thrift store. My friend Jim was still behind the counter. There wasn't any other customers so I started talking to him.

"Where's your dog?" he asked. "Did you give him to the cops?"

"Well, he ain't my dog in the first place and the cops wasn't that interested in the second place. But I got him a good place to stay so I can do some investigating. I guess that would be the third place."

"Ah," he said and nodded. "The murder."

"I ain't officially on the case. And maybe Tonto's a witness but maybe he ain't. Either way, he's probably lonesome to go home and the murder is the only clue I got to start me off."

"So the murder is a clue to help you solve the lost-dog mystery?"

"It ain't much of a clue. But it's the only one I got. I ain't got a legal yellow pad yet to write down my investigations. But if you could think of anything else from the news I'll try to remember it 'til I get home."

"OK, I'll try." Jim got quiet and stared at the wall across the store. Jim don't talk much unless he has to but his brain is real good. People think he's dumb, since he's quiet, but they're dumb to think that. They also think he probably can't drive a car since he only has one leg, but he's about the fastest car driver I ever seen. Sometimes you got to to wait to make up your mind about a guy. It's like an investigation. Sometimes the first clues ain't reliable. I didn't say nothing and let his brain work on remembering the news.

Finally he talked.

"A guy was killed outside the Halloween Bar. A young guy. He was some kind of scientist. He got into an argument with some old professor and they both got kicked out of the bar. They found his body on the sidewalk two blocks away. He'd been poisoned. They found the old professor outside the bar by the bike rack where he sometimes tied his dog. He'd been poisoned too. He was unconscious but still alive. They took the old guy to Saint Joseph's hospital. He's still there but with an armed guard. They figured he poisoned the other guy and accidentally got a dose himself."

"So why do they want to question Tonto?"

Jim thought for a minute.

"I have no idea," he said.

"That's OK. Thanks," I said. "That helps a lot."

"Good luck"

The thrift store was closer to Saint Joseph's Hospital than my apartment was, so I started walking toward the hospital. A detective don't need to know exactly what a clue is if he can figure out where it is and then go there. If you get close enough, the clues might find you.

A guy in a blue guard shirt was sitting at a desk in the hospital lobby. He looked serious, and he had big muscles under his guard shirt, but he also looked bored.

"How can I help you?" He asked like he said it a thousand times every day.

"I think I come in the wrong door," I said. "If a guy was supposed to make a delivery, where should he come in?"

"Back of the building," he said and pointed. "Back by the loading docks. What department do you need?"

"I ain't got paperwork in my pocket," I said which was the truth even if the whole truth was I didn't have paperwork anywhere and technically I wasn't making a delivery. "But I remember it was a professor and he got poisoned and I should give it to the guard outside his door."

He looked at me a little suspicious.

"Professor Reginald," he said. "But they won't let you see him."

"That's OK, I don't need to see him. I'll just leave it on the right floor and let the official staff take care of it. I think the paperwork said the sixth floor. So thanks a lot." I turned and started to walk out.

"It's the fifth floor," he said. "But they'll think you're another reporter and kick you out on your keister."

I laughed. "Yeah, I get mistook for a reporter all the time. I guess I'll have to let them kick my keister. If I even got one."

On the fifth floor it was easy to guess what room the professor was in, since a cop was sitting outside the door. I ignored him and walked past fast like I was going somewhere and didn't have much time. That's the same way you sneak up on a cat: you ignore it. I ignore Mortimer, my imaginary cat, all the time and it just makes him hang around with me more. I turned down a side hall while I was thinking up a plan. My plans is mostly foolproof, but they're even better if I think them up before I start doing stuff. I heard women's voices coming toward me before my plan was all the way thought up. There was a door marked "Employees only! Do not enter!" so I went in there. A light come on by itself and I could see I was in a big storage closet. There was green hospital uniforms stacked on a shelf and some bedpans in clear plastic bags, and some towels. I set my backpack down on the floor in a back corner, took off my shirt and put on a green hospital shirt. I turned my Denver Broncos baseball cap around backward and stuck most of my extra hair in there.

Even if my jeans was mostly clean and I was wearing a brand new hospital shirt, I figured someone might get suspicious if I pretended to be a doctor. And if they fell for it, about the last thing I wanted was for them to make me do a surgery on somebody. I think appendixes is just behind a guy's belt buckle, but they probably got rules for how you're supposed to take one out. I wasn't going to pretend to be a doctor, even if most of the TV shows with hospitals make it look easy. To make sure nobody pinned a doctor badge on me, I figured I'd do stuff like cleaning, which I never seen a TV doctor do. I picked up one of them brand new bedpans in the plastic bag it came in. Doing that give me another idea. I put down the bedpan and went back out into the hall.

A big, scary woman was standing there.

"So there you are!" she said. "I assume you're the new orderly." She looked at her watch. "About time! You must have been having a lovely dream."

"Yeah, I mostly have good dreams," I said.

She waved her hand to stop me from talking.

"I'm nurse Helga," she said. "And I'm your boss."

"Pleased to meet you, ma'am. My name…" She stopped me again.

"I don't need to know your name," she snapped. "You won't last long enough to be worth it. You're Orderly Number Ten. Got that?"

"Yes ma'am. I was just…"

"I post assignments on this bulletin board every day. So in the future just check that. Since you're new, I'll tell them to you today and we'll see how you do. Got that?"

"Yes, ma'am. I was just going…"

"There's a bad mess in 523. Bathroom looks like somebody blew up an outhouse. Cleaning supplies right behind you in the storage room. You've got a half hour and I want it spotless. Then report back to me for your next assignment. Do I need to repeat any of that?"

"No, ma'am. I been cleaning apartments in my building for a long…" But she was already walking away and not listening.

I smiled. My plan was working perfect, even if I didn't know I had one. Cleaning bathrooms is a lot easier than appendix surgery. Well, I think it is but the whole truth is I don't know it for sure.

OK, that bathroom was about as messed up a room as I ever seen, but it was like anything else. You figure out the first thing to do, then you do it, then you figure out the next thing and do that. It ain't the most pleasant work in the world, but then it ain't appendix surgery either so I felt lucky.

When I was done I went and found nurse Helga.

"All done," I said.

She looked at me hard and I thought maybe she was on to me

"You're done? Really?" She didn't say it like a compliment for doing my job but more like she was about to tell me what I done wrong.

"What about the towels? What about the sheets?"

"Well, they didn't look too bad."

"This is a hospital, Number Ten. Not a flea-bag motel. We don't leave germs from one patient to feed on the next one."

"That's real smart."

"Can you operate a washing machine? Does that fall within your limited capabilities?"

"Yes ma'am, it's one of my best things."

"Good. Get a laundry hamper from the storage room. Gather up all the towels and linens from that room and take them down to the basement and launder them."

I looked around and maybe I looked lost.

She pointed. "Service elevator is down that hall. Code is 4651. Do you need to write that down?"

"Nah, I've got a good memory."

"Fine. We're slow today so you can stay down there. Fold everything when it's done then put them back in the closet of the room. Remember, don't open the dryer until it stops. It's got an ultraviolet disinfecting cycle and it'll sunburn your eyeballs."

"Yes, ma'am. I don't want no tan lines on my eyeballs." I thought that was funny, but she didn't even smile. I think she was out of the smiling habit. Or maybe she had a hard day. You can't hold it against a person if they don't smile since they might have extending circumstances.

I didn't have no trouble washing the sheets and towels. The machines was big stainless steel ones. It was the first time I used a washing machine where I didn't have to put in coins or tokens.

When I was waiting for the dryer to finish, I was thinking up the next part of my plan. Being an orderly seemed like a good job and was probably even better if they paid you to do it. But it wasn't getting me much closer to solving my mystery. I needed to get into Professor Reginald's room. But if I tried, the guard would think I was a reporter and throw me plus my keister out. I needed a plan.

The good thing about deciding you need a plan is that once you do, one will show up in your brain. When the towels was dry and sunburned, I folded them back into the hamper, which was like a plastic barrel with wheels. I took it up the service elevator and rolled down the hall and past the guy guarding the professor's door.

In a minute I come back the same way and stopped by the guard. I tried my best to look confused.

"Excuse me, sir," I said.

41

"Nobody gets in this room," he said without even looking up from his magazine

"I just got a question," I said.

He looked up and seen the laundry hamper. "What do you want?"

"I'm kind of new here," I said. "Well, brand new since this is my first day. I don't remember where room 523 is."

"He looked at me more careful like he thought I was a James Bond spy or something. After a minute, he must of decided I wasn't James Bond. He shrugged.

"You're heading the right direction," he said. "Take that first side hall and you'll run right into it."

"Thanks," I said. "I'd ask nurse Helga but she kind of scares me."

He smiled. "She kind of scares everybody," he said.

I went where he told me, which I already knew where it was since I just cleaned it. I put the clean sheets and towels right where they was supposed to be. I figured I done enough for one day. Nurse Helga knew who I was, and so did the guard, which was a good start. I hadn't put in a full shift, I knew that. But then they wasn't paying me nothing either so that seemed like a fair deal.

The next day I showed up early so Nurse Helga wouldn't think I overslept again and wasn't reliable. If the real Orderly Number Ten showed up while I was working we'd both have some explaining to do. But maybe he wouldn't show up at all, or if he did maybe he'd get bonus points for me doing some of his jobs for free so he wouldn't be mad.

But my main idea wasn't to do another guy's work for him. My main plan was to investigate the professor so I could see if Tonto was his dog and why somebody kept trying to hurt him.

I went into the storage room. Yesterday it wasn't locked but today it was. It had the same kind of combination code lock as the service elevator. I tried the same code as the elevator and it unlocked right away. That seemed like a security risk, using the same code two places. At first I thought I should report that but then I thought, hey, Maybe I'll need to open some other door or elevator or something so it was better for me if they didn't fix their security risk right away.

I took a brand new bedpan out of its plastic bag and headed back to Professor Reginald's room. The same guy was guarding the door reading the same magazine as yesterday. I stopped in front of him.

"Nobody enters this room," he said without even looking up.

"I know that, sir," I said. "You told me yesterday. I ain't gonna break no rules, not even for Nurse Helga. But one of us needs to bring this new bedpan in and clean out the old one."

I held it out for him. Now, cleaning bedpans ain't a prize job for anyone. If you don't know what I mean, you can look it up somewhere. That's all I'm gonna say. The guard stared at that bedpan and then looked up at my face, and then back at the bedpan.

"It's OK," I said. "I'll guard the door for you. I bet you can be done in ten minutes, fifteen tops. Should I sit in your chair or stand by it?" I moved the bedpan a little closer to him. It was brand new and clean enough to eat lunch off of, but he wrinkled up his face like he was already smelling something bad.

"You're not a reporter, are you?" he asked.

I had to laugh at that one.

"Well, a big newspaper wanted me to write words for them. Only they got rules about guys with loitering tickets so I had to say no. I think I hurt their feelings."

He nodded and thought for another minute.

"OK, you can go in and do your job. But don't disturb the patient. He's mostly unconscious and when he's awake he's incoherent."

"That's probably why he needs the bedpan," I said. The guard grunted and looked down at his magazine. I went in the room.

There was only one bed in the room and Professor Reginald was laying in it. He was a small, thin old white guy with wrinkled skin and long white hair. He had a beard that was also mostly white about four inches long. He looked like he was asleep. But sometimes people pretend to be sleeping so they don't have to talk to anybody. Especially if the people who want to talk are mostly cops who think you done a murder.

I sat on the edge of the bed and started to talk to him in case he could hear me

"Hi, Professor Reginald," I said. I talked soft so the guard outside the door didn't hear me. "My name is Jumper. I ain't really a hospital orderly and I ain't a cop either. I found a lost dog on Colfax Street. He looks a lot like your dog only he ain't got a collar so I ain't sure. I would of give him to the cops as a dog of interest, only the cop was more interested in a girl so I didn't. But a guy in a pickup truck tried to run him over so I put him in protective custody…"

The professor's eyes popped wide open and he stared at me. His mouth moved like he was trying to say something only he couldn't squeeze no words out.

"Do you want me to get a nurse?" I asked. "Or maybe the guard?"

He shook his head "no" real slow and tried to talk again, only he said words I ain't ever heard. "Polonius," he said real soft, which obviously ain't a word. He frowned and shook his head no. He tried again, "Iago," he said or something like that and frowned some more. "Brutus!" he said and his eyes got brighter for a second.

"Is your dog's name Brutus? Is that what you mean?"

He shook his head no and looked frustrated. "Brutus," he said again and then he closed his eyes.

I stood up. Maybe the guy spoke some language from a different country, like maybe Canada, which is why his words wasn't words to me. But at least he was awake now some of the time.

"You probably need to rest," I said. "I'll try to come back tomorrow if the real Orderly Number Ten don't show up. Whoever's dog I got, I'll keep him safe til I figure out the mystery." I think he nodded like he understood, but I ain't sure.

"Man, that was a bad one," I told the guard and held out the bedpan. "I got this thing mostly clean, but it still smells a little so I won't bring it too close to you. We're gonna have to run it through a carwash if we ever want to use it again. And it looks like it's my job the rest of the week. Unless you changed your mind and want to take my shift?"

"There's not enough money in the whole hospital to make me take your job."

"Well, OK then," I said. "I gave you your chance. See you tomorrow."

The name tag on his shirt said "Mitch." I figured it would be good to memorize that, since people like their own name and they like a guy better if he remembers it. He sort of nodded, which was like saying goodbye plus have a nice day if you didn't know somebody good enough to use lots of words.

A very old letter: (continued)

As to your darling puppies already birthed, they
may wake again to the gentle nurture of a kindly
eam or two, whose pups shall in kind be blessed
with the fire of their own new oncles. The sleek
and solitary wasp may wield a fearsome lance, yet
nameless bees— who shake their humble weapons
in secret communion— compose more magic
nectar.

(To be continued...)

Chapter Three

That night I had more cleaning to do, even if I wasn't in the mood after my hospital shift. Mr. Silver had got real excited about kicking his birdseed out of the cage and there was seeds on the floor ten feet away. I got my good broom and I started sweeping. The broom's handle was broke in half, so somebody threw it in a dumpster but all the straws was like new. I ain't a guy to complain about a free broom with mostly perfect straws even if it's short. Mr. Silver kept honking and whistling at me when I swept his birdseed on the floor into a pile. He was about as mad as if birdseed was his best Mona Lisa painting and I was screwing it up by sweeping.

"You ain't setting a good example for Tonto if he gets to come back and visit. I told you to model good behavior like the social workers say."

Mr. Silver squawked out some curse words real loud and flapped his wings.

"Hey, settle down! I should feed you to Mortimer, who is a black cat you can't see even in the daytime."

He squawked some more. My imaginary cat didn't scare him much.

"You're a scrawny bird," I told him. "But I bet you'd make a good soup. I ain't bluffing. I already got potatoes and carrots. Plus an extra onion from cleaning 24B. Most of it ain't gone soft yet."

I put the birdseed I swept up into a mayonnaise jar.

"You'll get this same food tomorrow, even if it's been on the floor. Birds eat stuff off the ground all the time and I ain't rewarding you for making a mess by giving you brand new food."

"Shove it up your ashtray!" he squawked.

"Maybe a little cabbage," I said. "Potatoes, carrots, onion, cabbage, and parrot. I'm getting hungry already."

"Flushing bull sitter!" he said, only he was a little quieter this time. The idea of parrot soup was starting to get through his little brain. Everybody likes soup unless they're in it.

I went out on my balcony to practice my jumping. The air was cool and black since it was night, but it was an easy kind of black. A Spring black, when the air ain't so heavy like a hot summer night but it also ain't chilly and too thin like in Winter.

There's a two story garage building with a flat roof below my balcony. It ain't that far a jump so it's about a perfect distance to practice night jumps. Mr. Levi, the guy who owns my building owns the garage too. He stores boxes of stuff in the upstairs part and keeps three old cars he tells himself he's gonna fix up someday on the downstairs level. There's an old mattress on the roof. If there ain't a light on in the windows, nobody's inside to hear me and it's a good soft place to land. I climbed up on the railing and balanced for a little while. Then I jumped.

I always aim for the center of the mattress since I give myself bonus points for accuracy which makes it more like an Olympic event. It's only about one story from my balcony rail to the mattress. That's way too far to jump if you're a beginner. You'd break your ankles or your leg. If you land funny and fall, you could break your neck and kill yourself. But I been jumping every day since I was a little kid and I built up my bones and muscles. I done bigger jumps and never even got a blister. Me being careful ain't the same as you being careful. Plus I got a good aim. Jumping off balconies and tree branches ain't the right sport for most people, but it's about my favorite thing.

After I land, I climb up the downspout to start over. I mostly jump when it's kind of dark out since some people might think it was weird for a guy to climb up a rainspout if they seen me. All them people who think it's weird never done it before so you can't hold it against them.

While you're in the middle of a jump, it's like you're flying. I can't say it a better way. You could be an angel, or a monkey flying through the Wizard of Oz movie. Afterwards, climbing back up for the next jump makes a guy feel calm.

I do my best thinking when I'm jumping and this dog mystery needed some Columbo-sized thinking.

I learned some stuff at the hospital even if I didn't solve the mystery of who lost Tonto. Professor Reginald was a good suspect for the murder, since he knew the victim and they had an argument. But that didn't mean he knew Tonto. If his brain got better and I could get in his room again, I'd ask him more dog questions.

I also learned that if you carry a bedpan around, people think you're working. They don't even ask you questions. Burglars must not break into hospitals to carry bedpans around very often.

I made a note in my brain to remember that.

The next day, Professor Reginald seemed a little better. He pretended to be asleep when I first got there but it didn't take him as long to pretend to wake up. He still seemed mostly crazy, which could be a side effect from the poison. If medicines can have side-effect, poisons probably do too. Mostly it was hard for him to remember enough words to make sense. He seemed OK for a sentence or two and then went all loopy on me. I heard that some old people forget how to talk like a normal person. They know there's a word, but they can't grab it out of their brains. Except they still remember songs they knew when they was a kid. The professor seemed like that. It was like he was trying to say stuff by using them old songs, only they was songs I ain't ever heard before.

"How are you feeling today, sir?" I asked him, for one example.

"Like a midsummer nights dream," he said, which is something a crazy guy would say. "My head is a donkey. The fairy queen throws pots at puck."

49

So none that made any sense, which you figured out right away. But at least he was saying more words at a time and that seemed like a good start. He just couldn't make his mouth say correct words. Maybe it was the poison talking and he'd get better, but maybe he really was a crazy guy who murdered somebody. If you want information from a crazy guy, about the worst thing you can do is tell him he's crazy. He'll just say, no, I ain't crazy. Right there you jumped over the whole talking-with-a-guy bucket and landed in the arguing bucket which is hard to pull your feet out of. I figured we should start to talk about some easy stuff to get comfortable before I asked him about his dog.

"There's a guard outside your door," I told him "His name tag says Mitch. The cops think you done a murder."

His eyes got wide, like this was the first time anyone mentioned that to him. He tried to say something but all his words was stuck inside him. He held up both his hands in front of his face with his fingers spread wide apart. He stared at them, then turned them around and stared at the backs.

"Spots!" he said. "No damned spots! Do you see spots?"

"No sir. You got nice hands."

"And there in lies the tale. No damn spots! Signifying nothing."

"Sure, I say that all the time," I said.

He stared at the wall for a minute. "Why?" he said.

"I don't know. I was going to ask you why you done it too."

"Why do they think… think… why?"

"You was arguing with the guy. Then you both got poison doses. That's a pretty big coincidence."

"Who?" he asked, but his eyes look scared like he already had a good idea.

"Some forensic scientist. I don't remember his name."

"Isaac!" he whispered. He opened his mouth a couple of times but no words came out. Then he whispered some more, "Lord what fools…" he shook his head but the word he was looking for didn't shake out. "Fools these…" He tried one more time, real slow. "Lord what fools these policemen are." Then he lay back, all tired out.

"Why was you arguing?" I asked.

He looked at me for a minute trying to decide if he should answer. Or maybe he was trying to remember the words. He looked right at my Denver Broncos cap which I was wearing backward to keep hair off my face. Suddenly he could talk a little better.

"I'm…" he pointed at my Broncos hat.

"Isaac… Raiders."

"Well, now it all makes sense," I said. "You're a Broncos fan and he likes the Raiders. I probably would of murdered him too."

"I didn't murder him. We were working on… something." He rested for a minute, then he went on. "Our project was important. But who would murder someone over an old letter? It makes no sense."

"You can't talk to a Raiders fan," I said. "They're all crazy. They think the Raiders is a real team."

He nodded. "Incorrigible!" he said. "Gridiron xenophobes!" Then he stopped. "But Isaac Goldfarb had a good side. He was a good scientist."

"That's cool," I said. "I ain't ever talked to a Raider fan except to call each other names. I bet it would be weird."

He nodded. We talked a little more to get used to each other. When he was awake, his eyes was real alert, looking around like a robin hunting worms. But it was hard to talk to him. He'd start off on some ordinary sentence but

51

then get lost and throw in words he made up and names of guys nobody ever heard of. He might start off with real words like "that cop is carrying a lot of baggage," but then he'd say, "Something in his origin story is an albatross in the ancient mariner sense." You can't tell me that would make sense to anybody.

After a while, we'd done enough talk about easy stuff and the professor looked sleepy. So I asked him the big question.

"Is your dog's name Tonto?"

His face got sort of sad and he shook his head no. Then he closed his eyes and looked like he was asleep again. He was really good at looking like he was asleep.

"OK, Professor Reginald," I said and stood up. "I better go now. I don't think you can help me much with my dog mystery, so I ain't got much reasons to come back in. Except Nurse Helga scheduled me for a shift tomorrow afternoon and I don't want to explain I ain't really Orderly Number Ten. So maybe I'll come in again. We don't have to talk about murders, in case you might be a little sensitive about that right now. Some guys think the Broncos should draft another corner even if we already got about six. So maybe you got an idea about that."

I went out the door into the hall.

"See you tomorrow, Mitch," I said. The guard didn't say nothing but he sort of waved. I could have been a wastebasket walking past him. If you're a detective, having people not notice you is a good step.

As I was walking home I got an idea. Professor Reginald lost a dog and Tonto lost an owner. If neither one of us solved our mysteries, maybe Tonto would like to go live with the professor. And he'd probably let me come visit. As long as the professor wasn't in jail.

As soon as I thought up that idea, the professor's murder case got about as interesting as my dog mystery. If I could help the professor stay out of jail maybe I could fix him and Tonto up on a blind dog date. And maybe they'd really like each other.

I didn't see no hidden flaws in that plan.

A very old letter: (continued)

No word must be spoke of this for fear both our lives and litters be in mortal peril. Words might twine like roses yet be called not roses; the name itself may be their poison. Let Burb and Ned strut across the planks while WS pulls the strings and collects the coin. We three shall sing in the shadows, hid safe from slings and insults. With the boon of thy dear company as the honey on the cake, how can I aught but agree?

(To be continued...)

Chapter Four

The next day, Mitch the hall guard didn't look up at all, he just nodded when I went in the hospital room. The professor looked even more asleep than before, but I'm wise to con men. Having a roommate like Mr. Silver taught me you can't believe words just because they sound like they mean something, but being quiet don't always mean something either. I don't think parrots understand half the stuff they say. Plus, my cat Mortimer taught me you can't trust invisible stuff any better than stuff you see even if it's purring in your ear. Detectives have got to be careful. Some people believe stuff they can't see and words they don't know more than real stuff. I sat down on the edge of the bed and started talking to the professor soft and calm.

"Yeah, the Broncos went to Syracuse College to watch that fancy corner work out. Seems like a waste to me. We got more good corners than we need. Plus Syracuse ain't sent many good players to the pros after Floyd Little. I never seen Mr. Little play, so he don't count."

The professor opened his eyes.

"Orderly Number Ten," he said.

"Yeah, that's what they call me here."

"There was a witness."

"A witness to your dog escaping?"

He stared at me for a minute and I wondered if the poison screwed with his hearing.

"No. A witness to my little contretemps with Isaac. They probably saw whoever put the poison in our beer."

"Well, that would be good too." The professor was making more sense today, even if he was still making up some of his words.

"Her name tag said Esmeralda. I commented on it."

55

"Not much reason to lie on a name tag," I said.

He opened his mouth and tried to say something easy like "no" but it wouldn't come out. Like maybe he used up all of today's words and had to wait til tomorrow to get his tank topped off again. He shook his head. He was getting more frustrated. After a minute he said, "Such a one is a natural philosopher. Wast ever in court, shepherd?"

"Only for loitering tickets. The judge give me probation and community service." I felt sorry for the professor. It would be weird if you couldn't remember how to say easy stuff so you tried to talk in goofy old song words.

"I told her 'one drop of wine is enough to redden a whole glass of water." he said. He waited for some more words to come out of his brain. He swallowed a couple of times. "She said, you ordered beer, not wine. So I said 'One moment a maniac at another a queen.' She stared at me."

"Well, that ain't a real ordinary thing to tell a waitress," I said.

He acted like he didn't hear me. Since he had some more words ready to go, he said them fast like he was afraid they'd spoil. "I asked if her parents liked Victor Hugo..." He got stuck there for a second and stopped. Then he said. "Just stoic silence, speechless... ruin stared straight back ... eyes are nothing like the sun..."

"Well, they probably got you on some strong medicines," I said. "Medicines can have weird side effects."

"Because her name was Esmeralda!" he said. "Sanctuary! Don't you see?"

"If the name choices for a girl was Esmeralda and Victor Hugo, I think they made a good choice."

"One who does not weep does not see," he said, sounding tired. He lay back against his pillow and shook his head. "I reach in my pocket and find only reality."

"Well, if I understand you right, that waitress might of seen the real murderer, right? The police should question her. Did you give them that clue?"

He shook his head no. "They are fools. And a fool doth think himself wise but a wise man knows… No, I am here with thee and thy goats…"

"I bet a goat would be a good pet. Maybe I'll go to that bar. If Esmeralda's working, I'll talk to her real casual and maybe she'll say more clues."

"May the saints be your friends, and bless you. May the monsters be your friends and watch over you."

Then he closed his eyes and this time I think he really was asleep.

I found Nurse Helga on a whole different hall. She was mad at one of the other orderlies and was shaking her finger in his face.

"Excuse me, ma'am," I said, as polite as I could. She turned to me and I thought she was going to point her finger and start yelling at me next.

"It's Orderly Number… number nine, right? Can't you see I'm busy?" The guy she'd been yelling at backed away and made his getaway down the hall.

"Yes, ma'am. I'm Number Ten. I wanted to tell you I got appointments tomorrow and can't come to work. Maybe I could do extra work the next day to make up."

"Number Ten, eh? Everybody seems to like you. They say you get here early and do your job without much drama."

"Thank you, ma'am. I always try my hardest."

"OK, fine, thanks for telling me. But I hope you don't plan on having unexpected appointments very often."

57

"No, ma'am. I ain't planning on more unexpected appointments."

She looked at me funny, like she thought I was joking on her, but then she decided I wasn't. She kind of shooed me away with her hand and I left.

A very old letter: (continued)

But haste! Industrious K, once your trewe frend, under stern duress hath cast upon your name, and perhaps his own, a fatal blight. We know not that poor soul's intent beyond mortal frailty, but the badge of Arius pinned to thy back makes a target not soon erased. Tarry not, for the outrageous arrows, loosed of late that seek thy heart, they do flie swift. Chew the scenery but one more time, I beseech thee, and only in a play of our design. Then absent thyself from the common plega and conjure in yon bushy grove.

(To be continued...)

Chapter Five

"Hey, Jim. Did you ever go to the Halloween Bar?"

It was late afternoon, the thrift store was out of customers and Jim looked bored. It was an easy question but Jim likes to think of his answer to every question, even the easy ones. I waited while he thought. Finally he worked out his answer.

"Twice," he said. "So I guess I'm a regular."

"Well, they think that's where the poisoning happened"

Jim nodded. "Your murder investigation?"

"It's really my lost-dog investigation. I might have to solve the murder case to get to it."'

"That bar is a little ways away."

"Yeah. We can't always choose the scene of our crimes."

"And you'd like someone to drive you there."

"I've got some cash saved," I said. "I could buy each of us a beer."

Jim thought some more.

"My shift ends at five. Can it wait til then?"

"Sure. I ain't got much appointments scheduled today. I'll look at your pots and pans department."

When it was exactly five o'clock, Jim closed up the cash register.

"Somebody said something about a beer," he said. He locked the doors and we went into the parking lot.

It was about 5:16 when we got to the Halloween Bar. The sky was still light, but inside it was dark as a movie theater. It took a minute before we could see. There wasn't too many customers, but enough it didn't seem empty. Some of them was dressed up in costumes. There was a witch at the bar drinking with a storm trooper from Star Wars. One young woman was dressed ordinary except she had wings on her back like a butterfly. She was talking with a guy who was dressed up like a hobo in old clothes with some rips in them. But then, he might have been a real hobo and not an accountant in a hobo outfit. You can't tell about people by their costumes.

"I see why they call it Halloween Bar," I said.

There was plenty of empty tables. Beer signs on the walls had different colored lights and once we got used to it we could see OK.

"Where do you want to sit?" Jim asked.

"Detectives like to sit at the bar," I said. "Lots of people say things to bartenders and if you're nice to them they tell you stories. Only we gotta pretend we ain't detectives or the bartender might stop talking."

"I'll try to pretend not to be a detective," Jim said. "It will be hard, but I'll try."

Jim walked by using a crutch to help since he only had one leg. At the thrift store he sometimes got around with a cane. And sometimes he just hopped on his one leg. He was a good hopper and he could hop around as fast as most people walk.

"How come you use the crutch instead of the cane?" I said.

"It's a better weapon if you get caught in a bar fight," he said. "Plus, people see it right away and cut you some slack. If you ever want to date an attractive woman, use the crutch, not the cane."

"I'll remember that," I said. "But in this bar, they might think it's part of a costume."

"Yeah, they might think I'm pretending to only have one leg. I get that all the time."

The bartender was a lady. Her name tag said Pamela.

"What'll it be, boys?" she said and put a round cardboard coaster down in front of each of us.

"We'd each like a beer, please," I said. "Only I don't know brands so good. What do your customers like, Pamela?" Sometimes the best way to start being friends is to ask somebody to help you. Not a big thing, since that would be weird. But people like to help with little things, like telling you what's a good beer, and in about five minutes you feel like friends. That's a good detective trick I learned from about every TV show I ever watched. They also like if you call them by their name.

She looked at us careful, like we was dogs in a dog contest and got judged on our tails and if we walked like the kind of dog we was supposed to be. Even if our costumes was just the clothes we wear every day, she was probably used to guessing about customers who dressed different from that. She figured out right away we wasn't secret agent spies or Wall Street bankers so she smiled. She had a good smile, with lots of teeth. I bet guys told her all their secrets when she smiled at them.

"Cripple Creek is a good local beer. It's our happy hour special. Two for the price of one."

"Sounds good to me," I said, and Jim nodded.

She brought us two beers and set them on the coasters. "You got two more free beers waiting for you," she said. "That's how happy hour works here. Don't let me forget." Then she winked at us and smiled again.

"Thanks, Pamela," I said and paid her with dollar bills.

"That was nice of her to tell us about happy hour," I said. "Since we're strangers here she could of got away with telling us regular sad-hour prices."

Jim smiled.

"She's smart," he said. "That's how you turn strangers into regular customers."

We drank our beers slow and watched the other customers. Some people wore costumes, but lots of people were in regular clothes. Unless they was really vampires or werewolves and regular clothes was their idea of a costume. Mostly they was young guys in suits who just got off working at a bank or sales office. A few guys looked about as broke as Jim and me and they wasn't pretending. They was also drinking their beers slow. Some of the poor guys had quick eyes, like birds. Their hair might of been messy and maybe they had scraggly beards, but they was on the lookout for a deal: a guy they could beat at a game of pool for a dollar, or some old guy who forgot his wallet on the bar when he made a bathroom run.

There was more waitresses than they needed to sell beer to such a small crowd. They was all young and they laughed at the customers' jokes. If you laugh at a guy's jokes he tips you better. The whole place was a party where the main party game was trying to make a buck.

"This don't seem like the place a professor and a scientist would get together," I said.

Jim looked around. "I thought that too. On the other hand, if they had science secrets or literature secrets, nobody here would want to steal them. Maybe it was a convenient place to meet and it feels safe. At least all those car salesmen over there don't look worried."

When we was about done with our beers, the lady bartender came over again. "You guys ready for that free beer?"

"It's about my favorite kind, Pamela," I said. She brought the beers and set them in front of us.

"Is this the bar where that guy got poisoned?" I asked, trying to sound as casual as James Kirk on a new planet.

She looked startled for about a half second, then wiped some spilled beer off the bar.

"No one knows where he got poisoned," she corrected me. "But yeah, this is where they were earlier in the night."

"Wow," I said. "I bet that was scary."

"Not really," she said. She kept wiping off the bar with a white towel even if it looked dry to me. Bartenders like to talk to people and we was about the only guys sitting at the bar. "Those guys came in here two or three times a month. Kind of an odd pair; that old professor with all his big words and the young guy with his big smile. He was some kind of scientist."

"They must of hated each other kind of bad to do a murder."

"No, they seemed to like each other. Always talking quiet like they had some secret plan." She smiled and looked at a bar sign on the wall. "Well, they got a little noisy after about three beers. It was like they finished their secret business meeting and started to talk about football." She smiled. "They did not like the same team."

"I thought everybody in Denver likes the Broncos."

"The young guy grew up in California and followed the Raiders. When he moved to Denver and the team moved to Nevada he kept following them."

"Yeah, teams is a hard habit to break. Somebody said Esmeralda was their waitress. I bet she's got some stories."

"Who told you that?"

"Some old guy," I said, which was the truth even if it ain't the whole truth. She suddenly looked at me like I was suspicious which was the last thing I wanted. "Maybe I heard him wrong."

"Esmeralda wasn't working that night. You seem awful curious…"

"Sorry," I said. "I didn't mean to sound curious. I just ain't ever been around someone who was poisoned. It don't seem all that ordinary to me."

"Look," she said. She stopped wiping the bar and crossed her arms across her chest. "I wasn't here that night either, but I heard what everyone told the cops. Sure they argued about football, like they always did. But they walked out together. Nobody died here in the bar and I sure don't want anyone to spread a rumor that they did. Do you understand?"

"We ain't gonna say no rumors," I said. "Jim and me argue about football all the time and he never poisoned me."

"Yet," Jim said. "Not yet."

I laughed. "OK, OK, I'll stop talking about that Alabama quarterback that's gonna be in the draft."

"Seems like a fair trade to me," Jim said.

The bartender looked at him hard, then looked at me hard. Then she turned and walked away.

"There's a problem," Jim said. I waited until the rest of the words of his idea come to him. Finally they did.

"If Esmeralda wasn't working that night, your star witness has a memory problem." he said. "Or a lying problem."

"Yeah, he could be confused," I said. "I don't see much alternatives to that."

Jim nodded.

"Plus, I forgot to ask her my main question," I said. "Which is, did the professor have his dog with him that night?"

We finished our beers and went out to Jim's red Mustang.

While we was driving home, we didn't talk much. Jim kept looking at his rearview mirror.

"Is there a bug on your mirror?" I asked, which was sort of a joke.

"Not unless you consider a pickup truck that's going exactly the same direction as us a bug."

That got my attention real quick but I didn't turn around to look. I seen enough TV shows to know that ain't a smart idea. If I was alone I might of decided to stop the car and then if they stopped too, I'd go talk to the pickup driver. I'm a fast runner for a grown up and even if there was two of them I could probably get away. But Jim ain't all that fast on one leg. I told him about the pickup truck I seen before that tried to run over Tonto and then tried to kidnap him.

"What do we do?" I asked him.

"They've probably been watching the bar," he said. "Waiting for someone to ask about the murder."

"And then follow them home," I said. "They figure it will lead them to Tonto."

"Maybe," Jim said. "Or maybe not. But I don't like being followed."

"Maybe they ain't following us."

"Let's be sure. Let's take this turn-around."

"It ain't a turn-around Jim! It's an intersection with yellow lights about to go red!"

"Today it's a turn-around." He sped up real sudden. I'd forgot he put an extra-big engine in the Mustang, until his speeding up pushed me back against the seat hard. The light turned red just as we went into the intersection. Then he hit the brake all the way to the floor and turned the steering wheel left. The car started skidding sideways and the tires was squealing against the street. The car kept sliding sideways and turning around til it was aiming back the way we came from. Then he must of slammed the clutch all the way in, moved the gearshift stick let out the clutch and hit the gas. I don't know how a guy could do all that with only one leg, and he done it all so fast I ain't even sure I got the order right. He must of hit the clutch and the gas pedal at the same time with one foot, but I hope there ain't a quiz since I was so surprised I was holding on to the door and not looking at what he was doing. In about one second the tires was spinning against the street and you could smell rubber burning. The car jumped like a kangaroo in a cartoon movie and we was racing back down the street. The pickup truck was in the other lane stopped for the red light but we went past it too fast to notice the driver. Some cars was honking their horns but there wasn't any police lights flashing so it didn't bother us much.

"Where'd you learn to drive like that?" I asked.

He waited a minute to answer. "Navy," he said. "Munitions delivery. Every vehicle I drove was always one spark away from being a massive bomb. Incoming sniper fire teaches a guy to think quick."

"I wish I could of seen you drive with two legs," I said.

After a minute he nodded. "Yeah," he said real quiet. "I was pretty good."

We didn't talk for a few minutes and he drove in a direction that didn't lead straight back to my apartment in case they was still following us.

"You know, Jumper, it's possible some people are more interested in the murder than they are in the dog."

"I ain't thought of that before."

"A good detective considers all the possibilities. Even the unlikely ones."

"I don't think Professor Reginald done the murder. And I don't think Tonto is his dog."

"Why not?"

"I asked him if his dog was named Tonto and he said no. So I think the dog snatching and the murder is two different crimes."

"Then why are you so interested in the murder?"

I didn't see much alternatives except to answer, even if the answer was dumb.

"The professor lost a dog. Tonto lost a human. So you know, if I can't find Tonto's home and the professor can't find his dog…"

Jim nodded. "You're going to hook them up." He thought for a second then he said,"Yeah, that makes sense."

"But only if the professor ain't in jail."

"That's good thinking, Jumper."

"Thanks."

When we got close to my apartment I asked Jim to let me off at the park instead. It's an easy walk to my apartment. If someone was still following us I didn't want to make their job too easy.

"Thanks for the ride," I said as I got out.

"Any time," he said. "Thanks for the beer."

A very old letter: (continued)

Despite Ovid, I dare not sign my name, but shall smear the parchment with a drop of my own blood as we discussed. Therein lies my pledge. None can fathom the source of any blood but he who holds the dagger. Only you, and I, and the gods will understand.

Yours, 17

Chapter Six

I waited until he drove away then I climbed the biggest tree in that part of the park. If someone's looking for you, they do most of their hunting in their brain ahead of time, thinking where a guy might be before they ever start their search party. Their first plan is to look for someone hiding the same place they'd hide, like behind a dumpster or in some bushes. They wouldn't climb a tree to hide, so they don't think of it, which was one reason I climbed up it.

The second reason is that I like to climb trees. When I was a kid, me and my buddies all liked to climb trees. But when people grow up, they get cured of climbing trees just like they get cured of whistling while they walk, and catching bugs under rocks, and skipping stones across lake water. It don't make much sense. When you finally get old enough to do both kid stuff and grown-up stuff, a lot of guys decide to only do grown-up stuff. Maybe I ain't old enough yet. I keep watching for signs that I'm getting cured of kid stuff, but so far it ain't happened.

The whole truth and nothing but the truth is I was in a mood to jump out of a tree. Jumping is my sport and it's how I keep in shape. Other guys keep in shape by whacking at golf balls or killing deers, but them ain't my thing. My mom said that right after I figured out how to walk I started jumping off the couch. I kept doing it over and over again. I jumped off stuff so many times my legs got strong for it. I was still a kid when I started jumping off the garage roof and off tree branches. Maybe if I'd got started by killing deers, that would still be my hobby, but there was more trees and garage roofs in our neighborhood than there was deers.

There's several tricks for jumping off a tree branch. If you ain't an experienced jumper, it ain't a good place to start. If you're sitting on a branch, you can push off and go. But if you ain't careful, you're likely to hit the back of your head on the branch that first jump, which might also be your last jump. To get a little distance, you probably want to swing your legs out hard right when you dismount. Only that makes a head bump a lot likelier, so you

69

got to push off with your hands at the same time. It ain't as natural as it sounds.

Or you might crouch and pounce like a lion on a TV show going after a rabbit. A crouch and pounce gives you some distance from the branch, but if you don't fix yourself in the air you'll be doing a hard belly-flop onto the ground.

For your first few tries, you probably want to hang by your hands, make sure you got a clean shot and then let go. You fall straight down, feet first, which is the correct way to fall. Then, when you land, don't lock your knees straight. Bend them a little so it ain't as big a jolt. This is one sport where it ain't as important how you start as how you finish. A good landing is one you can walk away from.

By now it was dark and some street lights had come on around the park. I like the cool shadows street lights make. Street lights let you see where you're walking on the sidewalks. But the grass and bushes farther away stay dark and as spooky as a fairy tale. I sat in the tree and watched the park for a while. Bats came out and went zipping around the lights, chasing mosquitoes and moths like little space ships from a foreign planet. The air was crisp as new lettuce and my branch was hid by shadows. There ain't many things as good as being invisible in a beautiful place. I thought I heard an owl asking who, who? But it could of been a car with a loose fan belt over on the street.

Night jumps is tricky since you can't see your landing spot as good. If you land on an old bottle you could twist your ankle or break your leg. You might be the smartest detective on the whole team, but if you break your leg, the coach will put you on injured reserves as quick as he can throw a penalty flat.

My first jump that night was ordinary. I done it from sitting. There wasn't much issues and I landed clean on the grass and started climbing the tree again. Olympic jumpers get bonus points for how high they jump or how far. High divers get points for doing fancy stuff in the air, but they jump into swimming pools which ain't the same. So far, nobody come up a point system for a guy who jumps off of stuff onto grass or parking lots, which is probably why tree jumping ain't an official sport yet. But a guy can tell if he done a good jump. If I do a good jump, I give myself bonus points which is only fair. My first jump was fine, but I don't give myself bonus points for "fine." That would be cheating.

My second jump I about killed myself. It was the same branch as the first jump, only I done a crouch and pounce. Just as I was pushing off, a cat run under the tree and stopped right at the spot I was aiming to land. Once you're in the air, you can't change your landing target much. I tucked my knees up to my chest like always so I'd turn in the air and land on my feet.

"Look out, cat!" I yelled. "Move! Move!"

But the cat sat down and turned his head like he was wondering where that voice was coming from. The only thing I could do was spread my legs apart farther and land with one foot on each side of him, but the ground wasn't level. When my feet hit the grass, that cat yowled like I punched him and he jumped straight up in the air about as high as my belt. Then he raced off into the dark bushes.

My knees was bent, like always, but it was a hard landing. I felt like somebody stabbed my left ankle with a knife and I fell to the ground. I watched the pain to see if it would go away like most pains do after a few minutes, but this one held on tight. I rolled around on the grass to see if any other position felt better, but they didn't. Maybe I really screwed up my ankle. Maybe that jump I just did was the last one I'd ever do.

When my dad was sick, every time he done something he wondered if that was the last time. His last peanut butter sandwich ever; his last sunrise; the last time he'd kiss mom. It was like he had a list of stuff and he kept checking them off. I didn't know he was dying, I thought it was just a silly game. When he finally died, I thought OK, Dad. Now I understand. You checked off all the boxes. I wondered if I just checked off one of my own boxes.

After a minute I sat up. "Mortimer!" I yelled at my imaginary cat. "You been sleeping on your duty shift, buddy! You was supposed to protect me

71

from real cats! I'm starting to wonder what's even the point of having an imaginary cat?"

Obviously, Mortimer didn't say nothing and I don't think he was even there. There ain't many feelings as lonely as when your imaginary cat ain't there when you need him. I lay there for a few more minutes until my ankle calmed down a little but it still hurt like heck. Finally I got up. If I limped, I could walk about as slow as a ninety-year-old guy. I limped home real careful. About every five seconds I looked behind me for pickup trucks but I didn't see none. If the guy in the pickup truck was still following me, I couldn't outrun him or jump out of a tree at him.

"At least," I thought. "I can probably still out-think him."

The next morning my ankle was swelled up like a big softball above my foot, but it didn't hurt as bad as last night. I left for my hospital shift extra early, since I'd be walking slow. I went into the supply closet where they keep the orderly clothes and changed. One good thing, when you know the key code for the elevators and closets, you feel like you're a rich guy who owns the hospital and you're stopping in to take a look at your kingdom. Maybe I'd only disguised myself as somebody kind of ordinary so I could walk around with regular people and listen to what they really thought, and nobody'd know I was the king. But now I was back in my castle with my knights and jesters and cooks all waiting to serve me. Or, in my case, with janitors and nurses and doctors who was all my servants.

The idea of being a king with a hospital kingdom went out the window as soon as I went around the first corner of the hall. Holly, my friend from the apartment building, was walking toward me. She works as a nurse at this hospital but she ain't usually on this floor, so seeing her surprised the heck out of me.

I think she was even more surprised to see me there, dressed up like an orderly and pretending to be the king of the hospital. She stopped cold and her mouth opened all the way. In about two seconds, she put her hands on her hips, which is always a clue that she's feeling serious and it ain't a good time to try and joke on her.

"It ain't what it looks like," I said, which might be true if I knew what it looked like.

"What in the world...?" She started to ask me but was too surprised to finish.

"I'm sort of a substitute honorary orderly. Kind of an apprentice. Nurse Helga calls me Orderly Number Ten and she says I do a good job."

"But the application forms... the background check... the literacy... I mean the reading tests?"

I laughed like them wasn't a big deal.

"Sure there's lots of extra stuff if you want to be official..."

"You don't even have a bank account. How do they pay you?"

"If I decide I want to be official and get paid I'll have to cross them tees when I get to them. They ain't near as strict if a guy just cleans up stuff."

"I see. But why?"

"You remember Tonto?"

"The dog you found?"

"Yeah. I can't keep him in our building which I gotta thank you for reminding me of. So he's gonna need a new home. And there's a guy staying here who lost his own dog, only he's got some complications. If he gets better and fixes his complications, him and Tonto might hit it off. So I'm thinking it would be cool if I help him fix his complications." I was proud of thinking up all that, since it was mostly the truth, even if it ain't the whole truth.

"I see."

"It's nice to run into you, Holly. But I gotta go or I'll be late for my shift." I started to walk away.

"What's wrong with your foot?"

Like I said before, you can't get nothing past Holly.

"Twisted my ankle. A cat ran out when I was in the middle of a jump so I landed funny."

"You come up to my floor right now. I'll meet you at the desk and tape it up."

"Thanks, but I don't want to be late."

"Did I say something you misunderstood to be a question?"

"No, ma'am."

"Five minutes," she said and then she turned and walked away.

Holly's floor was number seven. It had its own little waiting room with a desk when you got off the elevator. There was six chairs for waiting in and old magazines on a table. A TV was up near the ceiling. It had an animal show on but the sound was turned all the way down. It was showing a tiger creeping up on an antelope, which is always interesting but I wouldn't show animals being mean to each other in a hospital if I was king of it. I sat in one of the chairs and started watching it anyway. As soon as I did, Holly showed up. She pointed at me.

"You," she said as firm as a gym teacher ordering you to do pushups. "This way." She started walking away and I limped after her. That antelope was on his own.

I followed Holly into a little side room.

"Sit up there," she said. There was a long table with a cushion on top and some brown paper on top of that. I sat down. Holly had a roll of brown cloth tape that was stretchy. "Take off your shoe and sock," she said. I started to follow them instructions but she stopped me. "No, you can leave that one on. Just the one you hurt."

"Right."

While I done that, she said, "Now you sit still and don't talk. I don't think I want to know any more about Intern Number Ten, or Tonto, or jumping onto cats."

"I didn't land on the cat…" I started to say but she put a finger in front of her lips and said "Shhh!"

So I sat there and watched her tape up my ankle.

Watching women is weird. You probably seen shows where little lizards change their color. Women is like that. If she's nice and smiles at you a lot, after you watch her for a while she looks younger and prettier. If she's mean, it don't matter how nice-looking she was when you first seen her. After a while she looks like the wicked witch of Oz.

Holly starts off looking pretty just sitting there not doing anything. If you seen a picture of her you'd think she could to be in a magazine ad or on a jar of honey. But she was also about as nice a person as could be and she smiled all the time. She concentrated like my ankle was the only thing in the world and in about two minutes she looked like Miss America to me.

She also looked like she knew some secret ancient medicine, like maybe from the Aztecs or the hippies. Her hands pulling that tape around my foot was a voodoo magic trick.

"There," she said and she stood up. "Put your sock and shoe on again.

After I done that I stood up.

"Wow," I said. "I can't hardly even feel it."

"That's sort of the point," she said. "No jumping for a week. Maybe two."

"Yes, ma'am."

"Now get out of here before I send you a bill."

I walked to the elevator and hardly limped at all. I got to the bulletin board the same time as Nurse Helga was walking away from it.

"Number Ten!" she said when she seen me. "Glad to see you could make it today. No important appointments?"

"Nah, they all got cancelled…" I had a funny thing to say about appointments but she stopped me with her hand.

"Don't need your life story," she said. "Assignments are on the board." And then she walked away.

My assignments was easy and I done them fast so I'd have extra time with Professor Reginald.

"Hi, Mitch," I said to the guard. He waved his hand a little and kept reading his magazine.

The professor looked asleep, but then he mostly looked asleep. Sometimes I heard other orderlies or nurses talking about him. They all said he ain't ever been conscious again and the cops wasn't sure he ever would, since the other guy that got poisoned died. The doctors couldn't find no reason that he never woke up or talked, except that poisons is funny and you can't ever tell how a guy would deal with it. But he'd fooled me that first time into thinking he was a mummy from Egypt who hadn't woke up since they locked him in a pyramid. So maybe he was still fooling everybody.

I done the regular jobs you got to do every day in every room, like cleaning the bathroom and wiping down any place a guy might touch. I talked to the professor while I worked in case he could hear me.

"Esmeralda wasn't working that night," I said. I talked quiet so Mitch the guard wouldn't hear. The professor opened his eyes.

"Yes, she was," he said. I was proud of him for using real words, but he was sticking to his story which maybe wasn't the whole truth and nothing but the truth.

"Well, maybe the bartender lied," I said. "Maybe she's best friends with Esmeralda and don't want to get her in trouble."

The professor tried to say something but his brain didn't remember how to talk again. He squinted up his face and tried real hard, but there wasn't any words in his mouth. Then some words to another old song showed up and he said them "I reached for my pocket and found only reality."

"I ain't ever heard that one before," I said.

"Drink, poured out of a cup into a…" he stopped. He shook his head like I wasn't getting his message, which is the whole truth.

"Kind of sounds like one of them old Beatles songs," I said. He looked frustrated, like we talked different languages and he couldn't make me understand. It was like me and Tonto trying to talk.

"I bear the dungeon within me. Within me is winter, ice and despair…"

That one didn't ring no bells in my brain either. I could tell the professor was trying to tell me stuff but he might as well been talking Klingon. Plus, the words he did say made him seem as crazy as Mr. Silver the parrot who lives in my apartment. All his squawking put together wouldn't make one good line in a bad song. I figured if the professor was nervous, that would only make his talking get worse.

"Look, buddy," I told him. "I ain't with the cops and even if you made some mistakes I ain't gonna turn you in. As long as you don't turn me in on some old loitering tickets which wasn't really my fault anyway. I got a mystery about a dog and you might know some clue you don't even think you know. So maybe if you relax we could talk about some whole other thing and after a while we could get more serious."

He nodded and closed his eyes, not like he was going to sleep but like he was trying to relax.

"OK," I said. "But I gotta admit its suspicious a Broncos fan would be friends with a Raiders fan."

He stared at me and opened his mouth but no words come out. The he frowned and clenched his fist like he was going to try extra hard. When he finally squeezed out some words they come one a at time like each one hurt him to say.

"Isaac… idiot about football… But great…scientist."

"They think you killed him."

He concentrated again and closed his eyes

"No…" he said, then he swallowed hard. Then he nodded his head slow. "He was…helping me."

"Cool," I said. "I ain't' gonna ask what he was helping with since it ain't my business. Unless it helps me solve my whole other mystery, which I don't see how it would."

"Kit's… murder," he said.

"I thought the guy's name was Isaac Goldfarb."

He shook his head.

"Kit's murder," he said again. Then he kind of leaned forward off the pillow and whispered, "Fake."

"I almost killed a cat myself last night. It ran out where I was jumping. Mortimer must of been off duty somewhere. Maybe sleeping and dreaming of ripping up somebody's curtains. He ain't that reliable."

He held up his hand to stop me.

"Not cat," he said. It seemed like his talking was getting easier even if he still sounded crazy. "Kit. People wanted Kit dead," he said. "Edward helped him. I have proof…" then he lay back down and closed his eyes.

"I never heard of anybody named Kit except for an old TV show that had a cowboy named Kit Carson," I said. "I ain't got all the TV channels, but one time I let a cable guy into one of the other apartments and he showed me how I could watch some channels with real old shows. I like them old black and white cowboy shows since the people talk slow so you can understand them. Plus, it's easy to tell which is the good guys from the bad guys. But mostly life ain't like an old black and white cowboy show. For one example, it's got colors."

I hadn't heard of any murders of people named Kit. I was about to ask the professor about it, only he'd gone to sleep right in the middle of our conversation.

I gotta admit, I didn't have much good reasons to think the professor had clues about Tonto. But him saying he had proof about a whole different murder was interesting. Since everybody else thought he was in a coma, I might be the only person he said it to. When stuff happens that ain't very ordinary, like a guy talking about a murder, you gotta pay attention to it. Paying attention is the number one rule for detectives.

Chapter Seven

When I left the hospital I didn't walk toward my building since the guy in the pickup truck might be surveying the hospital. A block away there was a bus stop with a new bus pulling up. I have a pass for free bus rides, which Officer Mike and Linda's parents gave me as thanks for helping with an incident of a gang called The Bones. The bus was going away from my apartment which is what I wanted. I got in and watched out the window for pickup trucks. In about four blocks we got to another bus stop. I hadn't seen any suspicious trucks or cars, so I got off and waited for a bus going the correct direction. In about seven minutes one come along and I got on it.

Mr. Silver was squawking and cussing when I went into my apartment. He'd kicked most of his seeds out of his cage and onto the floor again. I was tired and not in the mood.

"Ah, man," I said to the bird. "I explained this to you a million times already. When your birdseed is on the floor it's like a big flashing sight that says 'hey mice, free food at Silver's Cafe.' And stop with all the bad words! What if some kid came to visit? His parents would throw you in the pokey and say I was accessorizing you after the fact."

I got my broom and swept the seeds up off the floor.

"Maybe I'll give this food back to you tomorrow," I said. "If you get hungry tonight maybe that'll help you learn your lesson. Or maybe I'll give your food to Mortimer. He ain't a picky eater."

But Mr. Silver's a bird who thinks he's a pirate. Neither pirates or birds is good at following instructions, so you can't really blame him too hard.

The next day I rode the bus to work, but I didn't get off until it drove a few blocks past the hospital. Then I walked back and went in the front door. My ankle hurt, but if somebody was surveying the hospital and they seen me coming, they'd think I lived a whole different direction than I really did. When you're dealing with suspected crooks, you gotta think like a crook, only better.

81

Mitch the guard only looked up for about two seconds before waving me into the professor's room. Professor Reginald looked just like he always did, somewhere between asleep and dead.

"It's me," I said. "Orderly Number Ten."

His eyes popped open and he looked at me careful, from my head down to my shoes as if he never seen me before. He looked more awake than I ever seen him.

"Your parents were unorthodox," he said. "Naming you Orderly Number Ten."

I laughed at that. "Nah, my folks wasn't all that religious. Number Ten is just what Nurse Helga calls me. My real name is John Cable but everybody calls me Jumper."

"Well, of course they do." He repeated my name so he'd remember it. "Jumper," he said and closed his eyes. "Pleased to meet you."

"You bet," I said. "Maybe you didn't hear the Broncos got us another new running back."

"Star-crossed, no doubt, like all his predecessors. Doomed like Sisyphus."

"That song must be before my time"

He sort of snorted and tried to say it a different way. "Destined for disability, disillusionment and departure to some Canadian gulag of gridiron despair."

"Nah, I think he mostly plays running back. Our last two RBs got injured and traded away. This one looks good. But then they all do at first."

"What's my current duration of medical incarceration?"

"I don't think you got anything bleeding," I answered.

"How long have I been here?"

"Oh, that. I think it's been about ten days."

He nodded. "Based on my level of peckishness, that sounds about right."

"You don't seem all that peckish to me," I said. "If I was in your spot I'd be mad and pecking at everybody."

He looked at me for a minute.

"I'm hungry," he said.

"That's usually a good sign," I said. "They been giving you food through tubes but it ain't the same. I bet the cafeteria would send you something."

"No!" he said, louder than he ever said anything before. I looked at the door, but Mitch didn't come in. The professor seen me do that and I think he figured out what I was thinking. He started talking again, but real quiet. "No. If they know I'm conscious they'll interrogate me. I'm not ready for questions. I need to figure this out myself. Judging by the inquisitors they've sent, I'm Sherlock Holmes in a room full of Inspector Clouseaus."

"I ain't heard any of their names except for Mitch out in the hall."

He sat up and rolled his head back and forth like his neck was stiff.

"You've got some mystery about a dog? Was it purloined?"

That sounded like some fancy kind of steak I never ate before.

"I ain't so rich I'd buy steaks for Tonto. But yeah, I got a dog mystery. He likes liver."

"Listen," he said, like he was about to tell me a secret. "If you smuggle me in something to eat, I'll try to help you with your dog mystery."

"I don't know. They probably got rules."

"Do you have a better plan?"

"I usually wait and pretty soon a plan shows up."

"Well, maybe one just did."

He had me there. Lots of times something good shows up but it don't look like what you pictured so you don't pay attention. Maybe you're sitting by a river watching the bugs fly around and you want a chocolate bar but when it shows up floating like a little boat, the wrapper around it has words in French, which you can't read, so you watch it float past. Then you go back to wishing you had a chocolate bar. I ain't saying every wrapper with French words is hiding a chocolate bar, but I bet some of them are.

"OK," I said. "I could maybe sneak you in a chocolate milkshake."

"The ambrosia of the gods!" he said,

"I don't think they got ambrosia. It's mostly chocolate or vanilla. I'll be back in a little bit."

He laid back down and closed his eyes.

The cafeteria was down in the basement, which I knew by the sign in the elevator. You could choose your own food and put it on a tray and pay at the end. There was a big menu on the wall and it had milkshakes on it, but you had to ask this young skinny guy to make it for you. He was standing by the wall moving stuff around that didn't need to be moved and hoping nobody'd call on him.

"One chocolate milkshake please," I said when he noticed me standing there waiting for him. He let out a long sigh, like he was real tired and I just asked him to build a pyramid from scratch without any helpers. But he made the milkshake and I paid the woman at the cash register. She handed me my change. I stared at it and said, "Wow!"

"Did I count wrong?" she asked.

"No, I ain't sayin' you counted wrong, since subtracting wasn't my best subject. And I ain't complaining. That's about the cheapest milkshake I ever bought."

She smiled. "We're a nonprofit," she said. "Plus, we charge the patients' insurance companies so much upstairs we can afford to give our employees a break. Not that any of that profit finds its way back down here."

"Can I come in when I ain't working?"

"Sure. Are you planning a romantic dinner?"

"I'm always planning a romantic dinner, just like Mr. James Bond. Only he's got better clothes so it works out more times for him than me."

"Yeah," she said. "The ladies love him for his clothes all right."

"Your microwave has a sign that says out of order."

"It's been broken for a month. Maintenance can't get around to it and the administration says there's no money to replace it until the end of the quarter."

"Did you try a new fuse?" It wasn't my business, but changing the fuse was the first thing a guy would try. The second thing is they'd raise their milkshake prices so they could pay to get stuff fixed.

"Maintenance tried unplugging it then plugging it back in. That's the limit of their engineering skills."

"It ain't hard to do if you got a screwdriver."

"I don't think anyone in this hospital knows how to operate a screwdriver."

"Fuses is cheaper than a cup of coffee."

"Maybe so. But by the time we submitted all the paperwork and got an authorization, microwaves will be obsolete. We'll all be heating our coffee with phasers and replicators."

I laughed at her joke and said thanks for the milkshake and then I went back up to the professor's room. It was easy to hide the milkshake under my orderly shirt.

"It's me again," I said. The professor opened his eyes and I handed him the milkshake. His hands was shaking when he took it so he held it with both hands. I'd already stuck two straws through the lid, since milkshakes is so thick you got to give your mouth a fair chance to suck some in. He had to work at it, but he was able to drink it.

"Glorious nepenthe!" he said. "A gift from Plutus!"

"I think his name was Chuck, but yeah, he makes good shakes."

"This establishment should abandon all pretense of curing the infirm and focus on its one salient positive attribute. This hospital can concoct a milkshake." He sucked in another mouthful and looked up at me. "Thank you," he said. "You may be Don Quixote to the world and perhaps the English language is your windmill, but you are the Samaritan today."

"Don and Samaritan is probably different orderlies. I'm Jumper, remember?"

"Indeed."

It took him a while to finish off that shake but I didn't say nothing. If a guy is liking something it's mean to distract him away from liking it. When he got to the last little bit, the straws made a gurgling sound, whistling up air along with the shake.

"Shh," I whispered. "Mitch will figure out you're awake."

"Good thinking," he said. I took the empty cup, rinsed it out in the bathroom sink, then wadded it up in my pocket. My idea of helping him with his murder case didn't seem like as good an idea today, since he thought I was Don and I thought he was mostly crazy.

"OK, then," I said. "I probably ought to go."

"Wait!" he whispered. "I may need a confederate."

"Sorry," I said "I got about six dollars in my wallet, but none of them is fake."

He pretended like he didn't hear that.

"I can't maintain this charade indefinitely. Once the authorities abscond with me, I'll be effectively incommunicado."

Some of them was probably real words but I had my doubts. He forgot how to talk once, so maybe he forgot again and was just saying sounds and thinking they was words.

"You probably need to get some rest," I said.

"I'll say it succinctly," he said.

I stared at him. He nodded and started over.

"I'll use little words," he said. "You needn't comprehend the entire tapestry..." he stopped and cleared his throat.

"Edward and Kit were kindred... they were buddies. They both had the same job, writing words. You know, like screenwriters for TV shows. But Kit wrote words that made people mad. Inevitably, the constabulary... That is, before long the cops wanted to arrest him. Kit had dinner with these other guys and somebody stabbed him to death."

"Wow," I said.

"That's the official story. But something else really happened. It's the literary equivalent of the old nostrums, ontology recapitulates phylogeny or luminiferous aether: an archaic idea without merit that nevertheless holds sway."

He said all that as serious as the Pledge of Allegiance, so I tried not to laugh.

"Isaac and I figured it out. Some bad guys decided to kill us to keep us quiet."

Making up that weird of a story seemed like a bad symptom of a poison side effect. Or maybe he was crazy to begin with. When you're talking to a guy who might be a crazy murderer, it ain't smart to argue. So I played along.

"Why?" I asked.

"Why the murder or why the cover-up?"

"Well, the guy who's after you is probably the guy who killed Kit. You figured it out and he didn't want to go to jail. When he found out you knew, he had to go after you. Seems like good motives to me."

"No, no. First, nobody killed Kit. They faked it. All the co-conspirators are dead."

"Then it maybe don't matter much except for their families."

"Oh, it matters a great deal. Working as a team, Edward and Kit launched an empire, only they kept it secret." He stopped for a minute. "Have you heard of Lennon and McCartney?"

"I think they was in the Beatles music group, wasn't they? My dad liked the Beatles. Was Kit and Edward in the Beatles?"

"No, no. That's just an example of two creatives collaborating and their synergy eclipsing their individual potentials..." He stopped, then started over. "Sometimes two is better than one."

"Like a good quarterback and good running back make each other look better?"

"Just like that."

There was some men's voices out in the hall talking to Mitch.

"They're here!" the professor whispered, all excited. "I have proof. It's a letter hidden in my house." He pulled a key out from beneath his pillow and handed it to me. He whispered real fast and told me an address. "You may be my best hope, my deus ex machina. I don't know who to trust. My nemesis likely comes from either the world of academia or from Isaac's world. There's a conference...if I were free, I might be able..."

The door opened and three big cops come into the room. The professor lay back down before they seen him. In one second he looked as unconscious as a dead guy. One cop had a bunch of papers. They all had guns in holsters.

"Orderly, you're dismissed," the first cop said and motioned for me to leave.

"Yes sir," I said.

The professor was rubbing his eyes like he just woke up.

"Where am I?" he said and his voice sounded sleepy.

"You're under arrest for the murder of Isaac Goldfarb," the cop said. "You have the right to remain silent..."

Mitch pushed a wheelchair next to the bed.

"The doctors say you're well enough for jail. They think you've been faking your coma."

"Coma? If music be the food of love..."

"Yeah," the cop interrupted. "If music be the food of love I want a ham sandwich instead."

I finished up my shift at the hospital and then took a bus the wrong direction for a few blocks and got off. Professor Reginald had got me interested in his murder case, even if I never heard of the music group Edward and Kit. Not knowing stuff is OK. When somebody says they know the whole truth, there's two choices: they're really dumb or they're lying. Or maybe both.

I skipped the first bus going toward my building to be extra stealthy if I was being surveyed. That give me an extra seven minutes to sit on the bus-stop bench and think.

The bus stop was across the street from a little hardware store. I can think as good looking at tools and wires and screws as I could if I was in a fancy office building. I could think in there for about five and a half minutes and still get on the correct bus.

The hidden flaw in that plan is that hardware stores is interesting. A guy might plan on five minutes, but if he ain't strict with himself he'll look up three hours later and wonder why it's dark outside and there's no more buses. I told myself I was on a case and had to pay attention. I didn't even look at crescent wrenches, since they always make me wonder how somebody come up with the idea to make the first one. I didn't look at drill bits or wood screws, and I got myself back to the bus stop right on time.

So here's what I was thinking. It wasn't a plan. A plan is like a puzzle where you figured out which pieces fit where and you just got to put them there. What I was thinking was the steps. It was like saying, OK, what pieces do I got, and are some of them straight on one side, and what are their colors, and then once you look at the picture on the box you can figure out how they fit together.

Holly was good with computer stuff. I could ask her to look murders of guys named Edward and Kit. That was one step.

Another step was I had a key to the professor's house. If I went there, maybe I could find the letter that proved his ideas. He seemed sure that was a big clue.

90

Third, I should go to the conference he mentioned, since maybe it had good clues, too.

All that should give me enough clues to decide who killed who and who was trying to put the blame on the professor. Then I'd tell somebody and they'd let the professor go free.

Once I done all that I could try to figure out who was trying to kill Tonto.

Then, if no one had found the professor's dog, I could ask him if he'd like to take care of Tonto. Even if his own dog had come home, maybe that dog and Tonto could be buddies.

I figured all these steps should take about two days.

I didn't see no hidden flaws, which you always got to look for.

Chapter Eight

I ain't gonna pretend I understand everything about microwaves. But sometimes you don't need to understand the whole thing to figure out one thing. A guy named Newton had an apple bonk him on the head, which a lot of people say is interesting. Mr. Newton didn't understand it all the way, but enough to figure out he'd be safer if he made his cookies out of figs, which is soft, instead of hard apples.

Microwaves is like that. Sometimes I get paid to clean out apartments when people move out. If their microwave is busted, they usually leave it behind. But sometimes they're easy to fix.

Lots of them have a little white fuse, about as thick as a pencil and an inch long. A bunch of screws hold the cover on the microwave, but once you take that off, the fuse pulls out of its little clip and you pop a new one in. It's like they planned on fuses breaking so they made them easy to change.

For a while, I had a nice little side business. I'd spend pocket change on a fuse. If it worked, I'd sell the oven for twenty bucks and everybody was happy. It's what they call capitalism.

Obviously, I'd bought some fuses at the hardware store yesterday. I only had a couple of jobs on my list as Orderly Number Ten, so I figured I'd have plenty of time to do my jobs plus fix the microwave in the cafeteria. Then I'd go to the professor's house and do some detecting. I wore old jeans with lots of white paint on them and a white T-shirt. I put a white baseball cap and my good jeans in my backpack. Since painters mostly paint walls white, they like to wear white clothes. To do my orderly job, I'd change into my good jeans and a green orderly shirt, but then I'd change back into jeans with paint on them. If you was surveying the hospital, you wouldn't see Orderly Number Ten leave the hospital. Only a painter.

I didn't recognize anybody who was working in the cafeteria that morning. There was only about six nurses eating donuts and drinking coffee.

"Somebody here report a broke microwave?" I said pretty loud.

93

The lady at the cash register looked surprised.

"Have the End Times arrived?" she said. "It's only been two months."

"I don't know what time it is," I said. "I ain't got a watch and I don't know when End Times comes on anyway, since I never heard of that show. But if it ain't time to look at that microwave, I won't complain. I'll just check off my list that I tried and go to my next job."

Now, I was dressed like a painter, not a guy who fixes stuff. But people don't pay close attention to stuff that don't matter to them. If some engineer was dressed like a computer salesman, nobody'd notice. Good disguises look ordinary. People don't even know they're disguises. My disguise of a white T-shirt and baseball cap plus jeans with paint on them was working as good as a pink tuxedo and Abraham Lincoln hat. Which them nurses would of thought was a disguise the first time they looked at it.

The cash register lady took me over to the microwave.

"I ain't making promises," I said. "I only said I'd look at it."

"Fine with me," she said. "I'm tired of looking at it myself. Happy to let someone else have a turn."

I unplugged the microwave and set it on one of the little tables and started to unscrew the cover. Two nurses was sitting at a table about twelve feet away. One had dark hair, the other one had tan hair with some white hairs mixed in. They looked at me for a minute, decided that nothing about me was interesting, so they went back to talking like I wasn't in the room.

"I'm glad the cops took him away," the older one said. She was the one with some white hairs.

"Why?" the dark-haired younger one said. "He wasn't even conscious. Easy patient if you ask me."

"He's a murderer! It gave me the creeps knowing he was in the building."

94

"He was only a suspect. Why would he kill that scientist?"

"I've heard rumors."

"You can't convict someone based on rumors."

"I heard they had a fight."

"Not a fight. An argument in a bar over football. Old professors don't murder someone over an argument in a bar."

"No, it was more than that"

"What do you mean?"

"There was a treasure," the woman whispered so quiet I could hardly hear. I was going to ask them to talk louder, only that might give them the clue that I was listening to them.

"A treasure? That old coot?" They both giggled.

"Well, not a buried treasure of pirate gold. I heard the professor found some old papers. He was doing some really boring research and these papers fell out of the stuff he was looking at."

"That's not much of a treasure."

"Could be," she answered. "Maybe it was a treasure *map*. Or imagine finding a letter from George Washington to a girlfriend no one knew existed. Someone would pay a lot for that. Or a letter from Elvis. I think the old guy discovered something like that."

"Where did you come up with that crazy idea?"

"The professor was starting to come out of his coma the last week or two." She waited a second before she finished. "He talks in his sleep."

"And you happened to be on duty?"

"Yeah. But he mumbles and I couldn't make out much. Mitch, the guard, told me the cops searched his house but they didn't find it. I bet he and Isaac were going to sell it to the highest bidder. Maybe the professor didn't want to split the money. I don't know. But whatever he found, they thought it was a lot more important than a football game. And more valuable."

By now I'd took out the old fuse and put in the new fuse, put the cover back on, and had put all the screws back. I was going back and tightening each screw a little so it looked like I wasn't done. I wished it had been a slower job in case them nurses gave me more clues, but working slow seemed like cheating. I put the microwave back where it come from and plugged it in.

I went back to the nurses.

"It might be fixed," I said. "Could I borrow your coffee cup to try it?"

The younger woman nodded right away "Sure, mine's getting cold." She handed me her cup that was half full of coffee. I put it in the microwave, hit the button that says "add 30 seconds." Its light come on and it started to hum. Before you knew it, it dinged and I took out her half cup of hot coffee.

"Wow!" she said. "Thank you."

"No prob," I said. "It was a easy fix. I guess I better go now."

"Wait!" the lady at the cash register stopped me. "Do you know anything about refrigerators?"

"A little," I said. "Only my work order don't say nothing about refrigerators. I don't want to get in trouble with Nurse Helga."

The lady smiled. "Helga is the one who complains her lunch doesn't stay cold enough."

"I don't know…"

"Listen. Sergeant-Major Helga doesn't need to know. Plus I've got a big slice of warm apple pie with ice cream on top for whoever can fix the darn thing."

About then the refrigerator started to seem interesting.

"What's it doing?"

"The freezer part gets cold, but the refrigerator part stays too warm no matter how much we adjust the controls."

OK, that gave me a good clue about the refrigerator, which was like a regular house refrigerator. They probably had a big restaurant fridge someplace for the cafeteria food and the patient food. I wouldn't mess with one of them. This was for the people who worked there to keep their lunch cold. It looked about as old as the one in my apartment and in all the other apartments I clean, so it wasn't a big mystery to me. And I ain't had any apple pie in a long time. Plus, I could fool with it for a while and maybe them two nurses would keep talking and give me more clues about the professor's case.

"It's probably the fan motor," I said. "Did it make some weird sounds?"

"It did for a while. Kind of a rattling sound but now it doesn't do anything."

I could of said they should try a couple easy things first. Clean the dust off the little copper pipes on the back. They get hot so the fridge can get cold. If dust covers them, they don't work as good, but lots of smart people don't know that. Second is to make sure nothing's blocking the cold air from getting from the freezer to the fridge. Most fridges only cool the freezer part and then blow air through an opening to the fridge. If you pile stuff in front of that opening, either inside the freezer part or the fridge part, the fridge won't get cold. That should be the first lesson in the class of "stuff to know if you own a fridge" but lots of people skipped that class.

But since they said it made noise before it stopped, I had a bad feeling. There's a little fan that blows air from the freezer into the fridge. If some ice got stuck on the fan it would bang around until the fan motor burned out and stopped. It ain't that big a deal to put in a new fan, but you got to buy one first, which I had not done. I could at least tell them if that was the problem.

The most honest thing would be to tell them to do the easy stuff themself. Only I was on a case, so I started doing the easy stuff without saying nothing. I didn't take off no bonus points on myself for rule-bending on being honest. Cheating is the opposite of playing Doctor Hudson. When you cheat, you try to get something for yourself without anybody knowing about it. When you play Doctor Hudson, you try to help somebody else when there ain't nothing in it for you. But you still don't want anybody to know about it. Keeping it secret is the only thing cheating has the same with playing Doctor Hudson.

You could say I was cheating a little, only I wasn't charging them and the hospital wasn't paying me so it didn't seem so bad. I pulled the refrigerator away from the wall and unplugged it. Them two nurses was still talking.

"So, where is this mysterious treasure?"

The other one leaned closer. "It's in the last place they'll look," she said. "That's what he said in his sleep."

Well, that got my attention, so I kept listening while I fooled with the refrigerator. There was a bunch of frost inside the freezer part, so I left its door open to melt it. While the frost was melting, I took a wet paper towel and cleaned dust off the little pipes in the back.

"I thought you said it was at his house."

"Yeah, he said that too. Maybe he's crazy."

By the time I got all the dust cleaned off the pipes, the frost was a little softer. The blades on the little fan had some ice stuck to them. That was the big problem. The ice chunks was keeping the fan from turning so cold air wasn't getting pushed from the freezer to the fridge. Maybe the fan motor got burned up, but you couldn't tell without plugging it in. Inside the fridge I could see the reason the fan got iced up. Somebody had stacked a bunch of little take-out boxes right in front of the opening where cold air was supposed to come out. That stopped the air from getting into the fridge, which made the freezer motor work harder and all that frost built up. If the fan was burned up, they'd need a new one, but at least they could tell their repair guys what to fix. No way to tell until we plugged it back in.

I got a clean paper towel, wet it with hot water and held it on the little chunks of ice until they come loose. Without the ice, I could turn the fan with my finger, which is a good sign. So I was done with the stuff I knew how to do, but I kept fooling around for a few minutes pretending I was doing stuff. Them nurses was still talking.

"What else did you hear?

"I think they were going to give a talk or something. Maybe tell the audience about their big secret. I think it was this weekend."

"Where?"

"No idea."

The two nurses got up and left. That wasn't much clues and they never mentioned a dog even once. But a good detective takes the clues he got and not just the ones he wished he'd got. I plugged the fridge back into the wall. The little fan started spinning right away. I had to smile at that. I closed its door and pushed it back against the wall.

"OK, ma'am," I told the lady at the cash register "I think we got lucky this time."

"It's fixed?"

"There wasn't much fixing, but I think it will work now. Maybe put a little sign in there so people don't pile their stuff by the cold air tunnel." I opened the door and showed her. "That's where the cold air comes in."

"Incredible!" she said. "You sit down at one of these tables and I'll get you that pie."

"Thanks, but could I get it some other time? I got appointments."

"Whenever you want. Thank you so much."

"Just doing my job, ma'am," I said and then I left. Saying I had appointments wasn't the whole truth and nothing but the truth. I just had some other stuff I wanted to do.

The thing I wanted to do is go to the professor's house. That was the main reason I wore my painter-guy disguise.

I only had about three chores on the schedule board, so I did them quick and then left before Nurse Helga could give me more assignments. I took a bus to the street the professor's house was on. It stopped about three and a half blocks from the house. Before I started walking I took my painter cap out of my backpack and put it on. I also took out the clipboard I got from the thrift store. I already put some of the papers I got at the thrift store under the clip to make it look official. They was blank forms with boxes to fill in, which was perfect.

"*So far as any one knows and can prove, Shakespeare of Stratford wrote only one poem during his life. This one is authentic. He did write that one—a fact which stands undisputed; he wrote the whole of it; he wrote the whole of it out of his own head. He commanded that this work of art be engraved upon his tomb, and he was obeyed. There it abides to this day. This is it:*"

Good friend for Iesus sake forbeare
To digg the dust encloased heare:
Blest be ye man yt spares thes stones
And curst be he yt moves my bones.

"*In the list as above set down, will be found every positively known fact of Shakespeare's life, lean and meagre as the invoice is. Beyond these details we know not a thing about him. All the rest of his vast history, as furnished by the biographers, is built up, course upon course, of guesses, inferences, theories, conjectures—an Eiffel Tower of artificialities rising sky-high from a very flat and very thin foundation of inconsequential facts.*" —Mark Twain 1909

Chapter Nine

The professor's house was in a really nice neighborhood. All the houses was small but they was made of bricks. Everybody had a neat yard with some big trees and bushes and different kinds of flowers in front. The little flower beds probably told you stuff about the owners if you knew about the flowers. One house had a bunch of red rose bushes, another one had a patch of yellow tulips. One had hollyhocks and daisies. They wasn't all blooming, since flowers got their own schedules for blooming, but it was easy to see how they'd look when it was their turn to bloom. If you pictured them all blooming, it was like walking through the Denver Botanic Gardens which has got more flowers than a big wedding. Three houses had little vegetable gardens with a couple of tomato plants and some basils and some other plants I ain't learned yet.

I walked up the six concrete steps to the front porch. The house roof covered the porch so several people could sit on it even if it was raining. There was two pots of geraniums but their dirt was dry and the plants looked about ready to die. I was looking around for something to water them with when this lady come running from across the street, waving her arms over her head to get my attention.

"Who are you?" she yelled. "What are you doing here?"

She was maybe fifty years old and more on the heavy side than the athlete side. She stopped to get her breath, putting her hands on her knees and breathing hard. When she caught her breath she asked again. "What are you doing here?"

"Hello, ma'am," I said. "Nothing to worry about. Just a routine inspection."

"Are you with the police?"

I laughed a little at that.

"Do I look like a policeman?" I asked her, which wasn't a lie since it was a question. I learned that trick from watching politicians on TV. But I didn't wait for her to answer. "Nah, they don't send out officers for a routine inspection. If there's a gas leak and the whole place explodes, they don't want to lose official officers. Just guys like me. But then an officer wouldn't even notice these plants look sad. You ain't smelled any gas leaks, have you?'"

"No, but... "

"Well, if you do, don't try to fix it yourself."

You could tell she still thought I was suspicious.

"What exactly are you inspecting?" she said.

"It will all be in the final report," I said. "Which I should probably start on. Them geraniums can wait a few minutes more." I took a pencil out of my pocket and started writing on the clipboard.

"Now, ma'am, what's your name again?"

"I'm Jane Johnson," she said. "But you didn't answer..."

"And where do you live?"

She was surprised I was asking her questions. She pointed across the street and said her address.

"Have you seen any suspicious activity on the street?"

"What do you mean?"

"Like strange cars. Maybe a black pickup truck?"

"Now that you mention it, there was a black pickup truck the day after the...the incident. It was driving real slow."

"Did you report it?"

"A pickup truck driving slow? It didn't seem important."

"Yeah, most stuff ain't all that important 'til you think about it. You reported it now and that's what counts. The department will be very grateful for all your help."

"Can I go now?" she asked, which surprised the heck out of me. I wasn't making her stand there and talk to me. The good news is, she probably wasn't going to call the cops on me.

"Of course," I said. "Would you put your initial next to your name here so I can prove I talked to you?"

She took the pencil and initialed by her name. Then she looked at the form and frowned,

"This form is from the Health Department," she said.

I didn't know what to say about that. I ain't never actually read a form they made me initial, so I hadn't thought about the idea that somebody else would.

So I said, "What?"

She looked suspicious.

"This form is from the Health Department."

Having Health Department forms while I was dressed like a painter was a hidden flaw in my plan, but I thought quick.

"Yeah, the big shots like to save money so we all got to share our forms. Personally, I think homicide ought to have its own forms."

"That's outrageous!" she said.

"Tell me about it! If more citizens like you wrote letters to their council guy… OK forget I said that. We ain't supposed to say political stuff while we're working."

105

"Well, I surely will write a letter! And I won't say anything about you complaining."

"Thank you, Mrs. Johnson. If we have more questions we'll be in touch. But I really need to start my inspection." I put the professor's key in the door, unlocked it, and pushed it open a few inches. Mrs. Johnson was still standing there watching.

"I'm sorry," I said. "We can't let any civilians in. Crime scene, you know."

She looked disappointed but turned and walked away.

Inside the house it was dark since all the curtains was closed tight. I turned on a light and looked around.

It was a cool old house, with tall ceilings and wood floors. Bright colored rugs covered the wood in the middle of rooms. Some of the doorways had curved tops, like the outside of a watermelon slice after you eat the pink part. There was some lamps with stained glass covers and when I turned them on they looked cool. The walls was mostly an off-white color, like maybe Antique White, which I painted some apartments with when people moved out after their kids had colored pictures on the walls with crayons. The walls wasn't as smooth as modern walls made from drywall sheets, so they was probably plaster walls. When you clean apartments and sometimes paint them, you notice stuff like that even if it ain't important clues. But that ain't the main thing I noticed.

The house was a total mess, like a hurricane blew through it. The cushions for the couch was all thrown on the floor. Several walls had book shelves, but all the books was on the floor and open like someone threw them there. One book looked interesting. It was called The Oxford Book of Short Poems. One reason nobody likes poems is that they keep going on even after I'm done reading them. Short poems is a good idea. There wasn't no clues hid in the book but I thought, hey, maybe the professor would like something to read in jail or in the hospital. I ain't a big book reader, but some guys are and if you had to read poems, you obviously want short ones. I shoved the book into my backpack to give him. It might be a crime to take anything away but it didn't seem like a real big crime. Maybe I'd have to take my consequences, but if someone made a big deal out of it I'd give the book back, since there wasn't much chances I'd fall in love with reading it.

All the light switch covers was unscrewed and threw on the floor. If the cops done that, it was smart detecting, I thought. About the last place I'd hide something was inside a wall behind a light switch. If I ever wanted to hide something, that would be a good place, except now I knew the cops would find it anyway so I crossed it off my list of good hiding places.

Some pictures had been took off the wall and threw on the floor. The ones that had glass fronts had their glass broke and the picture pulled partway out.

One picture on the floor was of that Raiders football coach that everybody in Denver hated, since they beat the Broncos a lot of times and they don't play fair and they got ugly cheerleaders. This was a picture of their coach from a few years ago, that fat one who drove his motorhome to games since he was afraid of airplanes.

But why would a Denver Broncos fan have a picture of an old Raiders coach? Maybe it was a clue. I picked it up off the floor. When I seen it closer I could tell it probably wasn't a clue. It wasn't a picture on paper, it was a dartboard of cork with the picture printed on it. The old fat coach had plastic eyes with a brown ball inside each one. If you hit the board with a dart, the eyes would google-eye all over the place and look goofy. It would be fun to hit that coach in the nose with a dart. If I got to talk to professor Reginald again, I'd ask him where he got it since maybe one would look good on my wall too.

The back of the dartboard was smooth cardboard with a hook for putting it on the wall. It didn't take long to figure out where it was supposed to hang. There was a fireplace with a big blank spot next to it and a nail in the wall about the right height for a dartboard. The wall was covered in little dart holes. Most of them was right beneath the nail, where the coach's face went. If the professor's friend who was a Raiders fan ever come to visit it would be funny watching his face every time a dart hit the coach's nose or ear. I hung the dartboard up there and it looked cool. When I tapped it with my finger the old coach's googly eyes went every way they could and he looked like a idiot.

I took it back down and put it on the floor where I found it. Even if it wasn't a good clue, it was interesting, like them red hair rings Jim says is in old Perry Mason TV shows. Those are extra clues to make everybody guess wrong before we figure out who done the crime. I gotta admit, I never seen any hair rings on the show so maybe Jim was joking on me.

I looked in every room and in every drawer and on every shelf but I didn't find clues about a treasure letter. In the kitchen there was a tall refrigerator with a big freezer side. The name said it was a smart refrigerator. I think mine is a dumb refrigerator since it only knows how to go on or off. Sometimes I hide stuff in my freezer, inside frozen liver. The cops must of already thought of that, since it was all the way empty. If the professor hid his treasure letter in there, it was down at headquarters thawing out.

The inside of the fridge was interesting, even if it was empty. I never seen so many little lights and buttons before. It was about as fancy as the bridge of the Starship Enterprise. I almost said "beam me aboard, Scotty" but I didn't know what a really smart refrigerator would do if I said that. About the last thing I wanted was to land on some planet with dinosaur people, especially if they had lunch stored in that fridge and thought I ate it.

I closed the refrigerator door.

There was three bedrooms. The first one was the biggest. It had a bed and a dresser and a table next to the bed and a TV on the wall. The mattress was partway off, so the cops must of looked under there. The dresser drawers was all open and the clothes was on the floor. The clothes in the closet had all been took out and threw on the bed. The cops probably already checked all the shirt pockets but I checked them again anyway.

The TV was hung on the wall, but I could pull the bottom of it away enough to see there wasn't no secret treasure papers back there. There was some pictures in frames, but they was on the floor like the living room pictures. The cops had searched their hardest, since they even took all the pictures down. Then I thought, hey maybe it wasn't the cops doing the searching. Maybe it was the murderer. And maybe he was still watching the house. I decided to search a little faster. My ankle was almost healed, it only hurt when I took a step. But I ain't done any practice jumping since I hurt it and I couldn't of run my fastest if someone was chasing me. But then I thought, hey, I got nothing the murderer might want. No treasure maps and no good clues. A murderer might watch me in case I come up with good clues or even hair rings, but it would be dumb to do much to me and give theirself away.

I decided to search a little faster anyway.

The other two bedrooms was smaller. One had a bed and that's about it. It was probably the guest bedroom. The third bedroom didn't have a bed in, just a desk and chair and file cabinet. The file cabinet was empty. The cops took all the files to headquarters so they could check for clues and evidence.

The top of the desk had a calendar you could write appointments on. The professor didn't write out whole words, he gave himself reminder clues. One Sunday said "DB-SD early." Well that one was obvious and you probably figured it out as quick as me. The Denver Broncos was playing San Diego in the early game. Another was on a Monday "DB-KC-MNF" which was the Broncos playing Kansas City on Monday Night Football. One I couldn't figure out so easy was "I-noon-SCC." That was a stumper. I don't know why a Broncos fan would write down when Indianapolis played, but it's the only team I could think of. I don't pay much attention to college football, but there's several teams that could be "I," like Iowa or Idaho or Illinois. Thinking about the SCC part, I know one of the college conferences is the SEC and maybe that's what he meant to write. I wrote down the professor's notes on my clipboard.

There's good clues and bad clues and you can't tell which is which. A good detective don't play favorites with his clues, he lets 'em all play in the front yard and run through the sprinklers. Maybe one will start squealing and

109

waving his hands over his head shouting "Look at me! Look at me!" A good detective notices stuff like that and takes an extra look at that clue.

But most of the time, clues is shy. You notice them when they peek around a corner but then keep on detecting.

I looked at all the spots I could think of. I checked inside a sack of flour and a sack of sugar. I looked under his flower pots and in a sack of bird seeds for his bird feeder. I went outside and opened the top of the bird feeder. I looked under the welcome mat by his front door. Someone had already took the screws out of his microwave and looked inside it. They didn't even bother to put it back together. I took the cover off his furnace and checked the filter. It was big enough to hide a treasure map but there wasn't one in there. The filter was dirty and if I wasn't on a case I would of changed it for him. Anyway, the cops might think that was tampering with a crime scene so I put the cover back on.

"OK, Professor," I said out loud, even though nobody else was there. "You're pretty good at hiding something."

I went through each room one more time, closing any door I opened, making sure it all looked the same as when I got there. Then I went out the front door, locked it behind me and looked around on the porch. Nothing was suspicious. I stood there for a minute in case any neighbors was watching. A guy leaving real quick might as well have criminal written all over his T-shirt. I pretended to make some notes on the clipboard.

There was a little metal mailbox on the wall next to the door. If a guy was inspecting someplace, he'd probably check the mailbox, so I did. There was several ads in there. Three was to "resident" and a couple to the professor. None of them was bills or Christmas cards so I would of put 'em back, but a real inspector would collect them and turn them into headquarters. The cops might think they had fingerprints or forensics on them to investigate. A neighbor might wonder how come I put them back, so I put them under the clip of the clipboard.

Before I left, I turned on the water hose and watered the geraniums. Maybe that ain't something an inspector would do so the neighbors might think it was suspicious. But then a crook probably wouldn't either.

I coiled the hose up again and left.

.

"The poets make fame a monster; they describe her in part finely and elegantly, and in part gravely and sententiously; they say, Look, how many feathers she hath, so many eyes she hath underneath, so many tongues, so many voices, she pricks up so many ears!" —Francis Bacon

Chapter Ten

Back home, I looked at the notes I took on the clipboard which was mostly pictures of little stick-figure guys. No lights come on in my brain.

The ads that was sent to "resident" wasn't interesting. But one of the ads might be a clue. It was an ad for a conference called "The Forensics of Shakespeare" and it was addressed to Professor Reginald. I'd been thinking about forensics, the dead guy was in the forensics business, and the professor liked old stuff that guys wrote back in the dark ages. Since he was a reading teacher, he might even like Shakespeare. I read the ad three times in case there was a clue in there. The conference was this next weekend at the Stapleton Conference Center which I never heard of. The price to go was about as much money as a month's rent in my building. But that price was if you wanted to go and learn stuff. They'd probably give a good deal to someone if he promised not to learn nothing.

A good detective would go to that conference and blend in so nobody knew he was a detective.

It might be hard to pretend I was a forensic scientist or a reading professor, which is the two kinds of people who was going to that conference, since I ain't a scientist and books ain't my favorite things. It was a hard decision. Book guys make up stuff all the time, but scientists got to get stuff perfect or else their rockets explode, so I decided I'd disguise myself as a professor like Professor Reginald. It was already Wednesday afternoon, so I only had about two days to figure out my plan for blending in. But it was getting dark out and I was hungry so I figured I could start tomorrow.

I took a can of soup out onto my balcony, sat on my apple crate, and listened to crickets singing to each other while I ate my soup. Crickets only got one song, but it always sounds brand new. The main thing I needed was clothes that looked like a professor. First thing tomorrow I'd go down to the thrift store and see what Jim had on sale.

The next thing I'd need is some good words. Everybody likes people that's like theirself. One good clue about that is their words. If a guy uses plumber words, another plumber would say, "that guy is just like me and the guys in my shop." Guitar players say words like "more volume in the monitor." Any guy who says that real loud is probably a good guitar player and even the drummer knows it. Guys with fancy jobs recognize each other by knowing the same fancy words. To fit in with college teachers I needed some college-guy words. If I had extra time, maybe I'd throw in a few forensic words, which I knew from TV shows. Lots of times TV forensics guys say "contaminating the evidence" or "chain of custody." Their favorite is saying "D and A." One TV guy asked, "what about the proteins?" and it kept the other guys busy through two commercials. I said that one to myself about eight times and decided to save it for an emergency.

Reading professors was harder since there ain't many shows about them. Maybe that book of short poems had some good professor words. Tomorrow I'd read as much as I could before it made me fall asleep. Maybe I'd try to remember some poem words from it.

I didn't see no hidden flaws in that plan.

xxx

In the morning I fed Mr. Silver some bird seeds and read some of the poems to him. They didn't make much sense, since they was old, but Mr. Silver didn't care. I never seen a person or bird who was as mad as Mr. Silver all the time. His last owner never taught him manners. It would of been a quieter conversation if I practiced with Mortimer instead, only I didn't think of it. Mr. Silver squawked and cussed the whole time. Today I didn't even try to argue with him. I answered him with poem words so I could get them in my brain stronger. If I could say some poem words the guys at the conference would think I was supposed to be there. It would be like a disguise. Plus, any college words Mr. Silver learned would be an improvement even if the poems didn't make sense. The bird might be a nicer roommate if he was quacking out poems instead of naughty sailor sayings.

"Here's one you might like," I told him. "It's called the Ogre."

Mr. Silver shrieked and flapped, obviously insulted that he had schoolwork. "Your mother was a rotting seal!" he shouted out.

"The ogre does what ogres can," I told him back. "Deeds quite impossible for man."

"Worms'll eat your eyeballs!" he answered. "Worms'll eat your eyeballs!"

"They wrote this part just for you: drivel dribbles from his lips. OK, I ain't sure what that means but I bet you got drivel dribbling from your beak, too."

"Sheets for brains!" he screeched. "Sheets for brains!"

This was about the best conversation I ever had with Mr. Silver.

"How do you like your blue-eyed boy, Mr. Death?"

"Put it on a cracker!"

"Not even the rain has such small hands."

"Jesus mother flock and Mary!"

There was too many poem words for me to remember, especially since none of them made any more sense than Mr. Silver. But some parts of them sounded cool so I practiced saying them without the book. After about a half hour I figured I sounded like a college guy. But I also wanted some college-guy clothes in case my poem words didn't fool someone all the way, so I went down to the thrift store.

Jim was working today. "Hey, Jumper," he said "You still on the case?"

"Yes sir, Jim. I'm pretty much always on a case. I'm going to a meeting of college teachers so I want to look like one. I'm here to shop for that disguise. If you got something that makes me look like a Nobel prize winner, maybe I can use it at Halloween, too."

Jim thought for a minute. "I think these days college teachers wear whatever they want."

"Yeah, I bet that's right since they got good jobs they can afford to look poor if they want. But they mostly don't look as poor as me."

Jim smiled. "OK, college casual is the look you want. Khaki pants, a shirt with buttons on the collar and a sports coat."

"That sounds fancy, but you're the expert. Can I wear my sneakers with that? You know, my best ones that you sold me a month ago?" I was sort of joking on him, since all my shoes is sneakers.

"Sure, as long as they're clean. Let's see what we got in your size."

Jim knew where everything was in the whole store. He grabbed some tan jeans off a rack without hardly looking at them, and then found a light blue shirt that looked brand new. He threw them both over his arm like he was helping a big movie star shop at a store in Hollywood and he was gonna make a big commission. Then he walked over to some jackets.

"I think we got a jacket that would be perfect for you," he said. The coats was mostly all brown and tan, with a few black ones and they all looked about the same to me. Jim looked through them until he found a special one he liked. He smiled like it was a rare bottle of wine for his best customer and pulled it out.

It was a darker color of tan than the jeans and was made of heavy cloth. What was cool about it was that it had leather patches on both elbows.

"I wonder what they done to wear out both elbows," I said.

"Nah," Jim said. "They make 'em like that brand new. I had a teacher once who had a coat like this. Why don't you try on the whole outfit?"

"OK," I said. I took the clothes into the trying-on room. I walked out wearing them and Jim nodded his head.

"Yeah, that's a smart look," he said. Then he told me the price for all of them together which was a good deal.

"Smart is the disguise I was going for," I said. "I'll take 'em."

"You're not going someplace dangerous, are you?"

"Nah. It's a meeting of college teachers like Professor Reginald. It ain't like they're cut-throating drug dealers."

Jim nodded and thought for a minute.

"Except one of them might be a murderer."

"Yeah, but he ain't got good reasons to kill me. The cops'd notice that right away plus he'd blow his cover. Anyway," I said. "I'll be in my new college teacher disguise."

"Well, you be careful just the same."

"Yes, sir," I said.

The next morning I woke up on my couch like every morning. I didn't get up right away, but pulled my cover up over my chin. Mortimer, my imaginary cat, was still sleeping right next to me, so I talked to him for a minute.

"We got a big day today, Mortimer," I said. "We got to pretend to be different from what we are, which ain't all that easy. You can come along if you want, only no scratching or yowling so I get distracted from my acting. But if you get some good ideas, you should say 'em to me and not wait 'til we're home later and they don't do me no good. OK? Thanks."

I ain't ever talked to other people about Mortimer, but I think most people has imaginary cats they talk to, just like me. I won't hold it against somebody if they ain't got their own Mortimer. I'd just be sad for them since they're probably lonely and don't even know it.

I got up and put on my new clothes and combed my hair back from my forehead. In my light-blue shirt with buttons, and tan-colored jeans, and a sports coat with leather patches on the elbows, and my hair wet down and combed back I hardly recognized myself in the mirror. I put my backpack on over the coat. It didn't fit so good, so I loosened the straps and then it was OK. I practiced some of my poetry words, only this time to Mortimer instead of Mr. Silver. My cat liked them better than the dumb parrot had, which made it easier to practice. Then I left my apartment.

My apartment is on the third floor so there was three sets of stairs from my floor down to the street level. Each set of steps had one landing about halfway down it. I usually run up and down the steps skipping some and then jumping down to each landing from four or five steps up for practice. But I'd been really careful like Holly told me so I wouldn't hurt my ankle worse. I gotta admit, walking down them one at a time felt weird. It was like somebody told me, "OK, Jumper. Yesterday you was an ordinary guy who liked to run and climb trees and jump off of stuff. But today you're an old guy and that's a disease you can't ever get over. You got to walk slow and be careful and don't skip any rules. Most of all, you got to stop jumping."

But even if somebody tells you you're an old guy you maybe got some votes about it too. My ankle felt fine for several days and there wasn't someone in the stairway watching me to keep score. Maybe just one little baby jump, I thought.

I stopped going down the second set of stairs when there was three steps left before the landing. I stood there for a second to make sure my ankles felt perfect. Then I bent my knees to crouch a little. I took a deep breath. It felt good to be about to jump again.

"Just what do you think you're doing?" A woman's voice stopped me cold.

"Oh!" I said. "You surprised me, Holly. I didn't know you was there. You must of been practicing up on your quiet Indian-walking."

"I thought I told you not to do any jumping until your ankle healed."

118

"Well, the whole truth is, I ain't jumped once since you said that."

"And the 'nothing but the truth' part is you were just about to."

OK, so she Perry Masoned me into a corner. There ain't much use arguing with Holly once she starts to Perry Mason a guy. Then I remembered my new secret weapon. I decided to try some poem-words on her.

"All the black same I dance my blue head off." I said it kind of loud, as if it made sense.

"What?"

There wasn't no good answer to that one, so I said the blue head line again.

"Are those new clothes cutting off the blood to your brain?"

"Cloudy, cloudy is the stuff of stones," I said.

Holly stared at me and shook her head. Her pony tail swung back and forth. She'd forgot all about cross examining me and was wondering if I'd went crazy. That was a bonus to using poem words I never seen coming. Holly shook her head some more, then turned and walked down the hallway to her apartment.

I walked down the last three steps to the landing and started walking down the last bunch of steps to the ground floor. When I was three steps from the bottom I stopped and looked around again. Nobody was there, so I jumped. My ankle didn't hurt at all, so I went back up to the fifth step and jumped from there.

OK, a five-step jump ain't a big deal for a guy who practiced jumping every day his whole life. But even a baby jump feels cool if you been thinking you're an old guy with a bunch of extra rules.

"Thanks, Mortimer," I whispered. "That was a good idea."

Once I knew I could jump I didn't feel as much need to actually jump. After that second baby jump I walked out the front door and headed down the sidewalk to the bus stop.

"So I the pleasant grape have pulled from the vine;
And yet I languish in great thirst, while others drink the wine"
— Edward de Vere

Chapter Eleven

I had to take a regular bus to the main bus station and then get on a whole different bus to the Stapleton Convention Center. While I was riding along, watching cars on the road beside the bus and watching people on the bus, my brain went to solving clues.

I still didn't have a good idea about the professor's note that said "I-noon-SCC." If the 'I' was for Isaac, the dead guy, then maybe the professor was going to meet him at noon someplace. It reminded me of the great TV detective called Columbo. That's show is about as old as the Pilgrims, but it came on a station the cable guy set me up to watch for free, so I got to watch him investigating a lot of murders. If Columbo was on this case, he would have just one more question: why would you write a guy on your calendar if you was going to kill him before that day? That's a clue that the professor wasn't the murderer. And if he wasn't the murderer they should let him go. Then he could meet Tonto and maybe we'd all live happily ever after.

But what did SCC mean? I went through every football team I could think of. Then I went through every store I knew and every park and as many restaurants and bars as I could remember. Maybe it's a TV show, I thought, and they was going to watch it together. After I got home from this conference I'd use my whole brain on figuring it out.

The main Denver airport used to be called Stapleton until they built an even bigger one far away from town. When Stapleton was an airport, there was a bunch of hotels close to it and some of them did conferences. The Stapleton Convention Center was one of them old hotels.

I walked through the front door into a big lobby with nice carpet and really good air conditioning, which fancy places have. Cheap old hotels on Colfax Street use swamp-cooler air conditioning which make the air nice and cool but it smells like wet towels. Most of the old bars I ever went to had swamp coolers and they all smelled like that. I breathed in cool air that didn't have a smell and for a minute I was afraid people could tell I wasn't used to

Shakespeare of Stratford

Christopher Marlowe

"Yes, trust them not: for there is an upstart crow, beautified with our feathers, that with his tiger's heart wrapt in a players hide, supposes he is as well able to bombast out a blank verse as the best of you: and being an absolute jack-of-all-trades is, in his own conceit, the only Shake-scene in a country. Oh that I might intreat your rare wits to be employed in more profitable courses. Let those apes imitate your past excellence, and nevermore acquaint them with your admired inventions."

—Robert Greene, from his pamphlet "Greene's Groat's Worth of Wit" 1592

Edward de Vere
17ᵗʰ Earl of Oxford

Francis Bacon

this fancy a place. I almost went back outside to wait for the next bus back home.

Then I remembered my shirt had buttons and my coat elbows had leather patches so I was looking fancy myself. Maybe those college teachers was afraid they wasn't good enough either, especially if they wore the wrong clothes.

There was a guy behind a long counter. He looked bored so I asked him where the college teacher conference was.

"All the information should be in the registration package they sent you," he said without looking up. Not answering me was him saying he knew something I didn't, and it was my fault, like he was the teacher and I was the dumb student who should of read the registration packet since that was the assignment. Only I couldn't since I didn't get one. Not answering made him feel smarter. I didn't say nothing for a while since I already asked my question. The guy looked down at the counter and pretended to do stuff.

I wasn't sure how poem words worked exactly, but I figured hey, what the heck? I leaned forward so my face was closer to him.

"Which in the world is upside down, the fish hook or the question mark?" I said as serious as I could, like it was just as true as saying 'it's raining outside' or 'I like ice cream.' And then I waited for him to say something.

The look on his face changed right away. Instead of him being the smart guy who knew all the answers, now I was a guy saying stuff he didn't get. He didn't like that. He stared at me, waiting for me to explain some more, but I used my right to remain silent. I looked at him hard, imagining my eyes was laser lights burning into his forehead. I waited for him to get the point, even if I wasn't sure what it was.

"Yes, sir," he said. "It's right down that hallway. Just follow the signs."

"Thank you," I said. "I'll tell your boss you done a good job."

"Thank you, sir," he said. He sounded relieved I wasn't going to get him in trouble with his boss.

That was a good lesson. If you say something that don't mean nothing, people might think you're dumb. Or, they might wonder if they're the one who's dumb, in case you know stuff they don't know. I ain't ever tried saying stuff that don't mean anything and pretending it did. Maybe football announcers do that. What if 'giving one hundred and ten percent' ain't fancy math after all and don't really mean anything? Since I always feel dumb around women, maybe I'd try some poem words as an experiment. But I only had a few and the first one that come into my brain was "the feelings you say you have, you don't have." Maybe that wasn't my best choice, so I decided to think about it some more.

I walked across the lobby to the hall he pointed at. There was a sign that said "Forensic Literature" with an arrow that pointed down the hall. At the end of the hall was two big wood doors with a sign on them that said the same thing. I pictured somebody inside the door taking attendance and checking off stuff from their list. I took my clipboard out of the backpack to look extra-smart before I went in.

Once I seen the people in that room I got more comfortable about blending in. There was guys from other countries in turbans and robes and women that was dressed like nuns and guys with long hair in jeans and T-shirts that looked as scraggly as me. You can't tell about smart guys. Some guy who looks like a hobo might have just discovered gravity on the moon or something. Einstein was pretty smart even if he never learned how to comb his hair. He would fit in here easy.

Like I had guessed, there was a long table with two ladies sitting behind it. They was probably about forty years old with some gray hairs. Their clothes was neat and clean with no wrinkles, like they ironed them today.

They both smiled at me.

"Welcome to the conference," the first one said. "If you pre-registered we should have your name tag right here. Last name?"

"It's Cable, but I ain't pre registered. I just wanted to talk to..." I paused and looked down at the clipboard as if I didn't know who I wanted to talk to. "A professor Reginald. Where could I find him?"

The lady's smile faded away. "Oh, dear," she said. "Haven't you heard? It's been in the newspaper for a week."

"What happened?"

"There was a poisoning incident. Professor Reginald has been in the hospital."

"That's terrible," I said and tried to sound surprised. "Is he OK? I come a long way..." Which was the truth the way I thought about it. Taking two different buses to get someplace was a long way compared to most of my trips. A "long way" could mean one thing if you just come from the moon on a rocket ship and it could mean a different thing if you just come from Nebraska or Boulder. It ain't a lie if someone had their own idea about long trips.

"They say he's recovering. We've had reporters from all over the country asking about him. What paper did you say you were with?"

Obviously I hadn't said a newspaper I was with. Maybe this was another time to try poem words.

"Where peat hags gape too black."

She stared at me for a minute, then her face brightened up. "Ah," she said. "That must be New Orleans. Shall I put down the Times-Picayune?"

Sometimes it's smart to not answer a question, especially since anything you say would be wrong.

"Is there someone else I could talk to?"

The two women looked at each other.

"He was working with Isaac Goldfarb. But he's..."

"He's the guy who got murdered," the other one said.

I shook my head. "I don't write about murders."

"It's just as well," the first woman said. "Plenty of reporters only interested in the scandal."

"Sure," I said. "I just want to know about his work."

OK, so that ain't the whole truth and nothing but the truth. But he was interested in the murder of somebody named Kit, which might have something to do with his professor-work, which might help me with my dog mystery, so that seemed like a good place to start.

"Doctor Goldfarb's assistant Suzanne Smith is here. She works with traditional forensics; fingerprints, DNA, that sort of thing. Most of our attendees are more interested in linguistic forensics. You know, the clues about provenance one can extract from the lexicon of a work. I'm afraid her erudite display won't have much traffic; she might be happy to talk to you. Or to anyone. She's at table number 203. Last row, back against that wall."

Obviously this lady was using poem words right back at me. I tried to remember more lines from the book.

"Where the toad lives on starlight," I said. "Where eagles would explode."

"Exactly," she said. "Yes, her table is a bit out of the way. Here, take this press pass." She handed me a name tag on a string to hang around my neck.

"Thanks," I said and put the name tag on. "I promise I won't learn too much since I'm just a visitor."

Suzanne Smith didn't look like most of the forensic guys on TV shows. She was maybe 35 years old and looked nice for a lady that old. Her hair was short and blonde, her face was tan, and she looked athletic, like maybe she swam a few laps in a pool every morning. She had on a silky, milk-colored blouse and a dark blue jacket and pants. Her table had about twenty stacks of brochures about science stuff, which she was moving around so they'd be really neat. A big-screen TV hanging on the wall behind her showed pictures of things you'd see in a microscope. The picture changed about every six seconds. There was a little stack of business cards on the table so I picked one up. It said "Suzanne Smith, PhD microbiological investigations."

She looked at me when I done that and sort of smiled. It was a nice smile, but kind of sad, like her brain wasn't really in the mood for smiling right now. Maybe she could already tell I couldn't afford to buy much forensics. She'd be polite but she wasn't going to waste her best salesman smile on me.

"Let me know if you have any questions," she said and went back to fixing her stacks of paper.

One thing I figured out is that people who write PhD after their name like it when you call them doctor.

"Doctor Smith," I said. "I was sorry to hear about your friend."

She nodded and half smiled again.

"Suzanne is fine," she said. "And thank you. Isaac... that is, Doctor Goldfarb was a fine scientist and a good man. We'll all miss him."

"Yeah, I think that's probably right." I waited a little bit since I didn't know exactly what I wanted to ask. This lady was obviously sad about her boss dying, so right away I figured she wasn't a suspect of interest. But she might know about the big secret her boss and Professor Reginald was working on. I decided she wasn't going to fall for poem words and asking her "what about the proteins" wouldn't help me much, especially if she actually answered it. I decided to ask her my main questions.

"My name is Jumper," I said. "And I ain't the best guy to ask science questions. I mean, I got a parrot-bird and I used to have a turtle and once I seen a dragonfly eat a bug. But that's probably easy stuff for you."

She smiled again. It was still a sad smile, but there was maybe a little Fourth of July sparkler at the edges of her eyes.

"Mr. Jumper, if you've watched a dragonfly eat a bug, you're way ahead of most of the English Literature professors at this conference as far as science is concerned. And I doubt any of them ever had a turtle. Now, how can I help you?"

"Well, I found a golden retriever dog named Tonto and was trying to find his home. I heard that Professor Reginald also lost a golden retriever. At first I thought Tonto might be his dog, but when I asked him he said no."

"You've talked with Professor Reginald?"

Right then I figured out maybe I said more than I planned to.

"Well, yeah. I thought if I didn't find Tonto's home and he didn't find his own Golden Retriever dog maybe they'd hit it off like old buddies. I can't have pets at my building..."

"When did you talk to him?"

Shoot, I thought. If the cops find out I was talking to their main suspect when they thought he was still asleep I'd be in a pickle. I only seen one way out.

"A graceful error may correct the cave," I said. I bet lawyers use poem words all the time to get out of pickles.

She laughed. "You've been talking to too many English Lit professors," she said. "In my branch of science we prefer facts to metaphors." She looked away for a minute but you could see her brain was thinking, like I'd asked her a riddle. "If he'd lost his dog, it was after the incident..." She thought some more. "After the incident, he was in the hospital. But he was unconscious...

Or at least that's what everyone thought." She looked at me harder. "Did you talk to him while he was in the hospital?"

I looked down at my sneakers.

"A guy might get in trouble if he talked to a suspect of interest before the cops could read rights at him..."

"The cops are idiots," she said and then she smiled a real smile at me as if I was about to order a dump-truck full of forensics from her. "Professor Reginald didn't murder Isaac. They were best friends. I'll never believe it. Not if they had a 99 percent DNA match and Perry Mason was an eye-witness."

That was about a perfect answer.

"Most people ain't heard of Perry Mason any more."

She nodded.

"Yes, that's probably right. When I was a girl I read all the old Perry Mason books."

"They made books out of his TV show?"

"Something like that. Now, how can I help you?"

"I ain't got much clues about Tonto the dog, or about the Professor's dog, but I bet the murder case has some clues. Sometimes questions is about as good as clues even if some of them is hair rings. My three best questions is first, what does "I-noon-SCC" mean? And what was the job them two guys was working on? And number three is why is somebody trying to kill Tonto?"

She nodded slowly.

"You know, Mr. Jumper, the cops should be asking those three questions. Are you sure you're not with the FBI?"

"Not yet," I said but I knew she was joking on me. "I think they got rules."

She nodded again.

"The easy one is I-noon-SCC. Professor Reginald and Isaac were supposed to give a talk today at noon right here at the Stapleton Conference Center. SCC."

"A talk about what?"

"Their project. Who really wrote the plays ascribed to Shakespeare. They thought it was important, plus it would be great publicity for Isaac's company. We're about to go public."

"I bet Shakespeare wrote them."

"It's been a controversy for nearly 400 years. In 1920 the Looney theory was that Edward de Vere wrote them."

"Well, if it was a loony theory back then it probably still is."

"Thomas Looney was the name of the guy who came up with the theory. The actor named Shakespeare didn't have much education, yet the plays seem very educated. Looney wrote a whole book about his idea.

"Edward de Vere was the 17th Earl of Oxford, so he had a great education. Plus many of the events in Shakespeare's plays were things that actually happened to de Vere. We know what books he read and where he traveled. There are many Oxfordians at this conference."

"I bet Shakespeare wrote his own plays. Just since a guy ain't gone to a lot of school classes don't mean he's dumb."

"Of course not, and maybe you're right. People who have your opinion call themselves Stratfordians, since the actor named Shakespeare lived in the town of Stratford.

"Some writers prefer pseudonyms. They crave anonymity in their private lives. They play a role."

"Like William Shatner and Captain Kirk?"

"Exactly like that. Sometimes we remember the character's name, but not the actor's. Spock is more famous than Nimoy. Consider this: in a Star Trek movie, one actor plays young Spock and another actor plays older Spock. I think Shakespeare is like Spock, a character invented by writers."

"Shakespeare was a Vulcan?"

"No. I mean they hired an actor named William Shakespeare to pretend to be the playwright in public."

"If you were a guy named William Shakespeare, it would be an easy job to play a character named William Shakespeare."

"I suppose so. Some people think a writer named Christopher Marlowe invented the character. Others think Edward de Vere did. Dr. Reginald believed Marlowe and de Vere invented him together. And he thought Bacon joined them. I'd love to be a fly on that wall: imagine it: Marlowe, de Vere and Bacon with quills flying!"

I started to say I don't like flies on my bacon, but I didn't. If you ain't sure you understand stuff exactly, it's smarter to keep your mouth shut. I learned that lesson about a thousand times.

"Over a hundred years ago, Mark Twain thought the Stratfordians were fools. To him, the idea of an uneducated actor blossoming into 'Shakespeare' was far-fetched and based on flimsy evidence, like a reconstructed dinosaur in a museum. He said the actor named Shakespeare was a Brontosaur: nine bones and six hundred barrels of plaster of Paris."

"I like Mr. Twain. He wrote about Mr. Huck Finn, which my dad read to me. Who did he think wrote the plays?"

"Twain was convinced Francis Bacon wrote them. Bacon was educated like de Vere; in fact, they grew up in the same house, with the same teacher. Bacon knew more science and, because he was a lawyer, he knew much more about the law. Twain said the precision of Shakespeare's legal references was proof enough. People who think like Twain call themselves Baconians.

"Others think Christopher Marlowe did. Those people call themselves Marlovians. Marlowe was much more poetic and imaginative with language than Bacon. He wrote some very popular plays, like Faustus. We know that Shakespeare re-wrote and refined at least four of Marlowe's plays. Marlovians say Bacon was far too rigid to produce the poetic lines of Shakespeare, but Marlowe was not. They've all got good reasons for their theories."

"Why wouldn't a guy want his own name on something? I bet Mr. Shakespeare got A pluses on all his homework. I'd want them grades on my permanent record."

"After what Coke did to Raleigh you'd be a fool to risk it."

"If he didn't like Coke, he should of switched to lemonade. That ain't even a brainer. I ain't ever heard of Marlowe except he had some cigarettes named after him which cowboys liked. Who did the professor think done the writing?"

"Professor Reginald thought that Marlowe faked his own murder and moved into Hackney House with de Vere under some phony name. He thought Bacon joined them and they wrote as a team."

"So they was like a committee," I said.

She smiled.

"Often, an assembled group sinks to the level of the least competent person. Committees can work like that. The smart ones have to dumb-down their vocabularies to accommodate the slower ones."

"Yeah, I seen that all the time."

"But when you get the smartest, most eloquent minds of their time together, sometimes something different happens. The whole group is better than any individual."

"Like a Super Bowl team?"

"Just like that."

"But nobody figured it out? That's weird."

"Haven't you ever done something and kept it a secret? I bet you have."

"Sure, that's the main rule of the Doctor Hudson game."

"I think these guys were smart enough to keep secrets. They re-wrote some of Marlowe's plays, addressed Bacon's favorite themes, and used incidents from de Vere's life. Isaac told me the professor had proof. Whatever their proof, it probably got Isaac killed."

"But Shakespeare lived a long time ago. Why would anybody care?"

"Shakespeare's name is still big business. There's an area in England that's famous for the Globe Theater where the plays were first performed. The restaurants have Shakespeare-themed meals, the hotel rooms are named after his characters. They still perform his plays there and sell souvenirs. It's a big tourist attraction."

"Like the bell museum in the mountains by Denver? My mom and dad took me there once when I was little. They had lots of bells, plus one big gong they let me hit. It was cool."

"Kind of like that," she said "but even bigger. Every year over eight million tourists visit the area because of Shakespeare. That's more than..." she stopped for a second to think of a good example. "That's more than the number of people who go to Denver Broncos games in a whole year."

Obviously, now she was just making stuff up to sound smart. But I didn't argue since telling her she was crazy might make her feel bad. Plus, she was a nice lady who I already liked.

"The professor was a Broncos fan," I said.

She nodded, then looked sad. "Yes he was. And Isaac was a Raiders fan. The cops think they got into an argument about football. Which they did every single week and twice a week during football season. But they were like an old married couple that squabbles about whose turn it is to take out the trash. It doesn't mean they stopped loving each other."

"Yeah, I don't think Professor Reginald killed him either. You must of worked with the victim a lot."

She nodded. "Yes, we were...very close."

The way she said it, there was more meanings right behind the words. Only I already knew Isaac was married to a whole different lady. That was a tennis ball I didn't want to chase into the tall weeds.

"So you say they had proof?" It was all I could think of to ask her about. I didn't care even a little bit about what guy called himself Shakespeare when he wrote plays. At the end of a TV show, when they show the credits, nobody cares whether it was wrote by Mr. Shakespeare or Mr. Bacon or Mr. Gilligan. Maybe they order MacBeth Chicken Nuggets in England, but giving food goofy names ain't much of a motive.

"Yes. A letter. That's about all I know."

"Do you think Isaac's wife would know more?"

She looked at me hard, like that idea made her mad. Then her face went back to normal. When she started talking again, she talked faster.

"No. That's one shrew that will never be tamed. He was divorcing her, he wouldn't share something like that with her. Which was fine with her. All she cared about was his income and his pension and his stock option in our company. The company built on Isaac's work and some of mine. No, she got what she wanted. She can retire comfortably as a merry widow. It's only the people who appreciated Isaac for what he was that are suffering. He was a smart, kind soul... but none of that matters to your investigation. I'm sorry I wasn't more help."

She brushed a tear from the corner of her eye and went back to neatening up brochures on the table as if really neat stacks could cure cancer or something.

In my brain I crossed Suzanne Smith off my list of alleged suspects. Then I thought of one more question. It made me feel like Columbo.

"Excuse me ma'am. I just have one more question." Saying that felt good and I seen why Columbo liked to do it.

"Yes?"

"The mystery of what guy wrote some plays might seem cool to college teachers. They'd look for clues by reading the words. They might say, OK this guy wrote with a southern accent only the real guy talked like Scotty on Star Trek. But Isaac used microscopes and blue lights and all the other stuff in these brochures. Why would he get interested in old plays?"

"Another good question. Maybe they thought they could find some physical evidence on the letter. I can't imagine what it might be. Maybe something about Marlowe's death."

"Thanks." I turned to leave and thought of another good question. Columbo only thought of his bonus questions after a commercial. I didn't have no commercials so I just asked it.

"What about a girl named Kit? Professor Reginald said something about faking Kit's murder."

She smiled again at that.

"Kit wasn't a girl. That's what his friends called Christopher Marlowe."

"The writer-guy you was just talking about? Why would somebody fake a murder on a writer-guy?"

"Back then you could get killed for liking the wrong religion, or the wrong politics. People thought Marlowe was a spy so he was already on shaky

135

ground. Then the police found an unpublished note questioning Jesus's divinity. Marlowe's former room mate, Thomas Kyd, told them the note was Marlowe's, probably after being tortured. The note was heresy, a very bad crime, and they issued an arrest warrant. Marlowe's enemies wanted him dead and that was all the excuse they needed. He needed to hide, but he couldn't hide and still release plays. Unless everyone thought he was dead and he wrote under a different name. It was the same problem de Vere had, except he was an Earl and had some money and position and a big house. Bacon had political ambitions; he couldn't write plays that poked fun at important people or teased the monarchy and keep his career. It was smarter for all three of them to write under a fake name."

"So why did everyone think that one guy was murdered?"

"After a long day of drinking and gambling at an inn, when it came time to pay the bill, there was a big argument. According to the professor, Kit's friends distracted the innkeeper for a few minutes, dragged in a corpse from the prison yard dressed in Marlowe's clothes, stabbed the corpse, then made a big noise like they were fighting. The innkeeper didn't see the murder, but he heard the argument. When he came into the room, he saw the body dressed in Marlowe's clothes and assumed it was him. The corpse had been stabbed in the eye, so nobody wanted to look too close at his face. That was the end of Kit Marlowe, the poet and playwright. The body was quickly buried in an unmarked grave, the court decided it was self defense and no one was prosecuted. Bacon was a lawyer who represented that area in Parliament."

"I don't think people would believe that story even if Mr. Columbo himself told it."

"You're right. No one believed Professor Reginald. But Isaac was intrigued. To him, it was a puzzle to solve, like any modern murder." She looked at her watch. "It's almost noon. Since Isaac won't be giving his presentation, I think they're going to present his widow with an award. It will be in Ballroom B if you want to see her."

"Are you going?"

She shook her head. "I'd love to, of course. But these brochures aren't really organized yet, are they? Ballroom B is down that hall." She pointed.

"Thanks," I said. "I'll tell her hi for you."

"Don't bother," she said. "We're not close."

"OK," I said. I walked down the hall toward Ballroom B. I whispered as I walked, "Mortimer, I hope you're keeping a list. We got the mystery of Tonto to solve, plus the mystery of the Professor's dog, plus the mystery of Isaac's murder. But now we got another mystery which is older than America about some writer guys stabbing each other in the eyeball. If Columbo had that many cases he'd have to make it a two-part show to be continued next week. This ain't a good time for you to take a nap."

Mrs. Isaac Goldfarb was younger than I pictured, maybe about thirty. The paper said her husband was ten years older than that. She was serious, like a lady in the army who gives orders to do pushups. Her hair was short and dark brown and only long enough to cover her jaw on the sides of her face. She had on a black suit that fit her about perfect. She was talking to a guy about her same age, a skinny guy with really short hair and a little pointed black beard on his chin. He wore a turtleneck sweater; his tan pants looked about like mine. He reminded me of Maynard G. Krebs, a beatnik on an old TV show called Dopey Gillis. I could tell who she was since everybody wore name tags. The beatnik had a name tag which had flipped around so I couldn't read it.

When the guy with the little beard seen me, he looked surprised, like I reminded him of somebody from a different old TV show. For about a half second he opened his eyes extra wide. But I never seen this guy before, and I ain't been in TV shows. Everybody looks like somebody else you might know so you can't hold it against them. He decided he didn't know me either and his face went back to normal. He leaned over and whispered something to Mrs. Isaac Goldfarb. She smiled as sweet as a baby and said, "You talk way the hell too much. When will you learn to just shut the flock up?" I figured whatever the guy said was going to cost him fifty extra pushups. The man turned and walked out of the room. Cool, I thought. This is my chance to ask her questions, only I hadn't thought of any good ones.

Before I could go up to her, an old guy with a big nose and wrinkled skin come up beside me and started talking. His hair was mostly white, it wasn't combed very good, and it went over his collar in the back.

"I don't believe we've met," he said, holding out his hand to shake. His voice was deeper than I expected. "I'm Andrew Pottington, poetics of the late Romantic period, plus, of course, the works of the bard. Please call me Andy. It's a pseudonym I share with E.B. White, but not President Jackson." He laughed as if that was a joke, which it might have been in some country. There wasn't much point in lying.

"My name is John Cable, but everybody calls me Jumper."

Andy laughed at that too. "Well, of course they do," he said. "We dwell among swine who answer each question with 'oink.'"

I wasn't sure if he was doing poem talk on me, or was joking, or was another crazy guy. So I looked up at the ceiling and answered him in my best game-show host voice. "More geese than swans now live, more fools than wise."

Andy smiled and nodded. "Precisely!" he said. He had a bunch of words all ready to say, so he started to say them real fast. "I sense I have encountered a kindred spirit. I confess to being a closet Oxfordian. Of course, I spent most of my early career living metaphorically in Stratford, haunting the shadows of the Globe. I did my first thesis on the First Folio and was therefore, almost by birth, a Stratfordian. I suspect half the attendees have a similar origin story. I confess, I flirted with the Marlowe misfits and the Bacon boys. Every expert begins as a dilettante, right? In my dotage, I endeavor to feel equally comfortable in Bacon's parliament and the seedy plebeian ghetto of tradition with its sweaty, dusty cacophony of coarse fifteenth century rubes drinking stale beer in Stratford and howling at crude jokes. And, of course, also to feel at home in each of the many elegant confines owned by the Seventeenth Earl of Oxford.

"And where do you live, Jumper?"

"I live..." I started to say I live in a one-room apartment on the third floor of an old building near Colfax in Denver, but I stopped. Someone at this conference might be a murderer and a dog-napper. I should be more careful about giving away clues instead of getting them. I remembered more poem-words, so I said them.

"I live in the dust, in the cool tombs."

Andy nodded. "As we all do," he said. "Indeed, as we all do." He leaned close and whispered at my ear. "Steer clear of Row D," he said. "The Baconians are in a foul mood today. If they think you're an Oxfordian they'll pillory you as a mindless sheep. If they were more confident of their case, they'd be less abusive. In my unassailable opinion."

This was a guy who didn't need fancy questions to talk for a half hour like a TV preacher. But maybe he had a clue for me.

"Too bad about Doctor Isaac," I said.

He nodded several times like he was winding himself up to give a speech.

"Dreadful, of course. Simply dreadful. I'm afraid Professor Reginald lured him into a tangled web of dark ephemera with his theory. Absurd on its face, obviously."

"Obviously," I said, nodding along with him. "But maybe it had some good points."

"Superficially, yes. From a creative standpoint the synergies of collaboration explain the uniquely prodigious output ascribed to the bard. As Reginald said, 'a one-tine rake gathers few leaves.' The oeuvre itself is evidence. The bard collected an almost-impossible pile of leaves for one man.

"But one can't ignore facts. The name 'Shakespeare' doesn't appear on a title page until a few weeks after Marlowe's death. Marlovians have clung to that trivial coincidence for over a century. But the man was dead."

"Somebody should of noticed that," I said.

"Clearly," he said "And a subterfuge of that magnitude could not have passed without comment. Yet there is no contemporaneous record. Can you think of an analogy to that?"

I sort of panicked while he waited. Maybe he thought I had an analogy in my shirt pocket even if I ain't exactly sure what one is. I hoped he'd keep talking, but instead he kept waiting. My brain was going as fast as a hummingbird. Maybe an analogy is a kind of writer-guy. Or maybe he meant one actual writer-guy. A contemporaneous one sounds like an extra fancy one maybe with big yellow wings and a purple hat. I don't know so many writer guys, so I said the first one I thought of, which is a guy who wrote a story my father read to me.

"Mark Twain?" I said. His story was about Huck, who was really smart. I held my breath.

Andy stared at me. I figured I was busted and some security guys would grab my elbows and lead me out the door. Finally he said something.

"Interesting," he said, rubbing his forehead. "Quite insightful. Everyone knew Samuel Clemens wrote as Mark Twain, so of course there is no controversy, no documentation. Maybe both cases were only secrets from the authorities. In Clemens' case, the Union army he deserted. In de Vere's and Marlowe's the closed-minded authorities. You have an interesting perspective, Jumper."

I decided right then that if anybody else ever asked me for an analogy I'd say Mark Twain.

"I wonder who killed Isaac?" I said. It was hard to keep these professor guys going down a straight sidewalk.

"Ah!" he said. "The task of casting Claudius!"

"Claudius?"

"I only mention him because he used poison."

"Of course," I said nodding my head. I tried to look serious and sound smart.

"But we cannot ascribe motive based on the means. Romeo also used poison. I suspect our culprit is more akin to the elusive Iago. And our plot could be intricate, resembling Vonnegut's cat's cradle or a series of nested Russian dolls."

"Yeah," I said. "Made of nothing except loneliness."

"You could be right," he said, looking at the ceiling and thinking hard. "Perhaps not power. Romeo took poison as well, but for love. I suspect we're looking for an Iago."

"Iago," I repeated. "Interesting."

"So many plays across the eons, so few motives. Greed, jealousy, love, revenge... but of course you know that. I'm sorry to sound condescending. I have a class of freshmen this semester and they've taught me bad habits. You obviously know all the classical motives."

I was starting to run out of poem words. Talking to this guy used them up fast. I tried to remember another one.

"But I don't know who to pity. You know, for their small strategy."

He smiled. "You, sir, are an enigma."

"I don't mean to be. This coat is a little tight."

He laughed.

"Not at all, you are quite correct, the world is not literature and we are not critics. On the other hand, there are whispers and rumors...like...like..."

"Like Daddy loves his dollar?"

He thought about that.

"Yes, greed could be at the root. Very perceptive of you, Jumper. Isaac's firm developed some new forensic techniques. Something employing electron microscopy and telomeres I think. Don't ask me more. In that realm I am a child who has not yet learned to crawl. A new forensics tool would make his little company quite valuable. That might make his competitors nervous. Even murderous."

"That sounds like a good motive."

"Yes, but there are alternatives. Isaac worked with the police and even the FBI on several criminal cases. One was a crime syndicate run by a man named O'Malley. He's been indicted on campaign finance charges, awaiting trial for murder in Denver, and is under investigation in Texas. The death penalty remains quite popular in Texas. His organization has a reputation for, shall we say, efficiency. A guilty criminal might have wanted to interrupt Isaac's efforts. Avoiding incarceration— let alone execution—is a powerful incentive. But then, so is love. What do you think?"

It was getting hard to remember which poem-words I already used. Not too many used the word love.

"The winter of love is a cellar of empty bins," I said "In an orchard soft with rot." That had the word love and was one of my favorite poem-words since it sounded cool and I could remember it almost every time. Plus, I always liked apples, which grow in orchards. But Andy was asking me more questions than I was asking him, plus he wasn't giving me much good clues.

"OK, thank you very much," I said and turned away. Mrs. Isaac Goldfarb wasn't in the room any more and everybody else was having their own conversations with each other. Anyway, I'd used up all my poem words and got lucky no one figured out I just learned them. Talking about apples had made me hungry but I didn't remember to put a sandwich in my backpack. I already had more good leads that I could shake sticks at and my brain didn't have room for much more clues. I needed to think about them so it seemed like time to go home. If I was a TV detective I would of put a commercial right here.

I walked down the hall to the lobby and then out the door to the parking lot. The sun was bright and it felt hot on my face. I breathed in deep, then let it out and relaxed. I hadn't done much detecting work in there but it tired me out pretending to be somebody else. If any of them people at the conference was pretending too, they'd be tired all the time. I walked through a row of parked cars and thought.

"Hey, Mortimer," I said. "Do you got a list of all my suspects? Especially in the murder case with Professor Reginald?"

Mortimer don't say stuff out loud, so I thought up my own list. First was Professor Reginald himself. Even if I like him, I didn't have a reason to cross him off my list.

Then there was O'Malley, the mob guy who wanted to get his guilty verdict threw out over bad forensics.

Then there was the companies that was trying to beat Isaac's company. Them was all good suspects. But why was any of them mad at Tonto?

My best clue was Esmeralda, the waitress who gave them the poisoned beer. Either she done the murder or she might of seen who put the poison in the glasses. I decided to go back to the Halloween Bar and casually ask some questions. I wouldn't have to dress up and, if I had to use poem words on somebody, I could use the same ones I already used today. Them bartenders and pool shooters would think they was brand new.

I was so busy thinking all this that I didn't hear the pickup truck behind me. By the time I noticed the sound and looked back, that black truck was almost to me, driving way too fast for a parking lot and heading right to me.

143

There wasn't time to get out of its way. I was right next to a big old Buick car that was parked, so I done the only thing I could think of to do. I jumped about straight up and landed on the Buick's hood. The pickup truck didn't even pretend to slow down. It sped on past.

The incident surprised me, but even being surprised I seen one interesting clue: the guy driving that truck wasn't only trying to kill Tonto. He also wanted to kill me or at least scare me so I'd stop investigating. Which means that something I was doing was on the right track. For about three seconds I watched the truck race through the parking lot. Then I did the one thing that driver probably wasn't expecting.

I followed him.

"Money can't buy love, but it improves your bargaining position."

— Christopher Marlowe

Chapter Twelve

I jumped down off the car and started jogging. I didn't run my fastest, since even if I did, I could never run as fast as a truck. I ain't a cheetah-cat like you see on animal shows. Cheetah cats run about as fast as a motorcycle, but they get out of breath after four blocks. If a deer can keep ahead of him that long, it's safe.

I'm more of a wolf kind of guy. Wolves keep jogging after a deer all day. After a while, the deer gets too tired to care if it gets eaten and so that's what happens. I can keep jogging after a suspect for an hour, which is usually enough. Suspects always think a cheetah-cat is chasing them. When nobody's in their rear-view mirror they slow down. Columbo was more of a wolf kind of guy than a cheetah and he solved a bunch of cases. So I ain't complaining about being a wolf guy.

I could see the black pickup truck ahead of me in the parking lot. When my bus had drove past that part of the parking lot this morning I didn't see no exits. So instead of chasing the truck straight ahead, I went left through the rows of parked cars, since there was an exit over there. When I got to the exit, I crouched down behind a car and waited. In about six seconds the pickup got there too. He went out and turned right on the street.

I jogged a little faster to follow him so I wouldn't lose him. I didn't want him to see me in his rear view mirror, so I crossed the street. You don't have to be on the same side of the street to follow somebody, but lots of guys forget that.

I was about a block behind the truck when he had to stop at a stoplight. That give me a chance to slow jog and still keep up, plus it give me one more clue. When he braked, his left brake light didn't come on. That was lucky if you was following somebody. Even if he got a quarter mile ahead, I could tell which brake lights was his every time he had to slow down.

After a while, the truck turned left down a street with houses. I turned at the street before that and ran a little faster. His street had stop signs, so I had a good advantage. When I was about a block ahead I stopped and looked down the side street. In about eight seconds I seen the truck still going the same direction so I run faster to be ahead again. At the next side street I seen him again. My street was going the same direction as his street, one block over. I was still a long walk away from my home, but we was heading in the mostly correct direction. I wondered where they was going?

Then I had an idea. If they was looking for Tonto, maybe they'd go to the place on Colfax where I found him. It was a total guess, I ain't saying I used super-detecting on the idea. But sometimes a good guess is about the same as super-detecting, so I said what the heck. There was a bus stop about a block ahead of me, with a bus stopping there. I ran my fastest and caught the bus. I showed the driver my free-ride pass and he told me where the bus was going. It had a stop close to the spot on Colfax where Tonto and me met.

"Thanks, Mortimer," I whispered as I sat down at an empty seat. Catching that bus felt lucky.

I should change my disguise, I thought. I pulled a dark blue wool cap with a Broncos horse on it from my backpack and put on my sunglasses. I stuffed the jacket with leather elbow patches and the blue shirt with buttons into the backpack and zipped the zipper. Under the blue shirt I wore a black Grateful Dead T-shirt, so that's what I was wearing now.

When the bus stopped on Colfax Street, I put my backpack back on and got out. If them guys was looking for a really smart college teacher in a tan sports jacket they wouldn't see him. They'd see a Deadhead who was probably broke loitering in front of the stores singing Uncle John's Band in his brain.

It was a perfect disguise.

Three guys was leaning against the brick wall of a building, smoking cigarettes and flicking the ashes on the sidewalk. I went over and leaned against the wall right next to them. I pretended I was part of their rock band, and I was the guy who was late getting to practice. I ain't as expert at loitering as them guys, but I've got me a few tickets for it so I ain't a beginner either. I leaned against the wall real casual. Them guys looked over at me, decided I knew what I was doing, and nodded, so I nodded back. Then they went back to their loitering. I watched the street for the pickup, detecting with my whole brain, and pretended to loiter.

When the truck come down' Colfax it was going slower than any of the other cars, since the driver was watching for Golden Retriever dogs. The windows was tinted dark, so I still couldn't see inside. I pretended not to notice the truck and let it drive past. It got about a block to my left when it hit another stop light. I started to walk after it, trying to look like a homeless guy or a drug dealer who was out of customers instead of a college reading teacher. The main trick to that is looking like you don't have no assignment and are just walking wherever you want. Most of the time I can do that easy, but when you're chasing a suspect, sometime you forget and start watching real hard like a detective.

The truck slowed down even more on the block where I found Tonto. It went two blocks more then turned left. Colfax Street is all businesses, but when you go down a side street there ain't businesses, just old brick houses. The truck drove down that first street of houses, creeping careful and quiet like a nervous mouse when the cat's asleep. I followed a block behind, on the left side of the street, but it was obvious what they was doing. They was making a search grid so they didn't miss any blocks in case Tonto was still in the area.

Well, I knew they wouldn't find him since he was at Linda's house. Pickup-truck-guy was interested in Tonto the dog but that didn't mean he was an alleged suspect in Isaac's murder. Sometimes clues go to different crimes and you'd be a dumb detective if you didn't know that. Roosters crow in the morning and the sun rises in the morning but that don't mean the sun is taking orders from the bird even if that's what the bird tells you. Mr. Silver probably thought the sun took orders from him, too. But he also thought it was funny to kick his food out of his cage so I had to clean it up. Some birds is smart but also mean and not that funny. And sometimes two clues go to two different mysteries.

So now I had a choice. I could keep following the truck. Maybe I'd get close enough to see the driver or close enough to clean the dirt off his license plate. If I did, there was a chance he'd see me and decide to run me over again.

Or, I could walk home and make a new plan. I was already tired and hungry, plus making new plans is about my best skill. I was trying to decide what to do when I noticed I'd been walking toward my apartment while I was thinking. Didn't make much sense to turn around. When I'm trying to decide on a plan, if I keep walking, sometimes it's like I see a door ahead of me with the plan I was looking for holding it open saying, hey, what took you so long?

Mr. Silver was hollering when I went into my apartment.

"Sheets for brains!" he screamed.

"Settle down," I said back. "If you ain't careful I'll take you to the Halloween Bar tomorrow and leave you and your cage there."

"Muster clucking son of finches! Pluck you!"

"Yeah, even those biker guys at the bar might get embarrassed at your salty talk. But there's a whole big kitchen there and I can leave them my parrot-stew recipe right next to your cage."

"Pluck you! Sheets for brains!"

The old way of talking to the bird wasn't having much impacts, so I went to my new strategy.

"I might permit you to get the mange," I said. "Even if I ain't sure what the mange is, I bet you wish I wouldn't permit you to get it!" Those poem words shut him up as good as if they meant something. I cleaned up the birdseed on the floor by his cage, then I opened a can of soup and took it out to my balcony.

I listened to the crickets singing love songs to each other, ate my soup, and tried to think of questions to ask the bartender at the Halloween Bar tomorrow. I come up with a couple questions, plus I figured I could think of extra ones on the way down there. It seemed like a good plan. Sometimes good plans is like spider cobwebs that you don't even see until you walk into them.

"Thanks, Mortimer," I whispered. He was curled up on my lap purring like a Mercedes Benz car and watching me eat my soup. The crickets kept singing. The soup tasted good. You can't complain much about a night like that.

xxxx

The Halloween Bar was dark even if it was a sunny afternoon outside. Two guys was playing pool. Behind the bar, a TV was showing a tennis game. The bartender was a woman I ain't ever seen before. She was about thirty years old, with long blonde hair. She wore tight black pants and a white shiny shirt that was also tight. Nobody was sitting on stools by the bar. Maybe there was other customers in the booths back by the walls, but I couldn't see them since my eyes hadn't adjusted yet. I sat on a bar stool and the woman bartender come over to get my order.

"Howdy, cowboy," she said. "What's your pleasure?"

"Jumping, mostly," I said. "And the Denver Broncos of course."

"Cool," she said, nodding her head. Then she said real slow, one word at a time, "What would you like to drink?"

"Well, sometimes I like to drink a beer. But today I still got some thinking to do so I'd like a Diet Pepsi."

"One extra-virgin Pepsi coming up."

She brought me the Diet Pepsi in a tall glass with ice cubes.

"Don't think I've seen you before," she said. "You new to the area?" She reached out to shake my hand. "Or are you in disguise? You can't ever tell for sure who someone is at the Halloween Bar."

"I live over by Colfax Street," I said, and shook her hand. "Everybody calls me Jumper."

"Pleased to meet you, Jumper. I'm Esmeralda."

Well, that surprised the heck out of me. Esmeralda was the waitress who gave Professor Reginald and Doctor Isaac the poison beer and now she was standing right in front of me. I looked at the glass of Diet Pepsi she just gave me but I didn't take no sips.

"Esmeralda ain't that ordinary a name," I said.

She laughed. "Neither is Jumper. But see? It's right here on my name badge." She pointed to the tag pinned on her shirt. Now that my eyes was better used to the dark I could read it easy. I was going to ask her about the murder, but then I remembered something Officer Mike told me once. Sometimes the best way to get a suspect to answer a question ain't to ask them the question. If they want to hide something, they'll start lying right away. Instead, get them talking about a whole different thing. Officer Mike liked to explain things with little stories. The one he said that time was this: "It's like mules. The hardest part of getting a mule to go where you want is to get him moving at all. Mules weigh about as much as a car and they're stubborn as an Irishman." He laughed when he said that part. "An Irishman like me. No matter how strong you are, you can't pull him into the barn. But once you get him moving at all, in any direction, you've got a chance to steer him toward the barn. He'll think it was his idea."

"I ain't got a name tag," I told the bartender. "Anyway, my legal name is John Cable. People call me Jumper since jumping is my hobby. How did you get the name Esmeralda?"

"It's my legal name. It's from a character in a book my parents like. You haven't touched your Diet Pepsi."

The professor had joked on her name, but he said she didn't get the joke. His joke didn't make no sense, so I couldn't remember it.

"I ain't a big book reader," I said.

"They made a couple of movies out of it, too. If you ever watch 'The Hunchback of Notre Dame,' watch for the lovely girl named Esmeralda."

"Is it a funny movie?"

"Not really. A big ugly guy falls in love with a young woman. His job is ringing the church bells."

"I mostly like funny movies. And sometimes murder mysteries."

She smiled. "In the movies, they always catch the murderer. I think real life is a lot different."

You're probably thinking that Esmeralda was sure friendly, talking for this long to a guy she didn't know. I was thinking that same thing. But anybody could get bored standing behind a bar washing glasses with nobody to talk to.

Anyway, her talking about murders without me saying nothing seemed like Officer Mike's mule starting to walk around the lawn waiting to get led to the barn.

I was going to ask her a question about the murder night, only I didn't get a chance. She was watching me as hard as if she was the detective and I was the alleged suspect. She crossed her arms across her chest.

"OK, Mr. Jumper, or whatever your real name is. Why did you come in here? You haven't touched your drink. You don't look much like a cop, even an undercover one. And I've never seen you with O'Malley's gang. You can drop the 'dumb act' and tell me or I'll have a bouncer throw you out."

"I ain't acting. Sometimes I do detecting on the side, like a hobby. I just wanted to find out more about the night of the murder."

"Why?"

"I met a dog that I thought might be the professor's. It ain't his, but it got me wondering."

"So you decided to do some private detecting?"

"Yeah. Like what other customers was here that night? Things like that. I ain't thought of much good questions yet."

"Well, I can't help you. I didn't work that night."

"What?"

"That was my regular night off. Every Thursday I play Bingo with a bunch of old ladies in a nursing home. I've got a dozen witnesses."

"Bingo?" I was surprised since Bingo is mostly an old-people game and she wasn't that old.

She shrugged. "My mother liked to play Bingo so hanging out with these ladies feels like... well, it lets me pretend she's still alive. Any more questions?"

"I don't think so." I got up off the bar stool and started to leave, then I stopped. "Maybe one more question."

She stood there waiting.

"Who wrote that story about the bell ringer?"

"Everybody knows that one. He was a Frenchman named Victor Hugo and he lived a long time ago."

"Thank you, ma'am," I said. I walked out the door into the bright sunshine with more questions in my brain than I had when I went in. I tried to remember the joke the professor said to her. It was something about Mr. Hugo, only when he told it to her she didn't say nothing back, like she ain't heard of that guy. But today she knew about Mr. Hugo without looking it up or asking somebody else. She even knew the name of the book he wrote. So that didn't make much sense.

There wasn't a black pickup truck in the parking lot, so I started to walk to the bus station.

When you think of someone getting mugged, you picture a dark street at night, or maybe an alley you should of knew better than to go down alone. You might picture a slow, cold rain, and your shoes wet through to your socks and your feet cold and maybe the smell of an old bus with a smoky tailpipe driving by. Maybe the guys who mug you are from some other country and they talk with funny accents so it's hard to understand them.

That ain't the way it happened to me.

I was about one block away from the Halloween Bar when a guy stepped out from the side of a building and stood in front of me on the sidewalk. He was maybe 23 years old, with short reddish-yellow hair. He was taller than me and wore a green T-shirt with the name of a gym on it. The T-shirt was stretched tight over all his muscles. His arm muscles looked about as big as cantaloupes. He smiled and held out his hand like a crosswalk guard telling you to stop. "Mr. Jumper," he said and he kept on smiling. It wasn't a real friendly smile, more of a "happy-with-the-situation" smile, like an alligator might smile when a bunny falls into his river. "I understand you're quite the detective."

"Well, I ain't got my own TV show," I said. "So I ain't as good a detective as..."

Two other guys come up behind me and stood on each side of me. Them two grabbed my elbows and held them tight enough to hurt. They could of been the first guy's brothers, with matching muscles. The guy on my left wore a red T-shirt and the guy on my right wore one that was kind of shiny. Since they was in red and green and kind of silver, I almost said they was all dressed up for Christmas, but then I didn't say it. Guys can get sensitive if you talk about their clothes. They didn't pull my arms but they held tight so I understood I was held. The first guy nodded at the guy on my right who punched me in the stomach about as hard as he could. It surprised me and I didn't have a chance to tighten up my stomach muscles ahead of time so he got me good. It hurt like heck and I bent forward. I might of fallen forward except they was holding my elbows too hard.

"That was just to get your attention," the main guy said. "We don't want to hurt you."

The guy on my left laughed at that.

"Let me rephrase that. We'd be happy to hurt you but that's not our instructions. Not today. Do you understand?"

They'd knocked the wind out of me so I couldn't talk, but I nodded that I understood.

"Why are you interested in Mr. O'Malley?"

Right at that minute I didn't know who they was talking about, so the question didn't make sense.

"Who?"

This time it was the guy on my left who punched me. It wasn't a total surprise so I tensed up my stomach muscles some and it didn't hurt near as bad. But I bent over so they thought it did.

"Oh, that Mr. O'Malley," I said. "The businessman who everybody loves."

"That's the one. We're members of his club: The Irish Heritage and Benevolence Club. We take benevolence very seriously."

"Me too," I said. "I like all the kinds of envelopes."

"We hold people accountable when they get interested in Mr. O'Malley. Why are you asking about him?"

"I didn't ask about him. I was looking for the owner of a Golden Retriever dog I met and somebody said Mr. O'Malley might have clues. Since you guys are his accountants, I could just ask you. The dog's name is Tonto. Do you know him?"

"You're looking for the owner of a dog?" Green shirt laughed.

"It ain't funny. I bet his owner was real worried when Tonto ran off. If you ever had a dog, you'd know."

All three of them started laughing.

"It ain't a big deal now," I said. "Since Tonto probably went home on his own. But I liked him and it would be cool if I could go visit. Only I don't know where he lives."

So technically that wasn't the whole truth and nothing but the truth. But rules got to be more flexible when three blond gorillas are punching you in the stomach. I bet even the Pope makes exceptions to his own rules when guys is punching him.

"Let him go," the main guy in the green shirt said, "But listen, you. Mr. O'Malley is proud of his reputation for fairness and honesty. And he's proud of his Halloween Bar. If you ever have more questions about him, I suggest you be very careful. Do you understand?"

They let go of my elbows and I nodded,

"If he don't know Tonto, I ain't got a reason to ask questions. Maybe I'll cross him off my list and forget I ever heard his name."

"You're a quick learner," red-shirt guy said.

"Yeah, people tell me that a lot."

Then the three of them walked away, back down the sidewalk toward the bar, still laughing.

"Getting punched in the stomach is one way to learn clues," I told Mortimer. "It just ain't my favorite way." I could feel him snuggled up inside my shirt, so I felt better.

Them guys was like the scary blue genie who lived in a magic lamp. My dad always said, "If you don't want the genie, stop rubbing the lamp." I guess genies come in different colored shirts than just blue. I made a note not to ever rub their lamps.

I walked slow to the bus stop but my brain was thinking at light speed. The waitress Esmeralda told the professor she didn't know who wrote the bell ringer book, only really she did. It seemed a dumb thing to lie about. She must of told O'Malley's guys about me and they got interested since I was asking questions. Until they found out I was only interested in Tonto, which they obviously didn't care nothing about. But some guy in a pickup truck was all the way interested in Tonto, and now also in me. The cops thought Professor Reginald killed Isaac and poisoned his own self for an alibi. If this was a puzzle it was a thousand piecer and I ain't found any of the straight edges to start solving it.

I took the bus past my stop and got off at the next one in case someone was following me. Then I sat on the bench for a while thinking about my clues and watching for suspicious characters. Everybody looks suspicious after you get punched in the stomach, like every car looks brand new when it gets wet. Nobody seemed like good suspects.

After a while I walked home.

"The best composition and temperature is, to have openness in fame and opinion, secrecy in habit, dissimulation in seasonable use, and a power to feign if there be no remedy."
— Francis Bacon

View of the Rocky Mountains from Colfax Ave. In Denver

Photographer and date unknown

Chapter Thirteen

Holly lives in my building. I'm on the third floor in the back, she's on the second floor in the back. Neither of us can look out a window and see who's walking up to the front door from the street. But the hall on her floor has a window on the front side. I ain't gonna say it's true, but sometimes I think Holly watches out that window. If she wants to go all Perry Mason on me, there ain't a good way to sneak in the front door without her seeing.

I walked up the first flight of stairs and she was standing there leaning against the wall with her arms crossed in front of her.

"Well, well, well," she said. "Mr. Jumper John Cable. Have you had a busy day?"

When she uses my whole name I feel like I just got sent to the principal's office with no good excuses for whatever I done. My face got hot. In my brain, the judge had whacked his little hammer down on his desk and asked the court to order stuff. I'm on the witness stand trying to remember which of my stories might sound like "nothing but the truth so help me God." My first plan is always to get off the witness stand as quick as I can.

"It was ordinary," I said and tried to walk past her to keep going up the stairs. But she moved in front of me.

"That's nice," she said. "Ordinary is nice."

"Well, sometimes you like extra stuff to happen in a day so it ain't as ordinary. There ain't one correct answer."

She nodded.

"Orderly Number Ten didn't show up for his shift today. Nurse Helga mentioned it several times."

"He don't sound all that reliable."

"You're right. He seems very casual about his responsibilities."

159

I didn't say nothing. You always got the right to remain silent.

"Would you like to hear something funny?"

About as much as I'd like anything in the whole world, I thought.

"Sure," I said.

"A maintenance guy came to the cafeteria yesterday," she said. "Only no one recognized him. By their description, he looked a lot like Orderly Number Ten."

"That ain't all that funny. I heard a joke about a church bell ringer..."

"No. What's funny is that he fixed the microwave and the refrigerator. Yet the Maintenance Department has no idea who he is."

"There ain't a rule against fixing stuff, is there?"

"Sometimes I think our hospital has that rule. 'If it's broke, leave it alone.' But don't change the subject. You're up to something aren't you?"

"It would be easy to follow that rule. Most of the rules is a lot harder, which is why they made it a rule in the first place. Like, you can't eat your apple pie until you finish your broccoli. If everybody wanted to eat their broccoli first, you wouldn't need the rule, right? Since it's easier to leave something broke than take it apart and figure out how to fix it, there ain't as much demand for rules to not do stuff you don't want to do. So that would be an easy rule to follow. Well, it's been nice talking to you."

"What are you up to?"

"I was going to go feed Mr. Silver. He's that parrot that somebody left..."

"Jumper!" she said. She put her hands on her hips and stood blocking my path. Then she waited.

After a minute I figured I should say something.

"You probably mean my detecting business."

"I don't think you can call it a business if you're not making any money."

"Sure you can. Lots of rich guys get really busy playing golf and buying buildings but they don't even make enough money to pay taxes. A guy on the bus was telling all about that…"

"Don't make me ask you again! What are you up to?"

By now you figured out that if Holly was going full Perry Mason on me, my best choice was to come clean and tell the truth. OK, maybe not the whole truth but a lot of it.

"I'm mostly trying to find Tonto's owner, which ain't as easy as it sounds. But if I can't, he seems a lot like the dog that Professor Reginald lost, so that might be a good home. Only the professor's in jail on murder charges so even if they like each other, he can't have a dog in jail. I need to figure out who the real murderer is so the professor can go home. There ain't good alternatives to that."

She looked at me harder for a minute. She'd been so interested in figuring out my detecting that she hadn't looked at me close.

"You don't look so good," she said. "What happened?"

By now I'd already said so much truth there wasn't much point in making up a more interesting story.

"Some guys from Paddy-O'Malley's gang punched me a couple of times and I ain't all the way over it yet."

"Paddy-O'Malley! What did you ever do to him? In fact, why do you even know him?"

"I don't actually know him since we ain't met. His name come up from somebody else. It was just a misunderstanding. They thought I was

161

investigating him, but when I said I was looking for Tonto's owner they let me go and we all laughed about it."

"O'Malley is under indictment for campaign contributions violations. And under investigation for murder."

"These guys didn't seem like they wanted to make contributions."

"Paddy-O doesn't make contributions unless he's getting something himself. And this was a huge contribution in a national election a couple of years ago. He's facing a long prison sentence. If it turns out the money came from certain other countries, it could be treason. Do you know what the penalty for treason is?"

"I bet it's a bad one."

"Yeah. The worst."

I didn't know what the worst prison sentence was. Maybe no TV in his cell, or having to eat stuff that was healthy even if it tastes like mud. But a rich guy could pay extra to get candy bars and maybe some football games on TV. Jail sentences for rich guys is always better than for poor guys. So that don't seem like a good murder motive.

"Some of the witnesses have already had... mysterious accidents."

"I didn't even vote last time, since I had appointments. So Mr. O'Malley probably don't want me to have a accident."

"No, but he's nervous. People say the FBI has some serious evidence against him, but the forensics aren't conclusive. At least not yet. You stay away from him."

"Yes ma'am."

"Are you bleeding?"

"I don't think so. But after I feed Mr. Silver some bird seeds I might take a hot shower and go to bed early."

"Did you eat anything?"

"Nah, I been riding buses and walking home. I think I'll eat a can of soup on my balcony."

"I know your routine. You eat it out of the can, don't you? You eat it cold."

"It makes a lot of sense. There's no dishes to wash, no pots and pans to clean. If you lick the spoon real good you don't even need to rinse it off."

"You go take your shower. I'll bring you some real food."

I started to say something but she held up her hand and I stopped. Then I thought of one more thing, like Columbo and I opened my mouth. Before any words come out she held up her hand again.

"Yes, ma'am," I said.

If I live to be fifty, I'll never understand women. How can they go from being Perry Mason one minute and incriminating a guy to being the Good Witch of the West in sparkly clothes and bringing you food in about one second? If there was some alien creature on Star Trek that done that, nobody'd believe it. They'd cancel the whole series.

When Holly come back, she had a metal pie-tin with food inside.

"Thanks," I said. "What is it?"

"It's a casserole. Hamburger, cream of mushroom soup, with corn and mashed potatoes on top. I make a big batch, and then freeze it. One lasts me two or three meals, but this one is all yours. I already ate."

"It sure smells good," I said. "Next time I'll share one of my cans of soup with you."

"Thanks, but no need," she said. "I better go. You stay away from Paddy-O."

"OK. And if you hear of any clues, be sure to tell me."

She started to leave and then stopped.

"Did you hear about the article?"

"I bet you read more than me, so you might of seen more articles."

She nodded.

"That's possible," she said. "Somebody leaked some evidence to the press. The cops found a magazine article folded up in the professor's pocket."

"If he swiped an article from a library magazine he's gonna have extra fines."

"No, nothing like that. It was an article about hemlock in literature. When the EMTs were trying to revive him at the scene, they found it in his jacket pocket. The symptoms fit, so they decided to assume that was the poison. They got him some help quick and put him on a ventilator right away. Over a few days, his body was able to process the poison. When he regained consciousness, they moved him to the hospital wing of prison. Without that article, they might not have ever considered hemlock until it was too late. Probably saved his life."

"What's hemlock?" I asked.

"It's a poison," she said. "It's what Socrates..." she stopped. "It's a very old poison that comes from a plant that grows like a weed across parts of the country. Medics see it so seldom they don't think to check for it until it's too late."

"So it's a clue that the professor ain't the murderer, right?"

"Sure. Unless he gave himself a smaller dose and put the article in his own pocket so they'd think to treat him for hemlock. If you look at it that way, he seems guilty. What are the odds someone would get poisoned by hemlock when they had an article about it in their pocket?"

"About as good as the Raiders playing fair."

"It's a weird coincidence. There's no real antidote for hemlock. The article talked about hemlock in literature: Socrates, MacBeth, Tolkien. A professor of English Literature would know about it more than most people. It said that Tolkien fell in love with his wife when he saw her dancing in a field of flowering hemlock."

"That don't sound all that romantic."

"Everybody's different, Jumper. Of all people, you ought to know that. Enjoy your dinner. And stay away from ruthless gangsters."

And then she left and closed the door behind her.

"Yeah, Mortimer," I said after she was gone. "I think she's right about folks being different. I bet some guys have imaginary cows or pigs. I gotta admit, that would be weird."

Mortimer purred. He liked the smell of that casserole.

It's funny how, when somebody says don't do something, all of a sudden that's the thing you really want to do. When Holly said stay away from gangsters it made me think about Paddy-O and his crimes. And when his friends punched me and said not to think about him, he got to be a big flashing light in my brain saying, "Look over here! Look over here!"

If you think about it, with two different people telling me not to do something, I didn't have much alternatives.

It was about time for Officer Mike to be back from his fishing trip. Even if he retired from being a cop he liked to keep track of things and I bet he'd heard lots about Paddy-O. Plus, I knew the bar he went to sometimes. Maybe tomorrow night I'd go to that bar and have a beer or a Diet Pepsi myself. If he was there, we could talk real casual, kind of accidentally. Then, if he had clues, he'd probably say them to me and he wouldn't even know I was detecting.

I didn't see no hidden flaws with that plan.

"Then learn this of me: to have is to have; for it is a figure in rhetoric that drink, being poured out of a cup into a glass, by filling the one doth empty the other, for all your writers do consent that ipse is he: now you are not ipse, for I am he."

— Touchstone in Shakespeare's play "As You Like It"

Chapter Fourteen

The Speakeasy Bar was dark, but not as dark as the Halloween Bar. It also smelled better since it had good air conditioning. There was booths with red leather seats and backs and a long bar with a shiny top that looked like real wood. Past that was a big dance floor. They played music loud enough to make you tap your foot but soft enough you could talk to somebody. The songs switched from old rock songs like from the sixties and even older songs by guys like Frank Sinatra. People came to this bar if they like to dance to old music, which I already knew Officer Mike did.

The biggest difference was the Speakeasy Bar had as many women customers as men. At the Halloween Bar, the customers was mostly men and the bartenders and waiters was mostly women. Here, the customers were all ages and dressed nice. Not nice like they just got off from working at a bank or funeral parlor, but also not like they just crawled out from under a house where they was fixing plumbing.

Officer Mike was sitting at the bar with his back to me. He was easy to spot. If Officer Mike was an animal, he would of been a bear. His shoulders was as wide as a linebacker's. He was wearing a bright Hawaiian shirt with lots of big green leaves and bright blue flowers and some yellow things that might of been birds. Or maybe lizards. If Officer Mike was a little guy, some big dumb guys might say he was a sissy for wearing it. But nobody called Officer Mike a sissy even if he was old enough to be a school principal. His hair was a little longer than last time I seen him and it stuck out from his blue Denver Broncos baseball cap and touched the top of his shirt in back. Even from the back you could tell he was the only bear sitting at the bar. I went over and stood behind him.

"Mr. Bartender," I said. "Did you check this guy's ID? I ain't sure he's old enough to drink beer in a bar."

Mike spun around.

"Jumper!" he said. "Are you out of jail already?" He smiled since he was joking on me.

167

"I got 'em on the technicality that I ain't done no crimes."

"Not yet, maybe," he said "But I've got confidence in you, if only you'd apply yourself. Sit down."

There was a blank stool next to him and I sat down.

"Can I buy you a beer?" he said.

"Thanks, but I'll just have a diet Pepsi."

"Ah," he said. "So you're working on a case."

"Well, I was mostly in the neighborhood so it's lucky we run into each other like this."

"Yeah, that sure is lucky. You always seem to get extra lucky when you're on a case."

"So how was your fishing trip?" I asked him. "Was it lucky too?"

"It was extremely lucky for the fish."

He drank some little drinks of his beer and I drank some little drinks of my Diet Pepsi. I waited for him to talk some more, but he was good at not talking. After a while he put down his beer and looked at the ceiling like it was a TV special of elephants and giraffes doing something really weird, like making raincoats, and he couldn't stop watching.

"So, Jumper," he said while he watched the ceiling. "While I was off fishing did you meet anyone interesting?"

Officer Mike never went all Perry Mason on me trying to trick me into saying stuff I already decided not to say. I liked it that he already forgot about asking me about my detective case and just wanted to know how stuff was going with me.

"Well, I met an interesting Golden Retriever dog named Tonto. So I been trying to find his owner. I thought it might be a guy at the hospital but that was a red hair ring. It wasn't a time waste, since there was other interesting people at the hospital like Nurse Helga, and Mitch the security guard, and the nurses in the employees cafeteria. The cafeteria had a broke microwave but it was mostly a bad fuse. I was lucky to have a new fuse in my pocket."

I tried to think of all the interesting people at the hospital while I was trying extra hard not to say anything about Professor Reginald since I probably broke rules by talking to him.

Officer Mike looked down from the ceiling and took a sip of his beer. He nodded.

"Golden Retrievers are nice dogs," he said.

"Yeah," I said. "Dogs is smart, too. I never seen one who liked a murderer, for one example, and I watched a lot of TV shows with dogs."

"It's a good thing you don't hang out with any bad guys," he said. "Tonto might bite them in the ankle."

"Yeah, I was glad he wasn't with me when Paddy-O's guys punched me in the stomach."

Officer Mike looked surprised when I said that for about a second. Then he nodded.

"Too bad the guy at the hospital wasn't a good lead."

"Yeah, but he was a nice guy. He told me about this meeting of college English teachers, which was fun. Them guys talk a whole different language."

"You'd think they'd talk English."

"Mostly they do. Only they got all these extra words. Once they get going with extra words, pretty soon you can't understand anything they're saying."

"I wonder if I know Mitch, the security guard? Lots of cops get side-jobs working security."

"Mitch seemed OK. His job was easy, sitting in the hall outside a guy's room."

"Nothing wrong with easy jobs," he said.

"Yeah, they're about the best ones unless you get bored."

He nodded. "Any Broncos news?" he asked. "I didn't even turn on the radio while I was camping."

"I'm pretty sure we're going to the Super Bowl this year."

"We all think that, at least until the season actually starts."

"This is the best part of the season. It ain't as easy to think we're a Super Bowl team after we lose a bunch of games. Right now we're as good as anybody."

We didn't say nothing else for a minute while we took little drinks. Then he looked up at them elephants and giraffes on the ceiling again.

"Why did Paddy-O's guys punch you?"

I had to stop and think for a minute. Did I already give away too many clues? I couldn't remember saying any secrets. Before I could answer, Officer Mike jumped in with his own answer so I relaxed a little.

"I'm sure it was just a misunderstanding," he said.

"Exactly," I said. "They thought I was detecting on their friend when I was mostly trying to find Tonto's owner."

"I can see how that would confuse them. Especially Paddy."

The way he said the guy's name was interesting. Not like it was just some guy he read about in a newspaper.

170

"Do you know him?" I asked

He nodded and took another beer drink,

"For years," he said. "We went to high school together."

"Wow," I said. "I didn't know you was friends."

"We're not. We played on opposite teams. He's always been like..." he thought for a second. "He was always like the Raiders."

"It would be hard to be friends with a Raiders fan. They're mean. Maybe Raiders fans say that same thing about Broncos fans, only they'd be wrong."

"Yeah, O'Malley was mean. Liked to beat up on the younger kids. Tormented their animals, stole their lunch money. He hasn't changed much, from what I hear. Only now he's rich and can hire better lawyers to keep him out of jail."

I made a second note in my brain to stay away from him.

"I heard something on the radio when I was driving back from the mountains," he said. "Not sure I really understood it though. Maybe you heard about it too. Some Raiders fan got murdered by a Broncos fan. I thought that's what the radio said but I can't imagine a Broncos fan murdering somebody. Did you hear about that?"

"I might of heard about that, now that you say it. They got suspicions on a college teacher. I think maybe he teaches old books. Only he got poisoned too, which seems like a dumb thing for a murderer to do."

"I wonder if he's in jail?"

"Yeah, I think so. Once he woke up from his coma they moved him from the hospital to a hospital part of a jail."

"That makes me feel a lot safer. Those college teachers make me nervous. Like they're going to spring a pop quiz on me."

171

"Professor Reginald wouldn't spring no quiz on you. But he does know a whole bunch of extra words. I got suspicions that some of them ain't even real words. If a guy says made-up words it could make anybody feel dumb. You can't feel bad about that."

One woman was dancing on the dance floor all by herself. She kept looking over at Officer Mike and smiling. Sometimes he smiled back. He started taking bigger drinks of his beer. I think he was ready to stop drinking beer and talking to me about murders so he could go dance with that lady. Officer Mike loves to dance, which I already knew, and women liked to dance with him. Even if he was wearing a goofy Hawaii shirt.

"Listen, Jumper," he said. "I know you're not afraid of much, and you're brave in an emergency. But when it comes to murderers, well, sometimes it's best to let the police do their jobs. Especially when you don't even know who the murderer is."

"Yeah, I ain't gonna argue that one. Only I ain't really on a murder case, it's a lost-dog case. And them ain't near as dangerous."

"And you'd like me to keep my ear to the ground about missing dogs?"

"Yeah. Especially dogs named Tonto."

"Was that on his collar?"

"Nah. He wasn't wearing no collar."

"So how do you know his name?"

"Well, at first I guessed it. But then I tried all the names I could think of on him, like Lassie, and Rin Tin Tin, and Scooby Do, and Captain Kirk, and Han Solo, and Luke Skywalker, and John Elway, and Spock. The only one he liked was Tonto."

"I see. That's some smart detecting."

"Thanks. Some guy in a black pickup truck keeps trying to run him over. I think that's more a clue on the dog case than the murder case."

"Sounds right," he said. "Probably smart not to get in a fight with a pickup truck, either,"

I laughed at that, since he was joking on me. "I got one more question," I said. "Even if it ain't a clue. What do they do with a suspect's stuff?"

"His stuff?"

"Yeah, like if they search his house and there ain't clues and there ain't much valuables and maybe the guy don't have relatives. What if the guy has to stay in the hospital or in jail? What happens to his cups and his magazines and his frying pan?"

"I see. Well, if nobody claims it, the court would seize his assets. They'd appoint a receiver to sell it. He'd hire someone to haul away the junk."

"Somebody like me? I cleaned out a bunch of apartments for Mr. Levy."

"Sure, someone like you. Do you want me to put in a good word for you? You want the job of cleaning out somebody's apartment?"

"Thanks, but no. I was wondering for no reason."

The woman from the dance floor walked up to us.

"Hey, Mike," she said. "Are you going to make me dance alone all night? Haven't seen you in a while."

"Hey, Sugar," he said "I've been fishing for a couple of weeks. Now I'm catching up with my old friend Jumper. Sugar, meet Jumper. Jumper, this is Sugar."

She reached out her hand and I shook it.

"Pleased to meet you, Miss Sugar," I said.

"Likewise," she said then turned back to Officer Mike and waited. I think she was ending our meeting,

"Jumper," Officer Mike said. "If I hear anything about your case, I'll let you know. And you remember what I told you." He pointed his finger at me, like I was a kid who was in trouble.

"Yes, sir," I said. "I'll eat all my vegetables and look both ways before I cross the street."

Officer Mike got up and he and Sugar went out on the dance floor. I finished my Diet Pepsi and went home.

Chapter Fifteen

The next day I had to take a break from my detecting business to work on my can-collecting business. It don't matter how good you are at your main business, sometimes you got to do the business that makes you money.

Lots of people in Denver throw away their cans after they drink their pop. Sometimes they don't even get as far as a trash can. Any time there's a bunch of people there's gonna be used drink cans on the ground that somebody has to clean up. But you can get cash for every can you turn in, so collecting them is easy money. I always brought a big green trash sack with me when I was collecting, plus I always had an extra one folded up in my backpack.

Today there was going to be a fair or festival or something in downtown Denver, near the Capitol building. They had these things several times in the summer. I didn't pay enough attention to know if it was an art festival with lots of painters, or a food festival with tables trying to sell you broccoli and carrots, or a flower festival with pots of geraniums and daisies, since I wasn't going to buy nothing. The festivals always got a thousand people to come and buy geraniums or oil pictures or broccoli. Whatever it was, there'd be extra cans on the ground that anybody could collect.

I went there about an hour before it was supposed to start, since it's interesting to watch people set up their tables. They was mostly all nice and they'd talk to you if you said a question. If they was selling food, sometimes they give away free samples and sometimes they got a broken brownie or cookie they can't sell. I never ask, since that would be like begging, but if it's their own idea, I don't complain about getting half a broken brownie. A brownie you don't pay for is what business guys call "profit," the extra thing you get after you get paid for your work. The rest of us call them "tips." Free extra stuff is about the best part of working.

I started walking toward the Capitol. The air was still cool since the sun ain't been up that long. While I was walking, I heard some people arguing down one of the side streets. There wasn't much traffic so you could hear them clear as day. Some men was arguing with a woman and she was telling them to go away and get lost but the men just laughed. Then she got madder and said don't touch me, but the men laughed some more.

It wasn't any of my business so I could of kept walking. But sometimes when you hear stuff like that it means somebody needs help. My dad taught me the Doctor Hudson game, where you get points if you help someone and you get bonus points if you help without asking and if you never tell anybody about it. It's a fun game, but the "keeping it secret" rule is why lots of people don't play it. By telling you, I might be losing some bonus points but you can't spend your whole life worrying about bonus points.

I started walking down that side street until I seen what was going on.

First thing I seen was this wooden thing with big wood wheels. It looked sort of like a wheel barrow, since it had handles, only it was about six feet long. And instead of having the regular barrow part, the part you'd fill with stuff like dirt, it had a little wood house with a roof of red and white stripes, like a flag. On top of that was a sign that said "Kayla's Klaws." A young woman with straight, long black hair was standing beside it. She wore old fashioned clothes. Three teenage guys was pestering her but they probably didn't mean her no harm. They was just young and kind of jerks. She looked scared, and they thought that was funny. They'd get real close to her on all sides and say stuff and then she'd say 'get away from me' and then the guys would laugh.

One thing about the detecting business is that you ain't ever off duty. You're always looking for clues, even if you ain't on a case that day. You notice little stuff, which tells you what's going on. I was watching for clues with eagle eyes so I wouldn't step into hidden flaws.

The teenagers was all short and skinny with dark hair and good tans. They wore shirts from different football teams. The biggest guy had on a hoodie that was black and tan and said "Pittsburgh Steelers." I ain't a fan of the Steelers, especially when they play the Broncos, but they ain't evil like the Raiders. One wore a light blue T-shirt with a red square on the chest and a black cross inside that. It said "cemento cruz azul" which is probably a team in a small town that I ain't heard of. Lots of towns in California have 'cruz' in their names, for one example. I figured Cemento was the cement company that paid for their jerseys. The third guy wore a T-shirt that had big blue and white stripes running up and down. If I knew their team, I'd say something friendly like, hey, you guys got a good quarterback. Since I didn't know, I kept my mouth shut. That's a lesson I learned about a thousand times. All the clues said that these guys was probably just visiting Denver and they was too young to know this was mostly a Broncos town.

I ain't never seen the woman before, but them guy's didn't know that. I walked right up to her. There was a whole pile of sweet pastries on the cart that smelled fresh-baked with cinnamon and honey.

"Hi, Sis," I said to the woman. Then I looked at the guys. "My sister don't like people to stand that close to her. Would you please give her a little room?"

The teenagers looked at each other, then backed a couple of steps away from her. They kept grinning since they didn't know if I was dangerous or not. I was bigger and older than them, but there was three of them.

"How do you gentlemen know my sister?" I said.

"None of your fluffing business," Pittsburgh Steelers guy said.

"My sister's business is my business," I told him, as polite as if I was talking to a nun, but I didn't ask him again. No need to start an argument. I turned to the woman.

"I ain't never seen you in them clothes before," I said.

The three teenagers was quiet since they still didn't know what was going on. The woman didn't know exactly what I was doing either, but she pretended she knew me.

"I'm a medieval wench," she said. "It's my costume."

"I've heard of monkey wrenches and crescent wrenches," I said. "I never heard of a medieval wrench."

"Not wrench. Wench. It's an old word for girl. I sell bread and pastries, especially these sweet ones that look like a big animal foot. You know, bear claws."

"Oh yeah," I said. "I think you told me that." Having a nice conversation would be a good step toward everybody being friends and leaving each other alone without anybody getting their feelings hurt. Conversations is always better than fights. "Did I tell you I got a new dog, at least until I find his main owner? His name is Tonto."

The guy in the Steelers hoodie standing next to me grunted, like maybe he didn't like dogs, and I looked at him for a second. "Tonto's a good dog," I told him and I give him a big smile. Then I turned back to the woman. "What are you doing down here? Don't you want to be close to the Capitol building where there's customers?"

"Indeed I do. Only my wheel fell into this huge pot hole and I can't push it out."

I looked at the wheel. Sure enough, it was in a pothole that must of been a foot deep. I turned to the guys.

"Now I get it," I said. "You guys was going to lift her cart out of that hole to be friendly," I pointed at the cart. "Doctor Hudson would be proud. I'd sure like to watch that. I'll even help."

The Steelers fan said one of Mr. Silver's favorite cuss words. He was too skinny to look scary to me but in his own brain, he was as bad as Dracula. He was wearing brand new Nike sneakers that was named for a big-deal basketball player which made him feel both tougher and taller. The other two grinned bigger when he said that. Their sneakers was a lot more ordinary but they thought they was as scary as King Kong, too.

He said some more cuss words. My face started to feel hot but I ignored it since sometimes guys say stuff they don't mean any more than when a parrot says it. I was polite to him but he was obviously all the way mad for no reason. Even if I wasn't detecting I would have seen the clues. His face was red and his fists was clenched, which was confusing since I hadn't said anything to get him mad. I'd been as sweet to these kids as if they was little kittens.

I don't think the Steelers fan's brain was working at full speed since right then he decided that the smart thing for him to do was to punch me in the face. Only he made a couple of mistakes. First, he didn't plant his feet, so he was sort of off balance, like a rookie quarterback in a hurry throwing off his back foot. He couldn't get much strength into it.

Second, he wound up like a baseball pitcher does before he throws the ball. He might as well have put up a sign that says, "OK now, I'm about to punch you in the face."

You can't hold it against a guy if he makes some easy mistakes. I seen that punch coming from a mile away and ducked under it. When his punch landed on air, it threw his balance off even more. I pushed him just a baby-sized shove and he spun farther than he thought he was going to. Now his back was almost facing me, so with one hand I grabbed his belt right in the middle of his back and with the other hand I grabbed the hood part of his sweatshirt. The two other kids started to come toward us to help their buddy, but he held up his hand and stopped them.

"No!" he said. "I don't need your help with this old gringo!" The other guys nodded and stopped.

I probably told you that all my training for jumping made me strong. Before Mr. Fancy Sneakers Steelers Fan had a chance to turn around, I lifted him off the ground.

Well, that surprised the heck out of him. When he was a few inches off the ground he started waving his arms and legs around trying to get away, and trying to punch me all at the same time. Instead, without his feet on the ground to hold him steady, he fell forward. I held him in the air with his legs

179

off to my right and his head to my left. He looked like a fish trying to flop hard enough to get off a hook and back in the water. He yelled out some more of Mr. Silver's favorite words. His two buddies took a step toward us again to help him but he yelled out "no" and they stopped again. I swung him in their direction, like maybe I'd throw him at them and they stopped. They liked their buddy, but they didn't want to have to catch him.

"Did you want to get down?" I said. "Is that what I heard you say?"

He cussed some more and kept trying to punch at me, but he was confused from being swung around like a baby.

"OK," I said. I dropped him down to the sidewalk but kept holding his belt. He should of thought to catch himself with his hands, but he was too busy cussing to think clear.

"Ay!" he yelled when the sidewalk hit his nose. Even that didn't get him out of the mood for fighting. He tried to crawl away and then he tried to stand up but I was still holding his belt. "You'll be sorry you did that, you... you..." he said. Then he started shouting regular cuss words plus a bunch of stuff you could tell was cussing in a different language. So I picked him back up by the belt and swung him around a little so he lost track of where he was. While he was dizzy and confused, I held him a foot off the sidewalk then I dropped him again. He kept cussing until I done that three more times and then he shut up.

"I think you guys need to give me bonus points for not slamming you down real hard. Your nose will heal, once it stops bleeding. Now, why don't you lift my sister's cart out of the pot hole and we can forget any of this happened. OK?"

Nobody said nothing and I started to drop the guy onto the sidewalk again.

"OK, OK!" he yelled.

I set him down gentle but kept holding his belt.

"Now, a deal's a deal," I said. "But some guys don't keep their deals. So to be fair, let me give you all some advice. You might think you can run away and I won't catch you. But that would be wrong thinking. You ain't as fast as me and when I catch you you'll have to take your consequences. And if you run away to get out of a deal, there's gonna be extra consequences. There ain't no alternatives to that, which is the truth, the whole truth and nothing but the truth."

They all nodded and I let go of the guy's belt.

"You broke my nose!" the big guy said in his funny accent.

"Nah," I said. "Not yet anyway. You just got scratched up a little. If I'd wanted to break your nose you wouldn't be standing there whining about it." I pointed to the two wood handles on the lady's cart.

"How about if you take the handles," I said, as cheerful as I could, to the guy who was bleeding. "And you two take the sides by the wheels and lift."

Fancy Sneakers motioned to the others. They did like I suggested and the cart got back on good pavement again. They started to let go but I stopped them.

"Not so fast," I said. "My sister wanted to sell her wrenches down by the Capitol building and now she ain't gonna get there on time."

"They're bear claws, not wrenches," the lady said.

"OK," I said. "Anyway, why don't we lift her cart and carry it to where she wants it? Don't that seem fair?"

They didn't say nothing but they each held on to part of the cart and lifted it in the air. It was heavy, so they had to work hard. The lady walked ahead and they followed.

"I think we can go a little faster," I said, and they started to jog. They was breathing hard in about fifteen seconds but I kept suggesting for them to keep up the pace, and said encouraging words like "watch where you're going" and "look out for that curb."

When we got to the spot where she was supposed to park, they let go and looked at me.

"You guys done a good job," I said. "You'll be playing Doctor Hudson before you know it. And maybe next time you won't need so much Spring training to get in the mood."

"Thank you," the lady said and she give me one of them bear claw wrenches. It tasted even better than it smelled. Then she thanked each of the teenage guys and gave them each a wrench too.

They walked away fast and didn't look back.

"I'm Kayla," she said and shook my hand.

"I'm Jumper," I said back. "I hope you sell a bunch of wrenches."

"They're bear claws, not..." she said and then she stopped.

"Thanks," she said and she smiled about as big a smile as I ever seen.

I collected a bunch of cans that day. But if I didn't collect even one can, I ain't gonna complain about a day like that.

> *Were I a king I might command content;*
> *Were I obscure unknown would be my cares,*
> *And were I dead no thoughts should me torment,*
> *Nor words, nor wrongs, nor love, nor hate, nor fears;*
> *A doubtful choice of these things which to crave,*
> *A kingdom or a cottage or a grave.*
>
> — *Edward de Vere, 17th Earl of Oxford*

Chapter Sixteen

That night my apartment felt cold, so I put my second cover on the couch over the first one and pulled them both up to my chin.

"So, Mortimer," I said. He was already snuggled up against my chest, but he wasn't asleep. "We need to think about all our clues. Remember that time we put all our clues on three by five cards and sorted them? That's what we need to do, only we ain't got cards so we got to do it in our brains."

Mortimer purred. Some guys might have an imaginary cat that talks to them, but Mortimer ain't like that. Obviously, cats don't talk. I'd be suspicious of any imaginary cat that talks to people since that seems made-up. Mortimer don't need words. He just purrs and sometimes he yowls. If you ain't got one yet, imaginary animals can be any size. They can be strong as a dinosaur or quiet as an owl. In some far-off countries, parents tell their little kids what their imaginary friend is and they never know they got choices. I'm glad I live in America instead since I chose Mortimer and cats is cool. Mortimer don't do circus tricks or make jokes, but he helps me think and I feel better when he's around. Which is most of the time, as long as I remember to notice him. So now I told him all the clues I could think of.

"There ain't a good way to find Tonto's owner, since he didn't have a collar. That's my first clue. And I ain't got close enough to that pickup truck to clean off its license plate or see the driver and solve it that way. So, Tonto's case is a head-scratcher and we need to keep scratching our heads."

Mortimer didn't say nothing. We both knew that sometimes my best plan is to just wait and get lucky, even if you got to wait a long time for it to work.

"The murder case is about the opposite," I said. "There's clues all over the place like water filling up the bathtub and running on the floor. I'll tell them to you one at a time.

"We got Esmeralda the waitress who pretended she didn't know the guy who wrote the book she was named for.

"We got Professor Reginald who didn't have a good reason to kill Isaac and got poisoned himself. The cops think he's their number one suspect but I wouldn't of even picked him up for questions.

"We got Paddy-O, who I wish the cops would arrest before his guys punch me any more. He had good reasons but that's all the clues against him.

"We got the lady who worked with Isaac Goldfarb. Maybe if he was gone she'd get more of his company. I don't think it was her since she liked him a lot but you can't ever tell."

I thought about it to see if I was missing any suspects. You can't skip anyone until you got a good reason to. Who else had I met?

Well, Mr. Isaac's wife, for one. People kill someone they married in lots of stories. Then there was Professor Andy who liked all my poem words. It was sort of unusual that he come up to me and talked so much at the conference. He didn't seem much like a murderer but then none of them did. It could be some whole different person I ain't met yet.

I also met Mitch, the security guard, and Nurse Helga, and Sugar the lady who liked to dance, and Kayla who sold those bear claw things, and the guys who was pestering her. And the neighbor lady across the street from Professor Reginald's house. None of them had much motives.

I inspected each of my suspects several times in my brain. I was about asleep and starting to dream. It was a good dream about riding a circus elephant when I thought of one more suspect and woke myself back up. That ain't exactly right, it wasn't a suspect. It was a clue. No, that ain't right either. I woke myself all the way up and stared at the ceiling. It wasn't a suspect or a clue, it was more a question only now that I was awake I didn't remember it. It seemed like a treasure map which I should of put on my list, only I knew there wasn't a treasure map.

Maybe it was whatever Professor Reginald had found that might have forensics on it. Only the cops had searched his house and I searched it too. I don't think I missed any hiding spots, but maybe I seen a clue and didn't know I'd seen it. That happens on TV all the time.

I decided to do the whole search again from memory and see if I noticed something this time. That's always a risk; when I go back over stuff in my brain sometimes I get bored before I'm done and then I fall asleep. Which ain't bad, I decided. Either I'd think of the question that was keeping me awake or else I'd fall asleep and dream I was on an elephant and wouldn't have to worry about it.

I remembered going to the professor's house and going up the steps to his porch. I remembered his thirsty geraniums in pots. I remembered the neighbor lady coming up to me out of breath and wanting to know what I was doing. I remembered going in the front door and seeing all the stuff on the floor in the living room. I went through each of the rooms remembering stuff but there wasn't any questions waving their arms at me. Then I went back through every room, turning off lights and making sure I hadn't moved something that could be evidence.

The only thing I moved was that silly dart board with the googly eye Raiders coach. I'd picked it up off the floor and seen the nail it must of hung from because of all the dart holes in the wall. I had felt the cardboard in the back, and then I put it back on the floor right where I found it. "I should of threw at least one dart at that dumb coach," I told Mortimer, only I think he was asleep by now. "You know, while I had the chance." I pictured them googly eyes bouncing around like crazy goldfish eyes with a shark chasing them.

I started to go back to sleep. Then I opened my eyes wide open. It was probably a dumb question but it was waving its arms at me.

"Where was the darts?"

There wasn't no darts sticking out from the cork, or on the wall. There wasn't darts on the floor. I had looked in every drawer and shelf. There wasn't

185

a single dart anywhere in the professor's house. You don't get dart holes without darts. Why would a guy hide all his darts?

I said it again before I went to sleep so I'd remember it when I woke up.

"Why would a guy hide his darts?"

Chapter Seventeen

In the morning I still remembered my question only it didn't seem like a big deal any more. A guy could lose his darts or loan them to a buddy or take them to work in case he had a different dart board there. A question ain't always a clue. Sometimes you notice stuff that ain't all that ordinary but after you think about it, it seems ordinary after all.

Thinking about darts made me think of Professor Reginald's goofy dart board. That ain't something the cops could sell for much money so they'd probably hire a guy to throw it in the trash. That would be a shame since it would look good on my wall...

As soon as the idea of swiping the dart board for my wall showed up in my brain, I put my foot down on it. If a detective starts doing stuff just because it would be good for him instead of doing what was best for the case—well, the next thing you know the case goes out the window. He'd start looking for clues that do him the best favors instead of clues that lead to the best suspects.

But then I thought about little Linda, the girl who was watching Tonto without even getting paid. She wasn't detecting on a case, so she ain't got interest conflicts. She was a Broncos fan, so she'd think the dartboard was just as funny as me. If I swiped it to give her, that wouldn't change how I looked at other clues. Plus, it would be a good present for taking care of Tonto.

I liked that idea. I didn't have a good reason to break into the professor's house, since I already decided there ain't clues there. But breaking in to get a present for a little kid didn't seem so bad. They was probably going to throw it away anyway, plus pay somebody to do it. I'd be saving them the money of hiring a guy. I'd be doing them a favor even if they didn't know it. It would be a easy break-in since I had a key to the front door.

I could put on my old painter clothes, bring a big trash bag, unlock the front door, put the dartboard in the trash bag, and then leave again. If them geraniums was getting dry, I could water them. If Mrs. Johnson from across the street come over, I'd tell her hi and we could have another nice talk.

187

I didn't see no hidden flaws in that plan.

The next morning I put on my painters' clothes and put an extra trash bag in my backpack. But before I even left my apartment, Holly knocked on my door. She took one look at my clothes and got a Perry Mason look in her eyes.

"Are you doing some painting today?" she said. "I thought this was a can-collecting day."

"Just cause a guy's got painter clothes on don't mean he's doing painting. Sometimes I wear this same stuff if I'm cleaning an apartment, or fixing a plumbing leak, or pulling weeds for Mr. Levy. A pirate could wear a painter's hat but he'd still be a pirate. Clothes ain't a big deal."

She started to answer but stopped and shook her head.

"It doesn't matter," she said. "Linda called me with a message for you."

"Little Linda? The kid from the hospital?"

"How many girlfriends named Linda do you have?"

"She ain't a girlfriend. She's just a kid..."

Holly put up her hand to stop me from talking.

"Yes, it's little Linda from the hospital. Her message was this: Tell Mr. Jumper that me and my friend Fiona are having a garlic-planting party this afternoon in my back yard. We hope you can come. Signed Linda. P.S. There might be chocolate chip cookies..."

"What's a garlic-planting party?"

"I've never heard of it," said Holly. "But if I were a great detective, I might guess it's where little girls get together to plant garlic and eat cookies."

"Yeah, I was about to guess that too. Remember we done that turtle-release party with Linda? That was a fun day. I got an appointment this morning but I'm mostly free in the afternoon. Thanks for telling me."

"Someday you need to get your own cell phone," she said.

"It's getting high on my list," I said.

After Holly left, I thought about maybe skipping the dartboard part of my day. Lots of times, when you plan too much stuff for one day, one thing takes longer than you thought and then you got conflicts. But I was going to bring the dartboard to Linda anyway, so if I took the right bus I could go straight from the professor's house to Linda's house and save an extra trip. So in a way it was really doing less stuff in one day instead of more. Plus I wouldn't have to keep the dartboard at my apartment wondering how it would look on my wall. The idea had a lot of pluses.

I put a clean Denver Broncos T-shirt in my backpack. It was a cool one that said AFC Champions so it's special and I don't wear it that often. My white painter T-shirt would be good for breaking into professor Reginald's house but then I could change before I went to the party.

When I walked up the steps to professor Reginald's house I held a trash sack in one hand. In my other hand I had my clipboard and a sharp pencil. Mrs. Johnson come running across the street before I got to the top step. When she got there she was too out of breath to talk much.

"Mrs. Johnson," I said. "It's nice to see you again. Have you noticed any more suspicious activities?"

She nodded 'yes' real hard but she still couldn't talk. I set the trash bag down on the porch and held the clipboard like I was taking notes and waited. She put her hands on her knees and leaned over, breathing fast like she run a kickoff back for a touchdown instead of just across a street.

"I saw them!" she said and then she went back to breathing hard "Early in the morning! There were three of them! Teenagers! Probably never worked a day in their lives!"

"Can you describe them?"

"Of course I can! They were surly! Disrespectful!"

"I mean how they looked."

"They were wearing T-shirts. Two of the shirts had pictures of horrible rap groups I never heard of. The third one's shirt just had a rude comment."

"That's a pretty good description. Did you report them to the cops?" I flipped through some papers on my clipboard like I was looking for a police report.

"Of course I did."

"I don't see nothing in my files. But then headquarters ain't as good as it used to be. What was these guys doing?"

"They were knocking over trash cans! One after another! It's trash day so everyone had their containers out by the curb. These criminals knocked them down and kicked open the bags inside until trash was all over the street. Then they laughed and moved on to the next house. All the commotion woke me and I came running out, yelling and waving a broom at them. They're lucky I didn't chase them all the way back to the sewer!"

"So they got away?"

"This time they did. But they better not come back!"

"OK, I'll make a note in my report. But you should be careful in case it's a ruthless gang from some whole different state. Sometimes it's better to let the cops handle gang-guys."

She nodded. She'd mostly caught her breath again. She pointed at my green trash bag on the porch.

"So what are you doing here today?" she asked. I could tell she still wanted to go into the professor's house.

"I don't like to talk about official stuff," I said. "In case I ain't authorized. Let me ask you a question: did you ever have rats?"

Her eyes got wide. "Rats? In this neighborhood? I've never heard of such a thing!"

"I ain't saying there is rats and I ain't saying there ain't rats. I'm just saying that sometimes when a vacant house gets a problem it can spread to other houses as fast as water spreading out on a paper towel. If a house on your street had some little problem, I bet you want somebody to fix it before it got to your paper towel."

She nodded yes and backed away. She looked me up and down, like she thought she saw little rat eyes peeking out from my pockets and little rat tails whipping out from my socks.

"I told you we ain't supposed to let civilians inside a suspect house," I said. "But you been a good eyewitness. And I could sure use somebody to hold my collecting bag open so I can use two hands. Especially if we collect any live ones that want to wiggle and get away. You could sit on the couch, which I think ain't a bad problem spot yet..."

But she was already backing away even faster.

"No, no, that wouldn't be right," she said. "I don't want to get you in trouble. I'll just go back home..." She turned and walked about as fast as she could across the street.

The dartboard was still on the floor where I left it. I put it in the trash sack, then put the sack in my backpack. I looked around in case some clue just woke up and come stumbling out to say hello, but there wasn't new clues. I watered the geraniums in their pots, locked the front door behind me and started walking to the bus stop. At the bus stop, I changed from my painter T-shirt to my AFC Champion Broncos shirt. When the correct bus came, I got on and rode to a stop about six blocks from Linda's house and walked the rest of the way.

When I pushed the doorbell Linda's mom answered the door.

"Mr. Jumper," she said and give me a big smile. "Linda will be so pleased you could come. Come on in."

"Thanks," I said. "I never been to a garlic-planting party."

"Linda and Fiona are in the back yard," she said. "Before I take you back there, let me tell you what's going on."

"OK."

"Fiona's eleven, a few months older than Linda. Her mother died two months ago and Fiona's still taking it quite hard. And now her dad is getting transferred and they won't have a permanent home for several months."

"It ain't very easy losing your mom," I said.

"Yes. Linda told me about you losing your own parents when you were young. I know you understand how she feels."

"I probably don't really understand," I said. "I feel sad and everybody else has their own sadness. There ain't a good way to tell if somebody else's is like mine."

"I suppose not. Anyway, every year, Fiona's mom had a little garlic patch. Fiona helped her with it. But now, with them having to move away, she thinks she's leaving part of her mom behind."

"Gardens is mostly dirt and plants," I said. "They ain't got fingerprints."

"Of course not. You've got a very logical brain, Mr. Jumper. But a little girl's heart isn't interested in logic." She didn't say nothing for a minute, then she started talking again. "So we told her she could move her mom's garlic patch into our back yard, at least until she's got a more permanent home."

"You'd need a back-hoe and a dump truck to move a garden," I said.

She smiled. "We're not moving the dirt. Just the garlic."

"That sounds easier."

"Fiona will be living with us for a while until her dad gets settled somewhere. I think you'll like her. She's very smart."

We went back out the front door and Linda's mom walked with me to the back yard.

Linda and Fiona didn't see us for a minute. They was throwing a frisbee and Tonto was chasing after it. He jumped up in the air and caught it in his mouth before it landed. Then he started to bring it back.

Fiona was about as cute as Linda. She had mostly blonde hair with a little bit of red, which was twisted into two long pigtails. Her skin was pale but with lots of brown freckles. Both girls was wearing jeans and T-shirts.

"Linda!" her mom shouted. "Someone's here to see you."

Linda spun around and seen me. "Mr. Jumper!" she shouted. "You came!" then she started running at light speed right at me. "Come on, Fiona! It's Mr. Jumper!"

When she got to me she jumped right at me without slowing down, wrapping her skinny arms around my neck like a octopus and her little legs around my waist like boa constrictors. I dropped the trash sack and hugged her back, only there wasn't much chance she was going to fall off.

Fiona followed after her, but at a trot instead of a full speed gallop. When Tonto seen what was going on, he raced to me too with the frisbee in his mouth. He was a lot faster than any little girl, so he passed Fiona. When he got to me, Linda said, "Tonto! Leave it!" and he dropped the frisbee. Linda let loose of me and stood beside me. "Tonto! Sit!" she said.

Tonto sat with a big dog grin on his face for about one second and then he jumped up on me and started licking my face.

"Good boy," I told him. "I missed you too. Linda's been teaching you new words."

Linda shook her head. "Nope. He already knew all these words. I was the one who had to learn his vocabulary. Mr. Jumper, I'd like you to meet my friend Fiona. We've been best friends forever. Fiona, this is Mr. Jumper. I told you about him. He saved my life once. I know he looks like a grown-up but that's just his disguise."

"Pleased to meet you, Mr. Jumper," Fiona said and shook my hand even if Tonto was still leaning on me and trying to get all the attention. It wasn't that easy to shake hands while a big golden retriever dog was trying to slow-dance me. Fiona's lips smiled and she acted as polite as a TV game-show host, but the rest of her face was sad.

"Me too," I said.

"Fiona never heard of the Lone Ranger or Tonto," Linda said. "So she calls him Toto, Dorothy's little dog in the Wizard of Oz. The names sound kind of alike, and he comes when she calls him that."

"Tonto is smart," I said. "I bet he can translate lots of human words into dog words. In the movie, Toto pulled the curtain away from the wizard which was smart so that's a good name, too. Not as good a name as Elway, but I gave Tonto his chance and he didn't want that one."

"Throw the frisbee!" Linda said. "Tonto loves to play frisbee."

I ain't thrown frisbees that much once I got to be an adult, but it sailed like it was supposed to. Tonto raced after it and brung it back. After about eleven throws, I patted his head.

"You're a good receiver for a dog," I said. "Only I think we was going to have a garlic planting party."

About the same time as I said that, Tonto noticed the trash sack I dropped on the grass. He started sniffing at it hard, as if it was full of dog treats.

"What's in the sack?" Linda asked.

"It's a present for you only it's kind of dumb. Plus the guy who used to own it might want it back only I ain't had a chance to ask him yet. So it's a present, but it's sort of a loan of a present. I didn't want it to get throwed out."

"Tonto seems to like it."

"Yeah, I thought it was a clean sack but maybe it got used for something a dog might like. I don't think it's got germs."

Tonto barked at the sack.

"Next time I bring you something, I'll make sure to use a brand new sack."

"I'm sure it's fine," Linda said "What is it?"

I pulled the dartboard out and held it up. I tapped on it with my knuckle and the Raiders coach's eyes went totally googly. Both girls giggled and said, "Let me do it!" Linda tapped on the dartboard and then Fiona did and every time we all laughed.

"There ain't darts that come with it," I said. "Anyway, your mom might want you to grow a little bigger before you use real darts. I think some darts have sticky ends instead of a metal point." I leaned it against the fence.

"I love it, Mr. Jumper," Linda said. "It will be the best picture on my wall even if I never get darts."

Tonto walked over to the dartboard and sniffed. At first I thought he might lift his leg and squirt on it. Instead, he started barking at it.

"Leave it," Linda said, but he kept barking.

"Maybe somebody had a cat blanket in this bag and he smells that," I said. "The smell could of got on the dartboard."

"Leave it!" Linda said and pointed at the dog. Tonto stopped barking. "That's not like him. He's always a really good dog."

I folded up the trash sack and stuffed it int my backpack.

"Maybe he's like a vampire whose afraid of garlic," I said.

"Alliumphobia," Fiona said. "It's the fear of garlic. Maybe Tonto is extra sensitive."

"Yeah, or maybe he's a vampire dog. If he starts howling at the moon you better watch out."

"Tonto, sit," Linda said. He sat down without no argument, smiling with his tongue hanging out his mouth.

"You're a good dog teacher," I said. "How are you with parrots?"

"I could probably teach one to say 'Polly want a cracker.' That's what parrots say in old movies."

"That would be a good improvement. What's our garlic plan?"

She led me to the edge of the lawn. There was a strip of dirt maybe three feet wide next to the wood fence. They'd already drove in four short wood stakes on each corner of a spot about eight feet long. White string was tied to the stakes and stretched between them to make a little fence around the dirt.

"That's the new garden?" I asked.

"Yeah. There were marigolds in there but we got tired of them and mom said it would be a good spot for garlic."

"Is there steps we got to follow? I like garlic in spaghetti, but I ain't an expert on it."

"That's OK. Fiona knows everything in the world about garlic. Why don't you tell Mr. Jumper the steps."

"OK," Fiona said. She talked slow and her voice was soft. She mostly didn't look right at me but looked down at the ground, or sometimes up at my shirt. Shy people sometimes look at your shirt instead of your face.

"We have to dig up the dirt and break up the clods. If we have any compost, we enrich the soil. Then we plant the cloves in straight rows. The pointy end of the clove points up. Then we cover the cloves with dirt or compost. That's about it."

"What does a clove look like?"

Linda giggled. "I told you he was really a little kid in disguise. Fiona, show him a clove."

Fiona nodded. She had a cloth bag with a draw string. She opened it and pulled out a clump of something, that could of been an old dried-out wad of brown paper the size of a lemon. It looked as dead as sawdust.

"Is that a clove?"

"No, it's a bulb. There's maybe a dozen cloves inside it." Fiona pulled at it and got one clove loose and handed it to me. It was about the size of an olive and ordinary brown color. It did not look very interesting.

"Well, maybe it has a good personality," I said.

Linda giggled. Fiona reached out her hand.

"Let me show you," she said. She used her thumbnail to make a little cut through the skin of the clove and handed it back to me. "Smell that," she said.

I must of made a funny face when I smelled it since they both laughed.

"Kind of burns my nose," I said. "And my eyes."

"It doesn't take much to add flavor to food."

I blinked a few times until my eyes stopped watering.

"Maybe I'll let you guys handle the cloves and I'll handle the shovel," I said. "You got enough cloves to plant this whole garden?"

"Yes, sir," Fiona said. "My mom always let me help her with her garlic patch. That's where these came from."

"Are you sure they'll work? They don't look..." I stopped. I didn't want to say they looked dead since that might remind her about her mom.

"It's OK," she said. "They don't look alive, but neither do seeds, do they?" She wasn't shy when she was talking about garlic. "These will sprout new roots and leaves, which look like tall hollow grass. Mom would cut the 'garlic greens' into little sections a quarter of an inch long and sprinkle them on things like baked potatoes, like chives. In June, a thicker green stalk called a 'scape' comes up from the ground. The scape blooms and goes to seed, but it's hard to grow garlic from seeds. Farmers have grown garlic from cloves for so many years the plants have sort of forgotten how to do seeds." She stopped for a few breaths, thinking about seeds before she went on. "In late summer, all the top parts die and we dig them up. Every clove grows into a bulb with maybe ten new cloves inside."

"You plant one and get ten? So you can eat some and still have enough to plant your garden all over again? It's like a profit."

"Exactly. My mom loved her garlic patch. But now she's gone." She got quiet.

"I ain't sure someone is all the way gone if there's still stuff they loved," I said. "I think loves sticks to things, kind of like glitter does. Your mom left her glitter all over these garlics." I looked over at Linda. "Where did you say that shovel is?"

"It's in the shed." She pointed. "Right at the back of our yard. There's also a wheelbarrow in there and some little hand shovels. And there's a compost pile on the other side of the shed."

"So what are we waiting for?" I said, and started to jog to the shed. Right away Tonto barked and started chasing after me. Two seconds later them little girls was running after me too. I had to speed up to a full run or they would of caught me. Tonto thought it was like the frisbee game and he ran full speed even ahead of me.

The wheel barrow was bright yellow and looked as new as a picture in a magazine ad. The shovel had a yellow handle too, like they was going to be in a wedding and had to wear clothes that matched.

"Is your compost yellow too?" I said.

"Don't be silly! It's dirt-colored."

I pushed the wheelbarrow outside. The compost pile was under a blue tarp.

"I ain't sure the fashion cops will let us use compost from a blue tarp in a yellow wheelbarrow."

"Well then, let's not tell them."

I put three shovels full of compost into the barrow.

"Let's start with this much until we see how much we need," I said. "Fiona, have you ever drove a wheelbarrow?"

She shook her head no. "Mom had a cart, but she always pushed it."

"Well, obviously she did! Grownups always pick the funnest jobs for theirselves. I think you're big enough to get your wheel barrow license." We put the two little shovels on top of the compost in the barrow. "You stand here, with one handle in each hand. I'll hold on behind you until you get your learner's permit."

Fiona's eyes got big and bright when she started pushing. I held the handles right behind her hands, but I only held soft. She done most of the work and her face said she took it serious. It reminded me of when my dad let me push a wheelbarrow even if some people might of thought I was too little. We swerved around a little but the wheelbarrow never dumped over.

I took the big shovel and started to dig up the dirt where the garlic was supposed to go. The dirt wasn't that hard, since it already had growed flowers. Linda and Fiona followed behind me with their little shovels and broke up dirt clods til the whole area was smooth. Then Fiona took her little shovel and carved some valleys from one end to the other, about four inches apart. She was real careful, like she got bonus points if the rows was exactly correct and made the rows as straight as the lines on a football field. Fiona showed Linda how to pull the bulbs apart to get at the cloves. Pretty soon they had a nice pile of garlic cloves ready to plant.

"I ain't doing my fair share," I said.

"You already did the hardest part," Fiona said. "Let's do it this way. I'll stand in the garden and put the cloves down. They should be pointy-end up. Linda how about if you hand them to me one at a time? Then, Mr. Jumper, after I do a row, maybe you can cover them with compost."

"That sounds about as good as my own plans," I said.

Linda handed Fiona one garlic clove. She set it in the bottom of the little ditch she'd carved. Then she put three fingers down next to it and put another clove that exact distance away. They done the whole first row and then I used the shovel to fill the valley with compost. Fiona walked on that row like a high-wire circus lady to press down the dirt on top of the cloves.

"We're gonna need more compost," I said.

Fiona and me pushed the wheelbarrow and I loaded some more compost in it. I didn't have to help her push on the way back almost at all. We planted garlic cloves in the whole garden. Even if I knew there was garlics everywhere, it looked like flat empty dirt.

"It looks like a place a dog would like to dig," I said.

"Tonto won't dig in it," Linda said. "He learns real fast when I tell him not to do something."

"Hey, you farmers!" Fiona's mom called out to us. She was walking across the lawn carrying a tray. "Anybody want cookies and lemonade?"

"Yes, Mom!" Linda called out. "We all do!"

We sat on the grass and ate cookies and drank lemonade.

"It's pretty cool you planting garlic for your mom," I said. "I think you get Doctor Hudson bonus points."

"I don't understand."

"Doctor Hudson is a game I played with my dad. Only it's kind of a secret so I shouldn't of said nothing."

Linda punched me in the shoulder, only it was a little girl punch and she was just pretending anyway.

"Ouch!" I said real loud and grabbed my shoulder.

"You better tell us about this game, buster!" she said. "Or else I'll have to punch you again!"

"OK, OK," I said. "Only you can't tell nobody else."

They both leaned forward and listened with their eyes open wide open, like I was saying a ghost story by a campfire.

"Doctor Hudson figured out the secret to having good luck," I said. "My dad read about it in a book and he said it was a true thing. You got to do something nice for someone but you can't tell them and you can't tell anybody else. That's the game."

"Then what?"

"That's it. If you give a guy five bucks, he'll like it fine. If you want to make him feel extra good don't give it to him, put it someplace where he'll find it. He'll like the money just the same, but now he also feels lucky. He'll be smiling all day and you didn't say a word. Everybody likes a gift horse but it's better if you don't have to look one in the face."

"That's a weird game."

"If you do it right, something lucky happens to you. The hard part is you ain't supposed to do it for the luck, you're supposed to do it for that other person. You keeping your mom's garden seems like something you're doing for her without telling her. I think you get Doctor Hudson bonus points."

Linda frowned.

"I don't see any scientific reason that would work."

"Me either, but science ain't my best subject. Just try it sometime and see what happens. Only, since you can't tell the person and you can't tell anybody else, I don't think many laboratories done studies on it. That's also the reason it ain't a popular game. People like to keep score."

"Look what mom put in the cookie tray!" Linda said. She held up some pens. "They're tattoo pens! They look like real tattoos only they wear off in a week or two. Ooh, Fiona! Would you give me a garlic tattoo on my shoulder?"

They both giggled. Linda pulled up the sleeve on her T-shirt and Fiona drew a garlic bulb with green leaves coming out one end and a bunch of cloves bulging out. She drew it very slow and careful.

"It's perfect!" Linda said. "Would you like one?"

Fiona nodded and Linda drew the same thing on Fiona's shoulder.

"Wow," I said. "I remember you had natural gifts but I think you been practicing."

"Let's do Jumper!" she said. Before I could say the next word I had a little girl sitting on each side of me, giggling and drawing garlic pictures on both my shoulders.

"Did your parents leave you anything?" Fiona asked.

"They left me lots of stuff," I said. "I got an apple crate and I got the Doctor Hudson game. Plus I got some songs they used to sing."

"Ooh, teach us a song while we finish your tattoos!"

"I ain't the world's best singer," I said.

"That's OK. What's your favorite song?"

"Well, my mom liked one called 'It's a Marvelous Night for a Moondance,' but that one's kind of tricky. I probably can't do it here right now. You know, without my whole band. My dad liked to sing one called 'Daisy Daisy Give Me Your Answer Do.' That seems like a garlic-planting-party song."

So I sang it all the way through. When I was getting to the end, they started singing with me.

"Again!" Linda said. "We've almost got it."

So I sang it again only this time they both sang with me. We wasn't singing in soft little-girls-in-church voices. We was all using our big opera-star voices so it sounded extra cool. By the next time we sung it, besides all our opera star voices, Tonto was howling right along.

Then we all started laughing.

"We ought to do this every year" I said. "Like a birthday for being friends."

"April 19," Fiona said.

"Is that your birthday?"

"No, silly. It's National Garlic Day."

The Passionate Shepherd to His Love"

Come live with me, and be my love;
And we will all the pleasures prove
That hills and valleys, dales and fields,
Woods, or steepy mountain yields.

And we will sit upon the rocks,
Seeing the shepherds feed their flocks
By shallow rivers to whose falls
Melodious birds sing madrigals.

And I will make thee beds of roses,
And a thousand fragrant posies;
A cap of flowers, and a kirtle
Embroidered all with leaves of myrtle;

A gown made of the finest wool
Which from our pretty lambs we pull;
Fair linèd slippers for the cold,
With buckles of the purest gold;

A belt of straw and ivy-buds,
With coral clasps and amber studs:
And, if these pleasures may thee move,
Come live with me, and be my love.

The shepherds' swains shall dance and sing
For thy delight each May-morning:
If these delights thy mind may move,
Then live with me, and be my love.

— Christopher Marlowe 1590

"For murder, though it have no tongue, will speak
With most miraculous organ. I'll have these players
Play something like the murder of my father
Before mine uncle: I'll observe his looks;
I'll tent him to the quick: if he but blench,
I know my course. The spirit that I have seen
May be the devil: and the devil hath power
To assume a pleasing shape; yea, and perhaps
Out of my weakness and my melancholy,
As he is very potent with such spirits,
Abuses me to damn me: I'll have grounds
More relative than this: the play's the thing
Wherein I'll catch the conscience of the king."
— Shakespeare, spoken by Hamlet

Chapter Eighteen

One thing detectives do the same as criminals is return to the scene of the crime. The Halloween Bar was where the murder happened, so that's the scene of the crime. The cops probably went over it with a five tooth comb, but the best clues is ones that don't look like clues at all so they get missed the first time you look. I'm good at noticing stuff that don't look like clues. Most of the time they ain't clues even after you notice them, but it's better to have more clues than you need instead of not enough, so I always notice extra stuff.

I got there late in the afternoon and decided to detect on the outside first, before the sun went down. There was a sidewalk between the front door and the street. I walked down it real slow. Every time I took a step I stopped and looked at every inch of sidewalk, then I took another step. That might look weird, so if somebody walked past I pretended I was talking on a cell phone. A young couple walked toward me, so I put my hand up by my ear.

"Yes, ma'am," I said. "Mashed potatoes is about my favorite. And there ain't a Bronco game on that night so my schedule looks good." Once the couple got past me I stopped pretending to talk on a phone call until somebody else walked by.

There was some cigarette butts on the sidewalk, and one broke beer bottle, and the paper from somebody's taco dinner. The cops probably already noticed that stuff so there wasn't much point of me filing a report on it. There was a bike rack bolted to the sidewalk, but no bikes. The rack was dusty, since Denver don't get much rain. About four inches above the sidewalk, one of the metal posts had a section that looked clean, with no dust. It was only five inches of clean metal and I only seen it because the sun was low in the sky and hit it just right. I thought that's probably where some bicycle part hit the rack. As soon as I thought that, I put my foot down on the idea of explaining clues away.

You ain't supposed to be figuring out why something ain't a good clue yet, I said to myself. Just notice stuff to figure out later.

The sides of the building was going to be harder. There was six feet of dirt and weeds between the bar building and the buildings on each side. Obviously they didn't want drunks trying to sleep there, so they put up a ten-foot-tall chain-link fence. When nobody was watching me, I climbed it and jumped down the other side.

Maybe that fence kept out really drunk guys, but it didn't stop everybody. I counted 83 beer bottles if you include broke ones, and six old magazines that was getting moldy, and sixteen sacks from takeout food, plus so many cigarette buts I didn't even try to count. The weeds was as tall as my knees, so even doing my best detecting I might of missed some stuff.

Then I seen one thing that was interesting. It was a leather dog collar with a ten foot leash still hooked to it. There was a dog tag on it that said "Touchstone" which ain't a real word so it might be the name of the company that made the dog tag. Below that was the professor's name and address. I ain't ever seen a collar as thick as this one, so it was probably expensive. I put the collar in a clean trash sack in case it had evidence and put the sack in my backpack.

"Hey, Mortimer," I said. "I'm gonna have to tell Officer Mike that the cops have got lazy to miss a clue like this one." Then I kept on detecting in the weeds but I didn't find no more clues.

Behind the building was a parking lot and I couldn't see no fence stopping me that direction. I was done with this side of the building so I started walking toward the parking lot. I got almost to the end of the building when a door opened. I'd been detecting for clues so hard in the dirt I never noticed the door. The two guys who punched me walked out the door. In about one second they seen me and blocked my path.

"Well, well, well," said one. "Look who we found trespassing on Paddy-O's property. Are you still looking for a dog?"

"Nah," I said. "I'm looking for clues about the dog's owner."

"I guess we didn't get your attention last time."

They took a step toward me. I backed up away from the parking lot and toward the fence. I couldn't go too many steps back before I'd be up against the fence and trapped. I backed up slow so I could make my case for not guilty.

"Oh no," I said. "You got my attention all the way. I ain't even asked one question about Mr. O, just like you said."

They kept walking toward me and I kept backing up.

"I guess we'll have to try harder this time."

"Well, I hope you got a way to get my attention without punching me. For one example, jokes always get my attention if you know any jokes."

They smiled at that, the way wolves smile on a TV show when they surround a deer.

"Well, that's about the funniest joke I ever heard right there," one guy said.

By now I could feel my back pressed against the chain link.

"You get more friends with jokes than with punches," I said. "My mom said that all the time."

"Well, your mom ain't here, is she?" Then he said something rude about my mom and pretended he went on a date with her last night. I could feel my face getting hot, which always makes it hard to have a polite discussion.

"My mom's dead," I said.

"Well, that explains why she was so boring last night."

I could see they was both getting ready to punch me about as hard as they could. My arms was down at my sides. Some guys would of raised their arms to block the punches, but I grabbed the chain link behind me and held

209

it tight. When them guys pulled their fists back to aim, I lifted both my legs so my knees was almost touching my chest.

"You shouldn't of said that," I said.

Now, if this was a streaming TV show and I had a remote, pretend I just hit the pause button so I could tell you something. In case you don't remember, my main thing is jumping off stuff like garage roofs and trees. I train almost every day, doing about twenty jumps. After you jump you got to climb back up the tree or the garage so you can do it again. Obviously, I mostly do it since it's fun and it's my sport. But a bonus is that it's good exercise and after all these years, I gotta admit I'm pretty strong. Especially my legs.

There wasn't a way for them guys to know that. When my face gets hot and two guys is ganging up on me even if I didn't do nothing to them and they was talking bad about my mom—well, I wasn't using my whole brain. OK, so I probably wasn't using any of my brain right that second. I was just mad, plus I didn't want to get beat up again, so my best thinking went out the window.

So now, if I un-hit the pause button, you'd see these two guys with muscles as strong as dinosaur muscles grinning like circus clowns and winding up to punch me. And I'm backed up to a chain link fence holding on behind my back. My legs is lifted up with my knees almost touching my chest. Before they could get their punches off, I kicked both of them right in the stomach. It was like my legs was steel springs wound up tight and then I let them go. Their eyes got big and their mouths opened up like fish mouths on a hook and they stumbled backward and fell down.

OK, stumbled back ain't the best word since I kicked them so hard they kind of flew backward. I ain't never seen two guys look as surprised as them two. When they landed in the weeds I seen behind them that the door was open and an older guy was standing there. When he seen me kick those two guys he started laughing very hard. From the way he looked, I knew it was Paddy-O who these two muscle guys worked for.

I waved at him as friendly as I could. Then I turned around, climbed the chain-link fence in about three seconds and jumped down to the sidewalk on the other side.

"OK, you guys," I said. "I hope next time we meet you'll be more polite. You catch more flies with cupcakes than with dish soap, which my dad always said. I'd stay and talk some more but I gotta catch a bus on Colfax Street."

Then I started jogging down the middle of the street.

"Catch him!" Paddy-O shouted.

I stopped jogging when I got out of sight and stood close to the first building past the bar. I could hear them trying to climb the fence. Even just listening I could tell they was out of practice climbing fences. They was cussing as bad as my parrot.

"You idiots!" Paddy-O yelled at them. "He's heading for a bus stop on Colfax. Wouldn't it be smarter to chase him in a car?"

They cussed some more but I could hear them going through the weeds to the parking lot.

"Idiots!" Paddy-O shouted again, then I heard his door slam.

The building I was standing next to had a little entrance so the door was set back about two and a half feet from the sidewalk. I stood in there and waited.

In about one minute, they come roaring down the road to chase me. They wasn't driving a pickup truck, they was in a red BMW car going race-car fast. I seen the two guys through the side window as they zoomed past, but they didn't look my direction. It would only take them about eight minutes to get to the bus stop on Colfax, but the next bus didn't come for twenty minutes after that and I figured they'd park and watch for me. So I had about a half hour.

I walked back to the Halloween Bar and went in the front door.

I could tell where Mr. O's office was going to be on the inside since I seen him come out the door on the outside. It would be back behind the back wall of the bar area on the right side. The bartender was busy and the other customers was all talking to each other so I walked toward it.

The back wall was painted black so the black door wasn't all that obvious except for a white sign that said "Private!—Employees only!—Do Not Enter!" The door wasn't locked so I went through it. It opened up to a hall with doors on both the left and the right.

The first door on the left wasn't locked and didn't have a sign to keep out. That room had lockers against one wall, and a round table with six chairs around it. There was wood benches against one wall. One wall had a couch, with a lamp and a mirror. One wall had a board about three feet tall and four feet wide with a bunch of hooks. Most of the hooks had name tags hanging on them. It took a minute but I found Esmeralda. I took it off its hook.

"OK, so now I'm Esmeralda," I said. There wasn't nobody there to hear me except Mortimer and he was taking a nap. There was a detecting lesson right there: Anybody could wear a name tag but that don't prove it's who they are. And even if they said they was the person on the name tag, like I did, that ain't proof either.

Some of the lockers had locks on them, so they was probably where employees kept their stuff while they was working. I went back out into the hall.

The last door on the right had a sign that said "Private!—Do Not Enter!"

If they wanted these rooms to be private, they'd lock the doors, I thought as I opened it and stepped inside. An older guy with short gray hair was sitting behind a wood desk talking on the phone. Once I seen him up close I recognized him from TV news shows. I locked the door behind me.

"Hello, Mr. O," I said. "I think we kind of got off on the wrong feet."

He looked up, real surprised. "I'll call you back," he said into his phone. Then he turned to me. "You! What are you doing here?"

"I thought maybe we could have a nice polite conversation," I said.

"I doubt that," he said and stood up. He had a baseball bat in his right hand. He come out from behind the desk. When he was young, I bet people thought he looked like a bull. His shoulders was big and his arm muscles were good. He took a couple of steps toward me, whacking at his hand with the bat. I moved sideways a couple of steps. He even moved like a bull, I thought, rolling his shoulders and sometimes jerking his head up like he had horns and wanted to flip a rodeo clown in the air.

"We gave you every chance to escape," he said. "Whatever happens now is your own fault."

I kept moving sideways and he kept following me so we was circling his office. In about twelve seconds I was standing right next to his desk without much more room to move.

"To be real exact," I said. "Your guys didn't 'let' me escape."

He swung the bat at me like my belly button was a baseball and all the bases was loaded.

It shouldn't of surprised him so much that I done a standing jump almost straight up and pulled my knees up to my chest. The bat whipped through the air below my feet. I landed on top of his desk, which you could tell he didn't like. I gotta give him credit for quick thinking. In about two seconds he was taking another swing at me, aiming right at my knees.

Sometimes quick thinking ain't the best thinking. When he started to swing, I jumped over him. It was lucky his office had a high ceiling and I didn't hit my head on it. I landed right behind him.

He didn't understand what just happened. Maybe he closed his eyes while he was swinging the bat, which some guys do, so he didn't even see me jump. He stared at the top of his desk as if I'd used magic to disappear. Before he figured out I was behind him, I reached around and grabbed the bat and took it away from him.

"How did you..?" he started to say. He turned to face me. Then his brain put all the parts together and he seen I was standing right there holding his bat.

"It mostly takes practice," I answered him. "Now, you've had a couple of turns at bat. Fair play says I should get a couple of turns, too."

"What do you want?"

"If you're done with your bat exercises I could skip my turns for a minute. Maybe you could sit there..." I pointed to one of his visitor chairs. "And I could sit there," I pointed at another visitor chair. "You had a baseball bat behind your desk and maybe you got a gun in a drawer, which wouldn't be fair. So out here seems friendlier."

We both sat down. I laid the bat across my lap.

"What I wanted to say, if your guys had let me, is I don't think you done the murder."

"What?"

"Professor Reginald and Doctor Isaac Goldfarb. You had motives and opportunities and you got enough money to buy poison which is called "means." Once a guy has means, opportunities, and motives he should hire a good lawyer. But it don't make sense."

He leaned back and maybe relaxed a little.

"I don't understand."

"Well, you got motives since Isaac was working on forensics that might prove you was guilty of a crime. You got opportunity since it happened here in your bar. And the means is having enough money to buy poison."

"But you don't think I did it."

"Nah. Lots of guys have the same motives of not wanting better forensics. And lots of guys have money. But it don't make sense you'd kill a guy in your own bar. A smart guy would find some other guy with motives and do it in his bar. Like maybe if there was some other bar that always beat your bar in a pool contest or karaoke contest. A smart guy would do the murder in that bar instead of his own."

"Nobody beats us at pool," he said.

"That ain't the point. A smart guy wouldn't do it in his own bar. And Officer Mike says you're smart."

"Officer Mike?" He looked confused then he figured it out. "Old Turnip-Face-Mike? He said that?" He stared at the ceiling for a minute and his face changed, like a mean kid who picked on the other kids and was a loud jerk until somebody said he was going to the principal's office and he knew he had to take his consequences. He looked nervous.

"Him and me ain't ever talked about vegetables," I said. "He also said you're careful not to let crimes happen in your bar. Plus, there's the dog."

"The dog?"

"Somebody kidnapped Professor Reginald's dog from in front of the bar. Then they threw his collar over the fence which is where your buddies found me."

"Why?"

"It's got GPS. Once the cops think to check that, it would lead them right back here. Except I found it."

"Let me have it!"

"See, now that ain't your best thinking. The killer might of left forensics on it. If I give it to you, you're going to leave your own forensics on it, which is about as good as Perry Mason pointing at you and saying, 'There's the killer!'"

"I see."

"Of course, if you are the killer, you might as well take it. Your D and A stuff is already on it. You can say, oh, that got there after Jumper give it to me. But if you ain't the killer, and your forensics don't show up on the collar, it's going to point a whole different direction. It's about your best witness if you ain't guilty."

"But now it has your DNA."

"Yeah, probably. Only I ain't got means or motives or opportunity. I'm just a guy who found a dog collar."

"So you're going to turn it into the cops?"

"Well, you and me are. Or maybe we can take it straight to some forensic guys."

"How would we do that?"

"Do you have Officer Mike's phone number?"

"Yeah. But I never use it." He looked down at his shoes. "Our social circles have diverged."

"Well, why don't you call him now. Tell him you got his friend Jumper here in your office."

He wasn't convinced that was a good idea, but he called anyway.

"Mike? Old Turnip Face? Is that you? Paddy-O here."

There was a pause while he listened. He smiled a little then went on talking into the phone.

"Yeah, I was thinking we could go on a vacation together. Maybe play some pickle-ball on a cruise ship."

Another pause.

"I'll take that as a no. But seriously, I'm sitting here in my office with a friend of yours." He looked at me. "What did you say your name is?"

"Jumper," I said, and he said it into the phone.

Paddy-O smiled while Officer Mike made some comments I couldn't hear.

"No, no Mike. Nothing like that. Why would I want to hurt a sweet trespasser like..." he looked at me.

"Jumper," I said.

"Jumper," he said into the phone. "He's got a plan to prove my innocence and he wants you to help coordinate it." He listened to his phone for a little bit, then turned to me again. "So what is your plan? Turnip Face wants to know."

"If he can, I'd like him to come down here and take our statements and then drive me and some new evidence to the forensics guys."

He told Mike all that and then he listened again. Then he smiled.

"I don't think you need to worry about that," he said. "He outsmarted my two best...accountants. And sent them on a wild goose chase. Then he marched into my office and nearly took off my head with my own baseball bat. I think I'm the one who needs police protection." He listened for a minute. "Well, if you're already that close, we'll see you in five minutes or so."

When Officer Mike got there, he didn't knock on the door. He just opened it about as fast as a tornado would open it and stepped into the room. Paddy-O stood up. Officer Mike looked at him quick, then looked at me.

217

"Are you all right, Jumper?" he said.

"Well, I'm a little hungry..."

He turned to Mr. O. "What's going on here?"

"Calm down, Mike. Your friend here..." he looked at me.

"Jumper," I said.

"Your friend Jumper was snooping around outside and he says he found a dog collar. Thinks maybe it goes to a dog one of the poisoning victims owned. I haven't seen it."

Mike turned to me. "Why do you think it belongs to one of the victims?"

"Mostly since it has his name and address on the tag."

"That's a good clue," Office Mike said. "Where did you find it?"

"In the weeds next to the building. About twenty two feet from Mr. O's door."

"Interesting." He looked at Mr. O. "And you never noticed it?"

"We let the weeds grow out there. Discourages camping. So no, I never saw it."

"I met a forensics lady," I said and pulled Suzanne Smith's card out of my pocket and gave it to Officer Mike. "I think she'd help us for free. We ain't got good custody chains," I said. "A space ship from the moon could of dropped it in them weeds, so the main cop forensic guys ain't gonna be interested. But if Mr. O put it there, this lady could probably tell us. He says he ain't guilty, so he's OK with us bringing it to her."

"Is that your understanding, Pat?"

"Yeah. We've had our differences, Mike. You don't like how my... accountants figure my taxes. But I'm no murderer."

"I mostly don't like that you had promising career choices in music and electronics. Instead, you chose the easy way. Every time the easy way. The dumb way. The cruel way."

He turned to me. "Where is the collar now?"

I patted my backpack. "It's in a brand new trash sack inside my backpack."

"OK then. Let's take it to your forensics friend. I'm parked right in front."

"OK," I said and went out to the hall. Officer Mike waited a few seconds before he come out. I heard Paddy-O asking Officer Mike a question that didn't make no sense.

"You still ballroom?" he asked.

"When I get the chance," Officer Mike said. "You need a partner who likes that old music, plus you need the right clothes." He paused. "Do you still tango?"

Mr. O laughed a little.

"Bad knees," he said. "And you need a young partner. Not so many young women like to tango, especially with an old gimp like me. But yeah, every now and then."

"The world is changing," Officer Mike said. "We're two old dinosaurs waiting for an asteroid."

"Good luck, Mike."

"Good luck Pat. And for once in your life, try to stay out of trouble."

The Life of Man

The World's a bubble, and the Life of Man
Less than a span :
In his conception wretched, from the womb
So to the tomb ;
Curst from his cradle, and brought up to years
With cares and fears.
Who then to frail mortality shall trust,
But limns on water, or but writes in dust.

Yet whilst with sorrow here we live opprest,
What life is best ?
Courts are but only superficial schools
To dandle fools :
The rural parts are turn'd into a den
Of savage men :
And where's a city from foul vice so free,
But may be term'd the worst of all the three ?

Domestic cares afflict the husband's bed,
Or pains his head :
Those that live single, take it for a curse,
Or do things worse :
Some would have children : those that have them, moan
Or wish them gone :
What is it, then, to have, or have no wife,
But single thraldom, or a double strife ?

Our own affections still at home to please
Is a disease :
To cross the seas to any foreign soil,
Peril and toil :
Wars with their noise affright us ; when they cease,
We are worse in peace:
What then remains, but that we still should cry
For being born, or, being born, to die ?
                    — Francis Bacon

Chapter Nineteen

Officer Mike's car was a big SUV with extra big tires. He wouldn't start driving until I buckled my seat belt. He didn't say nothing until we got on highway I-70 heading west toward Golden, which is a town between Denver and the mountains. When he talked it was sort of like he was talking to himself, trying to figure something out.

"So Pat didn't see the dog collar and his goons must not have either. They would have burned it. The police also didn't see it. I'm sure they searched the whole area within twenty four hours of the incident." He waited for a minute. I didn't say nothing since he was still thinking. "Any first-year detective would have noticed a dog collar with a victim's name on it."

I wanted to say everybody makes mistakes but I didn't think he was done detecting in his brain so I kept quiet. Finally he turned to me.

"So what does that tell you, Jumper?" he asked.

I hadn't been using my whole brain on listening to him, so I had to go back and hear it all again from memory. I shook my head.

"It don't tell me nothing," I said.

He smiled. "Maybe you're not listening your hardest."

That was like somebody giving you a puzzle that everybody else can do but stumps you. I closed my eyes. I could feel the car bouncing a little and hear the tires humming and whining on the pavement. Sometimes I heard a car passing us going faster than the speed limits. We was almost to Golden when I got an idea.

"If the cops didn't find it right after the murder, and Mr. O didn't see it after that, and his accountants with big muscles didn't see it, but then I seen it easy that tells me something. It says it wasn't there. When they swiped his dog, they took the collar with. But then sometime later they brung it back and threw it into the weeds."

"Yeah," he said. "That's what it tells me too."

"But why?" I asked.

He turned and smiled at me. "I guess we're not done detecting, young man," he said.

A little west of Denver, just before the mountains, we took an exit then drove on some streets I ain't ever seen before. Finally, we pulled into a parking lot. The building beside it looked brand new. It was made of concrete and steel like lots of industrial buildings, only nicer. Next to the building was a strip of grass with bushes all trimmed to look exactly alike. We parked and got out. Officer Mike seen me looking around like I just landed in Oz and was nervous about flying monkeys.

"It's a research park," he said as if I'd asked a question. "New companies that raised a lot of seed money. They want to impress the IPO crowd."

"I didn't know seeds was so expensive."

He smiled and nodded.

The lady receptionist was probably twenty-six years old. Her clothes was neat and she acted professional.

"How may I help you?"

"We'd like to see Suzanne Smith."

"Do you have an appointment?"

"Nah," I said. "I ain't got much appointments today, which is why I'm free to see Doctor Smith."

Officer Mike nodded.

"No, we don't," he told the lady. "I'm a retired policeman and this is my friend Jumper. She met him at the forensics conference. We have some new evidence in the Isaac Goldfarb case we'd like her help with."

The woman nodded. She looked at me extra hard, like she thought I was one of them flying monkeys. But she called on her phone. Then she turned back to us.

"She'll be right with you. Please have a seat over there."

We sat on some chairs that was nice enough to be in a rich guy's living room. While we was waiting, a man and woman come in. They was busy talking and didn't look over at us. They also didn't stop to ask permission from the reception lady. They kept walking past her.

It took me a second to recognize that the woman was Isaac Goldfarb's wife. The man was her friend from the conference, the beatnik with the little beard who whispered something to her and then left. He was trying to convince Mrs. Isaacs about something.

"It wasn't a show," he said. "It was a documentary with secret facts the government doesn't want us to know. It was called Future Dog and you need to watch it. I tell you, they can implant trackers..."

"Be quiet!" she said. "You can't believe everything you see in a documentary."

And then they kept walking past the reception lady and down the hall.

"I seen that movie," I told Officer Mike.

"What movie?"

"Future Dog. It was cool. The dog was about as big as a horse and he could read your mind."

"I'll put it on my list," he said.

In a minute, Suzanne Smith came out. She wore a uniform that looked like what a hospital orderly would wear.

"Mr. Jumper," she said and shook my hand. "So nice to see you again." She turned to Officer Mike. "I'm Suzanne," she said and reached out her hand to him.

"I'm Mike," he said. We followed her down a hall to an office that was about the most ordinary office I ever seen. It had gray warehouse carpet, white walls with no pictures, and no window. She pointed at two chairs for us to sit in and she sat behind the little desk.

"You have new evidence?" she said.

"Maybe," Officer Mike said. "Jumper why don't you tell the story. Maybe the short version."

I pulled the plastic garbage bag out of my backpack. I took the hint about the short version. Some people keep talking after nobody's listening any more. Maybe they don't even notice they do it.

"I found a dog collar that goes to Professor Reginald's dog. If the murderer also swiped the dog, his forensics might be on the collar." I was proud about how short I made that story.

"Why didn't you take it to the police?"

Officer Mike answered right away. "We wanted the best."

She smiled at that. "A court might not accept me as a witness," she said. "The victim was my friend and coworker."

"We know," Officer Mike said. "But we don't think any court will convict someone based on DNA from a dog collar that's been sitting outside in the weeds anyway. We're not looking for legal evidence. We just want to aim ourselves in the right direction. And maybe exclude one suspect."

She nodded and thought for a minute. While she was thinking, I asked her a question.

"So how come you got better forensics that other people?"

Her face woke up a little at that question. She liked talking about her job better than talking about laws and courts. Only she obviously made up a lot of her words.

"We use a broader array of tools: multispectral imaging, computed tomography scans, headspace gas chromatography, and 3D modeling integrated by artificial intelligence using a dedicated program that Isaac developed and patented. DNA is great," she said. "It's like a whole, huge orchestra playing for an hour. If all the notes for all the instruments match, you can say for sure it was one specific symphony. But sometimes all you need is the first four note the flutes play. If there's only one symphony with that little phrase, you don't need all the other information."

"I ain't been to many symphonies," I said.

She smiled and nodded. Then she thought of a different way to say the same thing.

"A dog doesn't need to match every protein in a smell. One whiff containing two or three molecules tells him there's a cat hiding behind the curtain. A dog's sense of smell is ten thousand times as acute as a man's. We're sort of the dog sniffers of the forensics world. Unlike a dog, we can also see through the curtain. With Isaac's new procedure we'll be even better. Much better." She stopped and looked sad, thinking about Isaac.

"Cool," I said. "I always liked dogs. Will this GPS collar tell us where the dog went?"

"Depends on the model. But probably. "

"I seen a show where they used a needle to put a GPS chip in a dog. It was called Future Dog."

"That's different. That kind of chip can identify a dog just like a dog tag can. But so far, they can't put a geographical GPS tracker under the skin. Those need a bigger battery."

"In the TV show it worked."

"And maybe someday that will be possible."

"But it was on TV..."

"You can't believe everything you see on TV."

"Sure," I said "Everybody knows that."

"Maybe not everybody. But scientists and detectives do."

"So what happens next?" I said.

"We unwrap the clue," she said. "We'd usually vacuum all the air out of the plastic trash sack first and analyze that, but for your purposes that's not necessary. If it were going to be evidence, we'd collect it in a sterile room with no visitors. This will be more of a demonstration." She put on some thin latex gloves. Then she took the dog collar out of the bag and set it down on a big sheet of white paper.

I already seen the collar, but she looked at it hard and careful. It had the professor's name and address and the word touchstone and made in the USA and a serial number. It was dusty from being out in the weeds. She pulled out a little vacuum cleaner. "Next we collect the dust and pollen and any bits of hair that might be stuck to the collar. We'll be able to tell what kinds of plants the dog ran through recently, and probably identify some insects as well. There may be information about any human..."

The door opened and Mrs. Isaac Goldfarb come into the room. She looked mad.

"Exactly what do you think you're doing, Suzanne?"

"Just a demonstration," she answered. "My friends asked me to do a preliminary forensics exam on a dog collar that belonged to Professor Reginald. It's been contaminated by exposure to uncertain environments, so it probably doesn't have any evidentiary weight. But it might be interesting anyway."

"And who is paying the lab for this preliminary exam?"

"It should be very basic, and potentially quite useful. If we're lucky it might lead us to the person who murdered your husband."

"That's what we have police for. It's why we have the FBI. Our tax dollars pay for them. While I pay your salary."

"The Institute pays my salary."

"And as soon as we get past probate, I'll own the Institute. I'm sure you mean well, but I can't let you waste the Institute's time and money."

Mrs. Isaac Goldfarb picked up the dog collar and put it back in the trash sack. "I'll give this to the authorities. If they even want it."

"You just contaminated the evidence further," Suzanne said.

"You already admitted that it's not really evidence. Anyway, it looks like the whole regiment has already contaminated it. Now, if you two have no more business here..."

"I was going to ask Doctor Smith a couple of questions," I said.

"Not while she's on the clock," Mrs. Isaacs said. "I'm afraid I need to ask you to leave."

"They was short questions..."

"Now!" she said.

Officer Mike nodded and we went out into the hallway.

"I probably should of used some poem words on her," I said.

"She didn't really seem in the mood for poetry," Officer Mike said.

"You gotta figure she's still sad about her husband getting killed and she ain't thinking with her whole brain yet," I said. "You can't hold that against a person."

We walked down the hall toward the reception area. An idea was buzzing around my brain that I couldn't say in words. It was like a mosquito by your ears when you're trying to sleep. You know it's gonna get you, but it ain't landed yet.

"What is it?" Officer Mike said.

"I ain't sure. Except smart guys think everybody else is smart, too. Not quite as smart as them, but pretty smart. They do all their detecting by picturing what they would do if they was the crook. Columbo never went after a dumb crook in all his episodes. I ain't sure he could of won against a dumb crook."

"You think being smart is a handicap?"

"Not mostly. But maybe sometimes. A dumb crook might do dumb stuff the smart detective don't even think of. And dumb guys think the smartest detective is as dumb as them. We're lucky it's you and me detecting instead of Columbo."

"Yeah, I think dumb crooks probably do some dumb stuff," Officer Mike said. We walked down the hall. It seemed longer than when we came in with Doctor Smith but I wasn't paying close attention. "You're kind of quiet," he said after a while. "Are you detecting in your brain again?"

"Maybe," I said. "I wonder how Mrs. Isaac Goldfarb knew we was there?"

"I was wondering that, too," Officer Mike said. "It's quite a coincidence she'd march in right at that minute."

"I got an idea about answering that question," I said. "Plays is like people all pretending the same story, which ain't a lie. We could pretend we're in an episode where we found an extra clue the murderer don't know about. If somebody acts goofy over that episode, that's a good clue about them. And it's more like a play than a lie."

He smiled and nodded.

While I was telling him the rest of my plan, a guy in a blue security shirt came around the corner and stopped us.

"What are you doing here?" he said in a mean way. "Only authorized personnel are allowed in this area."

Officer Mike started to say something about he was a retired cop and we was with the forensic lady and we didn't mean to break no rules. I put my hand on his shoulder and he stopped. This was obviously a case that needed poem words. "In me she has drowned a young girl," I said in a serious voice. "And in me an old woman rises toward her day after day ..." I stopped for a second before I finished, "like a terrible fish."

The guard looked at me as confused as if I was speaking calculus. He wasn't sure if I was crazy or really, really smart, which is hard to tell apart. Lots of forensics guys in that building was probably smart, so he decided not to risk it.

"Fine," he said. "The exit is straight down this hall. But next time remember to get a visitor's pass."

"Yes, sir," Officer Mike said.

When we walked down the hall some more, he said, "I wouldn't have guessed you were a fan of Plath."

"Which path?"

"Sylvia Plath. She wrote the poem you quoted. It's called The Mirror."

229

"Oh, that. That's poem words. Everybody likes you better if you talk like them. I learned some poem words when I went to that conference so they'd think I was a college teacher. Which I ain't."

"Thanks for that clarification."

"If I see a terrible fish in my mirror, it's time to clean the mirror," I said. "I think Doctor Smith give us a clue before she even took the collar out of the bag."

"What was that?"

"She said you can't believe everything you see on TV."

"That's reasonable."

"But she also said some people do, which I didn't think of before. If a guy believed a terrible fish on TV was after him, he might do other stuff that don't make sense either."

We was about to walk past the receptionist. "Are you ready?" I whispered. He nodded.

So then I started talking to Officer Mike in a regular voice. "It's too bad we can't detect on that dog collar," I said.

He played along. "Doesn't seem right."

"Yeah, it was about our best clue. But at least it wasn't our last clue."

"What do you mean?" he said.

"I forgot to tell you before," I said. "But what if the waitress who gave them the poison beer wasn't really Esmeralda?"

He looked confused but didn't say nothing.

"What if she was just wearing Esmeralda's name tag?"

"I don't think the detectives found a name tag."

"That's 'cause it fell down. There's a little cabinet below the name-tag hooks. I seen a name tag behind it but I couldn't read the name on it. Then I had to go meet Mr. O and I forgot about it. If the killer wore that name tag, there might be forensics on it."

"That's good thinking, Jumper."

"Thanks. If you told the cops to come to the Halloween Bar tomorrow morning I could show them right where to look. They could take it into official custody with all the best evidence chains."

"Tomorrow?" he said and sounded confused since there was still plenty of time today to go out there if we wanted. Then he smiled as he seen my plan. "Would ten in the morning be convenient for you?" he asked.

"That would be a perfect time," I said.

The reception lady never looked up at all as we walked past her. When we got to the exit door, I waved at her. "Thanks for all your help," I said. "Have a nice day."

She waved back. "You too," she said.

"When a man's verses cannot be understood, nor a man's good wit seconded with the forward child understanding, it...

No, truly, unless thou wert hard-favour'd; for honesty coupled to beauty is to have honey a sauce to sugar."

—Touchstone in Shakespeare's "As You Like It"

Chapter Twenty

While we was driving to my apartment, I had a whole other idea. It was a clue I didn't see before but I didn't say nothing.

Officer Mike looked over at me and laughed.

"OK, what is it?" he said.

"What is what?"

"You should never try to play poker," he said. "When you get an idea maybe your brain whispers about it. But your face shouts like a Broncos quarterback barking out signals."

"Thanks," I said.

"So what's your idea?"

"It probably ain't anything. Sometimes you detect extra clues and you got to throw some away. I think this is an extra clue."

He waited. Lots of times the guys that are really good at talking back and forth are also good at waiting. I ain't practiced that part as much.

"There was a dartboard," I said and then I stopped. If you look at it one way, I swiped the dartboard without court approvals. Plus, maybe it was evidence so I tampered with a scene. Maybe it's a smart lesson to wait before you say stuff, but it ain't a lesson I learned yet.

"I changed my mind," I said. "It ain't a clue."

He nodded and didn't say nothing. After a while he started talking again.

"You know what the best thing is about being a retired cop?"

"Sleeping late?"

"Yeah, that's good. But the best part is I don't have to report every little thing. If a guy's got a busted tail light, I might point it out in case he doesn't know. But I don't have to mention it to the cops. I don't have to write a ticket. I get to keep secrets."

"Even if a guy swiped some alleged evidence?"

"That depends. Was it the murder weapon?"

"Nah, it's just a dartboard with a picture of that dumb Raiders coach from a while back. The one with the big RV. It has goofy eyes that bounce all over if you hit him with your dart. Professor Reginald had it in his living room."

"I see," he said. Then he waited some more before he said, "And maybe somebody broke into his house and took it?"

"I didn't break in!" I said. "He give me the key."

He nodded and kept thinking while he drove.

"So how is a dartboard a clue?" he said.

"It ain't."

"Maybe an extra clue?"

"I don't know," I said.

He waited some more. I ought to learn how to do that, I thought. I went back over our conversation. I'd tried my hardest to keep the dartboard a secret and all he done was waited for me to tell him. By now he'd figured out I had been inside the professor's house and swiped the dartboard. There wasn't much point in pretending some details.

"The board was on the floor. Either the cops or the perps threw it there, but it was easy to see where it was supposed to be. There was a nail to hang it from and a whole bunch of dart holes on the wall. I held it up and it fit perfect. But then I put it back on the floor."

"That sounds like correct procedure."

"That ain't the end of the story," I said. He didn't say nothing. The man was a ninja-expert at not talking.

"Remember that little girl Linda? I done art therapy on her when she was in the hospital."

"Of course I remember her. She thinks you make the sun come up every morning."

"Yeah, I do like to get up early. She's a Broncos fan and hates the Raiders and I thought she'd like that dartboard. The cops would of threw it out."

"I think I understand. Somehow, somebody—and we don't know who— gave little Linda the dartboard. But what's the clue?"

"The holes in the wall. There was a whole bunch of them. Darts went right through the cork front, through the cardboard back and made holes in the wall behind it."

"Well a lot of Broncos fans hated that Raiders coach. He beat us nearly every time we played. It's not a big mystery they'd throw hard."

"Yeah. So why wasn't there any holes in the cardboard back? Did the darts just go through it by magic?"

He nodded and thought for a minute. "Maybe we should go visit Linda," he said.

"OK."

We kept driving on the highway toward home and didn't talk much. Officer Mike watched his rear view mirror extra hard. I thought it might be a habit he got from being a cop. When we nearly got to the correct exit, he cleared his throat.

"Did you say something about a black pickup truck?"

"Yeah. It tried to run me over two times and the driver swiped Tonto so I had to jump out of a tree and rescue him. Why do you ask?"

"It's probably just another extra clue," he said. "There's been a black pickup behind us ever since we left the forensics lab."

I wanted to twist around and look, but I didn't.

"What if it ain't an extra clue?" I said.

"That's what I'm thinking. Why take a chance? Let's not go straight to Linda's house."

I nodded. One thing I always like about Officer Mike is he takes me serious. It would be hard to be friends with a guy who don't take you serious.

We didn't even slow down at the correct exit. About three exits later, he turned on his blinker and took that exit. Since I don't drive much, I wasn't sure where it went. He drove slow and careful.

"Interesting," he said. "For someone who's just an extra clue, he sure is persistent." We drove down a couple of streets with houses and lawns. "He stays two blocks back," Office Mike said. "Exactly two blocks." He stayed as calm as if he was sitting on his couch watching TV shows. After another minute or two, he said, "Let's stop in and visit with some of my friends."

"OK."

Two blocks later we pulled into a parking lot next to a two-story brick building. We sat there for a minute and I seen the black pickup truck drive past on the street.

"Look familiar?" Officer Mike said.

"I think so," I said. "Them black pickup trucks all look about the same."

He opened his door. "Come on in and say hello. Just in case we're still being watched."

"What building is this?"

"It's a precinct office. Parking lot's almost full, maybe it's someone's birthday. There could be twenty cops in there, if they've got snacks."

"A crook wouldn't want to go in there," I said.

"Not a smart one, anyway."

Inside the front door, a cop was sitting at a long counter. There was a gate on the end of the counter. Nobody could get farther inside unless the cop unlocked the gate.

"Is that Joe French?" Officer Mike said to the cop. That guy's face lit up.

"Did Hell freeze over?" he said. "I didn't think I'd ever see you back here."

"I didn't come to work, so it doesn't count."

"Well then, how can I help you?"

"You remember my friend Jumper?"

He looked at me closer and then you could see he remembered me.

"Why, of course I do!" He reached out to shake my hand. "This is Denver's own Columbo. That is, if Columbo liked to jump out of trees."

I shook his hand. "That's about the nicest thing anybody ever told me."

"Jumper and I were driving around, minding our own business..." Officer Mike said.

Joe French smiled. "OK, for the sake of peace and harmony I'll stipulate to that lie."

Officer Mike smiled.

"Thank you. Anyway, we noticed we were being followed."

"Seriously?" Joe French wasn't smiling so much now. He was all business. Officer Mike kept telling him the story.

"Yeah. A black pickup truck. It might be the truck implicated in a dog-abuse crime. And maybe even a murder."

"Did you get the plates?"

"Nah, he stayed too far back. When I turned into the lot here he sped on past."

Joe French nodded and thought. "But he could be waiting until you leave again."

"That's what I'm thinking. I thought I saw Nick's Harley out back."

Joe French nodded, like he understood some secret message. "When you guys drive off, if a plainclothes officer happened to follow you for a little ways on his motorcycle, well, who knows what he might see?"

"It couldn't be official."

"I understand. They'd never outrun Nick on his bike in city traffic. Listen, there's a bunch of guys back in the break room. One of the newbies got promoted and they're eating pizza to celebrate. You go back there, have a slice, say hi to the fellas. I'll take care of it."

"Thanks, Joe. Want me to bring you some pizza?"

"I already had too much, but thanks."

All the cops in the break room knew Officer Mike. They all shook his hand or slapped him on the back and joked on him for being old and retired. One guy give him a slice of pizza and said, "It's a lot easier to take my afternoon nap when Officer Mike ain't around."

"You never had much trouble napping when I was on the job either," Officer Mike said. Everybody laughed. Somebody handed me a slice of pizza on a sheet of paper towel.

"Thanks," I said. They was all real friendly except they didn't talk much to me. They wasn't being rude. It was like I was part of their gang and we didn't need to talk about it.

After about twenty minutes we was done eating our pizza.

"Great to see you guys," Officer Mike said. "But I've got to get Jumper here home in time to do all his homework."

"I'm pretty sure the dog's gonna eat my homework."

"Now, Jumper, remember what I said about that." His voice was stern while he was pretending I was a kid and he was my dad. "Remember?"

"You said don't let the dog eat your homework."

"That's right. You guys take it easy. Or however you can take it."

They all made wisecracks and we went back outside to his car.

"I don't see a guy on a motorcycle," I said.

"That's the whole idea. He'll stay back and watch. When he's sure we're not being followed, he'll come back to the station."

We drove several blocks back toward the highway. At a stop sign, a crazy looking hippie on a huge motorcycle pulled up next to us. His hair was wild and curly, his beard went down to his chest. He had on sunglasses and a black helmet with Grateful Dead stickers all over it. His neck was tattooed like a map of some place that ain't been invented yet.

"License and Registration," he said when Mike rolled down the window.

"Is that Easy Rider, always ready to rescue fair damsels and old retired cops?"

The hippie smiled.

"So your friend's a retired cop?" He said to Officer Mike. "I guess that makes you the fair damsel."

"I wouldn't want to be an unfair damsel."

The hippie nodded.

"Nobody's following you," he said. "Your driving probably bored them to death." He stopped for a few seconds. "I'd like to stay and catch up, but I got to go babysit some serious drug dealers."

"No problem. Thanks for the escort. By the way," Officer Mike said. "I think Jumper is going to catch a murderer tonight."

"Is that so?"

"Yeah. Down at Halloween Bar."

"You're going to catch Paddy-O?"

"Jumper thinks it's someone else."

"Is it one of their 'crazy dance' nights?"

"You bet. If you happen to show up, I'll make sure one of their channels is devoted to Led Zeppelin and the Grateful Dead."

Nick smiled real big and zoomed away and then we drove off.

"Sometimes you can't tell about somebody by the way they look," I said.

"You mean you're not the Pope?"

"Nah. But I can see how my disguise might of fooled you."

"I think it was your purity and virtue. Maybe we should visit Linda on a different day."

"I think that's a good idea."

"Next time, we'll have a plan."

"Cool," I said. "My plans is mostly foolproof."

Chapter Twenty-one

The Halloween Bar on "Crazy Dance Night"ain't like anything I seen before. When you first go in, there's a guy taking money and a lady handing out earphones. The guy didn't make me pay any money since Mr. O and Officer Mike told him I got in free. The earphones was interesting. They didn't go right in your ear, but on your cheek about a half inch in front of your ear. They also give me a little box, about the size of a pack of cigarettes or bar of soap. The box was connected to the bar's computer system by radio or magic or something and also connected to your earphones. There was a screen on the box where you could set what kind of music you wanted to dance to.

"Don't it get confusing?" I asked the woman. She smiled.

"Everybody can only hear the channel they're tuned to," she said. "So the room itself is quiet enough you could whisper to someone and they'd hear you. Makes it a lot easier to take drink orders."

"I don't get it," I said.

"All the channels are set to the same beat, the same speed. Everybody could clap their hands in time with each other. But one person might be hearing music from the 1940s and someone else from the 2020s. Everybody feels like they're dancing with everybody else."

"That's pretty cool," I said.

"Yeah, and the neighbors never complain. There's twenty channels all with different music. Mike set up a channel just for you with some songs he knew you like. It's the very last channel. He also told me to give this to you. She handed me a black pen that looked expensive.

"I ain't planning to write much," I said.

She smiled. "It's not really a pen. It's a voice recorder. He said you might want to record a conversation."

"It looks like a pen."

"That's what James Bond told me. Just put it in your shirt pocket. Don't need to turn it on or anything. It's recording right now. Mr. O'Malley sometimes records his business meetings. You know, for tax purposes."

"Wow!" I said. "Testing, testing, one, two, three."

"I think it's heard that one before."

The place was almost full and lots of people wore costumes. There was some witches in black pointy hats, and people dressed like tigers, and three guys dressed like Denver Broncos with women dressed like cheerleaders. Two young women, maybe 22 years old, was dressed in glittery outfits with short skirts. The guy who took money seen me watching them.

"Go-go girls," he said. "They'll tune to music from the 1970s, like you might hear on that old show Laugh In." He pointed to a wrinkled couple about 100 years old. The man was dressed in a suit and tie and she was wearing an ordinary black dress. "They'll be hearing the Mills Brothers and Glen Miller. But they'll be dancing next to that guy..." he pointed. "Who always plays Grand Funk Railroad. Younger people will be listening to groups I never heard of."

On the other side of the room was a guy in a cowboy hat. He had a short beard on his chin, like the guy I seen with Mrs. Isaac Goldfarb, but then the crowd got in the way and I couldn't see him.

When it was almost time for the music to start, some people come in from back by Paddy-O's office. This group was all dressed better than anybody else. I swallowed hard when I seen who they was, since it surprised me.

First was Paddy-O, dressed in a silky black suit. He ain't a skinny man, but the suit fit him so he almost looked skinny. Next to him was the waitress

I met the first time I come in here. Only now she had on a long black wig and a bright blue dress that looked like it was painted on her. The side of the dress had a slit from her ankle to where her pockets would of been if her dress had pockets. She wore real high heels.

Then come Officer Mike. He was wearing a fancy white tuxedo, and a black bow tie with a pink rose in the button hole of the jacket. He looked like a guy in one of them old black and white movies that has Humphrey Bogart in it where they dance in rooms with big fancy lights hanging from the ceiling.

The woman holding his elbow was what some guys call "drop dead gorgeous." She had on a long pink dress with puffy arms and was about the prettiest person I ever seen. It took me a minute to figure out why I knew her. It was Holly, the nurse who lives in my building. I ain't ever seen her in fancy clothes with nice makeup and lipstick. Her hair was pulled up on top of her head like a Christmas ornament. I could feel my face getting hot from looking at her.

They all walked right past me. When Holly walked by she looked over at me, smiled, and give a wink. Part of the plan was they'd all pretend not to know me, but she could of give anyone a wink without knowing them so that was OK. I was glad I was the one she winked at.

I turned on the little box that ran my headphones. There was twenty numbers on the screen. I touched number one and heard some old music with violins. I looked at all the dancers to guess which ones was listening to that song. I picked a couple that was slow dancing in the corner and looked like they just got married since they held on so tight. I pushed number two and heard a song about singing in the rain. There was an old couple, probably fifty years old that looked like that one fit them. Number three was "Ooh-ooh-ooh-ooh Staying Alive" which was in an old movie. I couldn't guess if anyone was listening to that song since the beat would of fit any of them. The next one was about having friends in low places. The cowboy and his girlfriend was doing a line dance that fit that one about perfect. One couple who looked as old as the pyramids was doing a real slow jitterbug, with the man sometimes twirling her around in slow motion. I guessed they was hearing Chattanooga Choo Choo or some other song from the Dark Ages which was on channel ten. All the songs sounded good, but I turned it off before I got through all the channels. Sometimes I get distracted, which music can do to anybody, so it was smarter to not have any music in my ears while I detected. But the dancers was interesting, so I watched them for a while.

The two go-go dancers faced each other and did the exact same moves, like they was seeing theirselves in a mirror. They moved like their bodies was Jello and they made sure the sparkles on their dress sparkled every place it could. An old hippie couple poked out their elbows at the air. They jerked and swayed like they was fish with hooks in their mouths. The man was Nick, the motorcycle cop.

Without any music, all them people in Halloween costumes dancing around looked like some old painting in a museum that come to life and didn't know what it was supposed to do. They was like bright-colored moths flying over a magical lake in a fairy tale, or like an old TV show with the sound turned off. It reminded me of one of the poem words I ain't got to use yet: "everyone was a bird and the song was wordless."

I liked the idea that everyone was a bird. But there was two star bird-couples.

Paddy-O'Malley looked like a crow in his shiny black suit, tango dancing with his partner like they was on a TV contest show. They both held one arm straight out pointing to one side and then danced over that way. They moved with quick, neat steps, like crows might move. Then they turned around just as quick and went the other direction, like crows who suddenly smelled some dead squirrel on a highway and wanted to go peck at it for lunch. They changed direction at the same time, like a traffic cop was giving them orders, and moved like they wasn't two people but one person with two backs, one shiny black and one painted-on blue.

Officer Mike and Holly was a swan dancing with an angel. They wasn't dancing so much as gliding like ice skaters over the floor. He was cool as

246

Captain James Kirk. For a guy with gray hair and a big belly he looked like he was floating across the floor on a magic carpet and telling Holly how to move with brain waves. They both smiled all the time and he kept looking right in her eyes. OK, that didn't seem too professional to me, but she ain't my girlfriend so it ain't my business. From the way she was smiling back, she thought it was fun and I could see why women liked to dance with him.

I ain't ever heard of ballroom dancing before, but I thought, hey, maybe I should learn to do that. I bet it ain't as hard as jumping off a garage roof.

The people was all moving sort of in time with each other, even if their dances was different. Without hearing the music, it was weird to watch. I could of stood there all night watching. But detectives got to remember to do their detecting first thing, like eating your vegetables before you get an ice cream sandwich.

I walked back to the corner where Paddy-O's office was and went through the door that said "Employees Only! Do Not Enter!" The room that had lockers wasn't locked, so I went in. I turned on the light and walked over to the board on the wall where the name tags was hung. I took the one that said Esmeralda. There was a wood cabinet on the floor below the name tag board. I pulled it away from the wall about an inch and dropped the Esmeralda name tag behind it. Then I pushed it back close to the wall.

Against one wall was a little couch about big enough for two people and a big mirror on the wall next to it. A light on a metal pole stood next to the couch, which lit up the couch and anyone trying to see themself in the mirror. I unscrewed the light bulb so the couch was a lot darker. Then I went over to the main light switch for the room.

"If anybody's listening on my fancy pen, I'm going to turn off the light and go wait on the couch. Over and out."

The room was about midnight dark when I turned off the light but I didn't have much trouble getting back to the couch. After I sat on it, I thought it would of been smarter to leave the pole light screwed in until I got back to the couch so I could see my way better, but you can't think of everything.

"OK, I'm on the couch now. Over and out."

Mortimer curled up on my lap, so I petted him a few times. Sitting there in the dark, in a nice warm room, on a soft couch, with my imaginary cat purring on my lap, it would be easy for a guy to fall asleep. And a couple of times I noticed I was thinking about stuff that would be good dreams, but I put my foot down on that idea. In all the old Columbo shows I never seen him fall asleep even once. It just ain't professional.

Still, when the light come on, it seemed extra sudden and I sat up straight. For a minute I didn't remember where I was but I didn't make any sounds.

A guy walked into the room and made a bee-line to the name tag board. He didn't look around even once. Since the room was dark when he opened the door, he figured it was empty so he didn't have a reason to look around. He pulled the little cabinet away from the wall and felt around behind it.

He was wearing a big cowboy hat and tight jeans and cowboy boots. I knew who it was the minute I seen him, partly since I was expecting him. It was the guy who always hung around Mr. Isaac's widow. He pulled the name tag out and put it in his pocket.

I stood up.

"Did you lose something?" I asked.

He about jumped out of his cowboy boots.

"I didn't see you..." he said. "What are you doing here? Who are you?"

"We already met. My name's Jumper."

"You startled me. I'm leaving."

He moved toward the door but I got in his way.

"I got a couple of questions," I said. "Like, why do you hate dogs?"

"I don't hate dogs."

"Trying to run them over with your pickup truck ain't a good way to show love."

"Do you have proof I tried to kill a dog?"

"Nah. Nothing that a judge would agree to."

"Then I didn't do it. Now I'm leaving."

He tried to move to the door again, but I got in his way again.

"Was it your idea to poison the professor? Or was that Mrs. Isaac Goldfarb's idea? She kind of seems like the smart one."

"Poison? I don't know anything about poison."

"Now, that ain't the whole truth and nothing but the truth. You and Mrs. Isaac Goldfarb poisoned her husband so she could get his company and be rich. Then her and you could live happily ever after. But I ain't sure why you want to kill his dog."

"I didn't poison anyone. When the professor fell down on the sidewalk, his dog started barking. She told me to take it somewhere."

"Mrs. Isaac Goldfarb told you to take the dog?"

"Just to protect it."

"I can see that. But then you saw Future Dog and got worried."

"Yeah. If that chip in his shoulder could connect me and the dog the cops might think I had something to do with the murder."

249

"Only you found out the chip inside him wasn't dangerous to you. Just the chip in his collar."

"The show had some bad information in it."

"So you threw the collar into the weeds behind Halloween's Bar."

"You can't prove I did that."

"You figured they might find it by the GPS chip in it and then everybody'd think Paddy-O done the poison."

"It makes sense. Only you found it before the cops did. Doesn't matter. That collar's nothing but ashes and dust now."

"I gotta admit, it was a good plan," I said. "Only there was a hidden flaw."

"What's that?"

"I'll tell you in a second. But first answer me this: why did Mrs. Isaac Goldfarb want to kill the professor?"

"I never said she wanted to kill anyone. But if she wanted to kill somebody, it would have been her cheating husband."

"Why?"

"His little company was about to go public which would make him very rich. But he was working on divorce papers. We found them in his office at the Institute. His wife would be left broke and that little assistant of his would be rich."

"Then why poison the professor at all?"

"If I was to guess about this little fantasy you're creating, I'd say to make him look like a suspect. He got a smaller dose so he was sure to survive. Especially with papers about hemlock in his pocket. The medics knew exactly what to do. The cops would say he gave himself a smaller dose so he wouldn't kill himself but he wanted to look like a victim."

"I ain't sure the newspapers said anything about hemlock, so that was a lucky guess you made. I can see how Mrs. Isaac Goldfarb wanted the cops to have lots of suspects to choose from. The professor, the waitress Esmeralda, and Paddy-O. And now you."

"Me? I'm not a suspect!"

"Maybe not yet. I might of said that wrong. You're like the third-string back-up suspect."

"You're crazy!"

"That's a whole different subject. But you know stuff a sidekick would know, like about what the professor had in his pocket and that he got a smaller dose. Plus there's Future Dog. Did she like that movie?"

"She thought it was the worst movie she ever saw."

"And you think she's gonna marry a guy who loved it? That don't sound much like any woman I ever met. Especially if she was gonna be rich and the guy don't have much money. Nah, that ain't the guy she marries. That's the guy she makes her third string backup suspect."

"You're stupid and I'm leaving."

"Don't you want to hear my evidence?"

"You don't have any evidence."

"She didn't tell you the truth and nothing but the truth on the dog collar."

He stopped moving toward the door but didn't say nothing.

"That GPS chip in the collar don't just say where it is right now. It keeps track of everywhere it goes."

He smiled. "Well, it's a shame that collar got accidentally destroyed then."

"Yeah, that's a shame. It was a nice one. But all that GPS stuff didn't get destroyed. It got sent back to the company headquarters where they made the collar. If you call them up and tell them the serial number they'll make a whole map for you."

"Did you write down the serial number?"

"Nah. That would of been smart though."

He smiled. "So there's no evidence at all."

"I didn't say that. I just said I should have wrote it down. But I didn't need to."

"You're saying you memorized the serial number?"

"Nah. Memorizing is hard. It's what they make you do in school when you want to put your head down on your desk and take a nap."

"That's what I thought."

"I ain't that good at memorizing. So I made up a story and remembered it. It's easy to remember a story."

"What story?"

"Darth Spock."

"Darth Spock?"

"Yeah. See how easy that was to remember? It's mostly just Spock only he's wearing a long black cape."

"And that's a serial number?"

"No, the serial number is the numbers 05041701"

"How do you get that from Darth Spock?"

"Well, Darth Vader wore a black cape and he was in Star Wars. 05/04 is Star Wars day. You know, May the fourth. Like in May the fourth be with you. And 1701 is the number painted on the Enterprise which I seen a thousand times. I couldn't believe what a easy number they gave that dog collar. Somebody at the collar factory was making a joke on everybody else. Darth Spock is an easy story to remember."

He looked mad and confused at the same time.

"So now let's get back to the truth and nothing but the truth," I said. "Let's pretend I called the dog collar company. If I done that on a hypothetical phone, what do you think they told me?"

He frowned. "She told me to take the dog to my house. After a couple of days I was supposed to throw the collar into the weeds behind Halloween's."

"Mrs. Isaacs told you to take the dog to your own house? That's kind of interesting ain't it?"

"Not really. She wanted me to keep the dog safe."

"For a third-string suspect you should start warming up your throwing arm. You might get some playing time after all. If she knew how that GPS thing worked, why would she want you to take it to your own house? And then make sure the collar got found near the scene of the crime?"

"She loves me, I tell you!"

"Yeah, love can make a person do weird stuff. I think it just made you confess to accessorizing a murder. We're gonna have to promote you to alleged suspect after the fact, plus at the same time as the fact."

"It doesn't matter. Nobody will believe you. You're an illiterate hick and I'm a well-respected and soon-to-be very wealthy businessman. Our attorneys will eat you alive."

"Oh yeah?" I said. "What if I recorded everything you said?" Then I made a little mistake. I tapped my shirt pocket where the pen was, but only for a second and he probably didn't notice.

Kind of suddenly, he looked over my shoulder at the door and threw both his hands up in the air.

"Don't shoot, officer!" he said, real excited. "I'll come peacefully!"

OK, I should not of fallen for that. I seen The Lone Ranger use that trick on bank robbers about six times. But you gotta admit, if The Lone Ranger used a trick, it was probably a good one. I turned to see which cop was coming in the door. Nobody was there.

But right when I turned, the cowboy punched me in the jaw and grabbed the recorder pen out of my hand. That surprised the heck out of me and I wasn't on my best balance. I stumbled backward and fell flat on my back. I tried to catch myself but it was too late. The back of my head bonked real hard on a wood bench and then everything went blank.

I ain't sure how long I was sleeping, but I had a nice dream. My mom was there taking care of me. She felt my forehead and tucked a blanket around me. The best part is she was singing soft, like you'd sing to a baby. She sang "It's a marvelous night for a moon dance..." It sounded so nice that even in my dream I closed my eyes. A cat yowled at me like I'd missed its dinner time, but Mom kept singing. The cat yowled some more and I realized it wasn't my mom singing, it was Van Morrison singing it the way he sung it on the radio.

"What are you doing here?" I asked him but he kept singing and the cat kept yowling. Even after I opened my eyes and seen I was on the floor of the locker room at Halloween's Bar he kept singing. I sat up and the back of my head hurt like heck. In a minute I figured out I was listening to the headphones. Officer Mike knew I liked that song so he put it on my channel. I must of turned it on when I fell. I touched the screen and Van Morrison stopped singing.

So the dream wasn't as real as I wished, but it was still a cool dream.

My head hurt extra hard when I stood up, but I wasn't wobbly or confused. I knew I had to catch that cowboy and get back the recording pen whether he wanted me to or not. And he had a head start.

I went down the hall to the main room of the bar. More people had showed up and the whole room was full of people crazy-dancing. Since you couldn't hear any music, it was like they all really was crazy. One time at school I got to look through a microscope at some pond water; this was like that. A bunch of weird bugs and worms waving their arms and tails at each other without no plan. Maybe them bugs in the pond water was dancing to bug music I couldn't hear either. You can't tell what music somebody else hears in their own brain.

The cowboy's hat stuck up from the crowd a little so it was easy to spot him. He and the cowgirl was line dancing toward a door that said Emergency Exit Only. There was so many people between us, my best chance at catching them was to blend into the crowd. Which meant I had to pretend I was hearing music too and dance through everybody.

OK, so I ain't practiced dancing much. When I was little, my mom tried to teach me waltz dancing in our living room. What I remember most is you had to count one-two-three over and over. It would of been dumb except she counted right along with me so it was a game. I started to dance through the crowd.

If someone was watching me they might think I was clumsy as a rhinoceros. Or else they might of thought I was hearing music in my head they ain't never heard. Like music from darkest African jungles, or maybe Tulsa. Or maybe they'd of thought I wasn't hearing nothing even if I was dancing like a drunk monkey. Maybe I was extra happy or had termites inside my jeans chewing on my leg. What people think about me ain't my business, so I don't waste much time wondering about it.

255

But nobody was looking at anybody else. They was all just dancing and wondering what everybody else thought about their dance. They could of been dancing in front of a mirror.

When the cowboy got close to the emergency exit, I seen one of Paddy-O's accountants standing in front of it with his arms crossed on his chest. The cowboy seen him too and changed direction. Now he and the cowgirl headed toward the main front door.

They got lucky that six people decided to stop dancing at the same time and go to the bar. For about three seconds there was a clear path before the crowd filled it in and the cowboys and his girlfriend quick line-danced through it. But by the time I danced over there, there wasn't an open space and I couldn't get through. I seen the cowboy hat over the tops of people. He was almost to the front door. I looked around for Officer Mike but I couldn't see him. I maybe could have yelled out his name, since I wasn't hearing music but that idea never come into my brain. The Halloween seemed like a place that don't have sounds except in headphones so you think sounds didn't work there.

There wasn't much chance I could catch the cowboy by going through the crowd. I looked over at the long bar which went almost all the way to the main door. The barstools was all full, but I seen something on the bar between customers that made me rub my eyes and look again.

Mortimer was sitting right on the bar, between drink glasses. He was licking his paw and then rubbing the back of his ear, which is how cats clean themselves. Nobody paid any attention to him and he ignored them back. Seeing him gave me an idea.

There was only a few people between me and the bar. I started to dance a little crazier than most of the customers, jumping up and down and waving my arms out wide. I kept counting one-two-three, so it was sort of like dancing. Even crazy-dancing people get nervous when they think somebody else really is crazy. Which obviously I ain't, but they didn't know. I moved toward the bar and the people in front of me backed away. Even the worst

Broncos running back we ever had could of walked through the opening they made and got a first down.

I had the plan that I'd get up on that bar and run on top of it toward the door. Even being careful not to kick over anybody's beer, I'd get to the front door about as quick as the cowboy. It might seem like a dumb plan to you if you never jumped up on a bar and ran from one end to the other. Any plan seems dumb if you ain't ever done it before. But in room full of people crazy-dancing while a cowboy makes his getaway, it's the only plan that come into my brain. I didn't see no hidden flaws.

In about three seconds I seen one flaw. There was people sitting on every stool and they was so close together I couldn't get next to the bar. There wasn't much time to politely explain that I wanted to jump up on the bar and could they please let me use their stool for about two seconds. Luckily, I'm a fast thinker. I aimed at one Godzilla-size guy sitting on a stool wearing a T-shirt that showed off his muscles. The back of the T-shirt said, "They Stole the Election." I don't care what you thought about the election either way. But most of the guys who wear that T-shirt ain't all that friendly to guys like me, and they're like big firecrackers with little bitty fuses. It's easy to make them jump up and do something.

I tapped on his shoulder. When he turned to look at me I waved my arms in the air and jumped up and down. He stared at me for a second then he turned back to his beer.

I tapped on his shoulder harder this time. When he turned to look, you could see he wasn't that happy with me. He said, "Get lost, loser!" then turned back to his beer saying some cuss words I ain't never heard before.

That give me a thought. I could hear him yelling at me just fine, since there wasn't no loud music in the room.

I tapped his shoulder again. This time when he turned around I said, "Your T-shirt ain't right. It was a fair election and your guy lost."

OK, that did it.

He come down off that bar stool like it had electric wires and it just shocked him through his jeans. He was red in the face and cussing his hardest. He made a fist and aimed it at me. Only he figured I was crazy and just as drunk as him so he didn't have no Plan B. When he started his punch I bent my knees and ducked down. Now I was crouched down like a monkey about to jump to a branch with bananas. His punch missed my head by a mile. Making the punch miss was just the first part of my plan. I was already crouched in a good jump position. Before the guy seen what I was doing, I done a standing jump right onto his bar stool. Then I done a little hop from there onto the top of the bar. I was careful not to knock into his beer glass, which was almost full. Spilling his beer would of been mean.

The guy had good reflexes, I gotta give him that. Before I could take one step on the bar he was already reaching for my ankles. That was smart of him, but he wasn't fast enough. I done a little hop to one side and he missed me clean. He tried again, only by then I was running on the bar. His hand slapped into his own beer glass. I didn't look back, but from the way he was cussing most of that beer landed right in his lap, and probably his election T-shirt too. I was sorry I hadn't took down his name, since I could of come back the next day and give him Mr. Silver as a free present. They would of made a good team, but that ain't the way life works sometimes.

I run down the top of the bar toward the door. I went as fast as I could without landing on people's hands or knocking into their drinks. People looked up with surprised faces as I went past them but nobody got mad. They thought it was funny.

The cowboy was getting to the front door when I got to the end of the bar. There was four couples between us. The cowboy would be out the door and maybe into a getaway car before I could get through all them people. Without people in the way, I could of jumped the guy easy right from the bar, but I didn't want to hurt anybody.

"Get down!" I shouted. "Get down!" I crouched ready to jump as if I was in a swimming pool pushing off one wall. Everybody ducked down except for two ladies who was talking to each other. They looked over at me and then went back to talking. The cowboy looked over at me and grinned, since he was taking one step through the door.

But before he could take his next step, a black cat climbed up his jeans and up his shirt and grabbed its claws into his chest. It yowled as loud as I ever heard a cat yowl, right at the guy's face. The man's eyes got big and he took a step back into the room and tried to push the cat off him. Now the guy was in the perfect spot for me to tackle him if them ladies wasn't standing in the way but they kept ignoring me. The alleged suspect would be out the door in about two seconds so I had to think quick.

"There's a spider on the ceiling!" I shouted. The ladies' eyes got wide and they ducked down low while they looked up at the ceiling without even thinking.

And then I jumped.

When you're in the middle of a jump, it feels like you're in a old black and white TV show where sometimes they do stuff in slow motion. About eight ideas go through your brain in the time it usually takes one idea. Colors is brighter and sounds is cooler. You think if a fly buzzed past you could reach out and pick him out of the air like he was floating on a string. That cowboy turned and looked up at me when I said the spider line. As I was shooting through the air like Superman, his eyes got big and he tried to turn away. But he was in slow motion and I was Superman so he didn't have much chance. When I was in the air about halfway to him, I changed from Superman mode into that new rookie linebacker on the Denver Broncos football team. He likes to jump at a running back as if he was flying and grab him around both legs right at the knees. If a linebacker's got your legs wrapped up like that you got to figure you're about to get tackled hard and you're going to spend some time in an ice-water bathtub.

The cowboy had the same idea about getting tackled and his eyes got even bigger. He tried to push the cowgirl away from him so he had more room to make his getaway but he moved about as fast as a feather falling out of a tree and I was a speeding locomotive. Mortimer jumped off him as easy as jumping off a chair.

I crashed into him and grabbed both his legs. I could feel his kneecaps through his jeans. As we fell on the floor I heard the football announcer in my brain saying, "Jumper makes another textbook tackle!" And the guy in the announcer booth with him said, "Yeah, that one's gonna leave a mark." The cowboy went down hard and he was too surprised to do much. He landed on top of the cowgirl so she started screaming about as loud as a Raiders coach when the refs call a penalty. The cowboy was still holding the recorder pen but he was distracted so I took it away from him with one hand while I kept hold of his legs with the other. Since I was on top of both him and the woman they couldn't get up. He tried to punch me in the back, which anyone would, but he didn't have a good angle to do much damage.

And then Officer Mike was standing over us in his white tuxedo.

"Children, please!" he said. "Behave yourselves!" He looked at me and smiled. "Anything interesting on that recorder?" he asked, as calm as could be. I handed it to him.

"Yes sir," I said. "Book 'em Danno."

I always wanted to say that. It's a line from an old show called Hawaii Five O which you're too young to have seen. Unless they remake it, but the actors would be old by now so that ain't likely. Trust me, it was funny when I said it. Officer Mike smiled since he's even older than me.

"And who is this with him?"

"That's the lady he was dancing with," I said. "She was just in the wrong place when it was his time."

Officer Mike reached down and grabbed her hair and all of it came out in one bunch.

"Mrs. Goldfarb, I believe," he said. "And wearing a whole new wig."

"I want my lawyer!" she yelled.

260

Mr. O'Malley came up to us. "Do you need any help?" he said. His two big accountants was standing right behind him.

"I can always use a little help," Officer Mike said. "I've got several cops outside waiting for these two but I still have a little business in here. You suppose your friends," he nodded toward the big accountants "could hold these two for a minute?"

Mr. O waved his hand and the two big guys came around us. One grabbed the cowboy's elbows from behind and the other grabbed Mrs. Isaacs. They was a little rougher than they needed to be and looked like they was having a good time using their muscles on smaller people.

"I think Jumper here just proved you innocent of murder," Officer Mike said. "I gotta take these two down to the station and help them get booked. Do you suppose you could arrange to bring Jumper and our friend Holly home?"

Mr. O shrugged. "Only if they'll ride in a Lincoln Continental."

"It don't have Raiders bumper stickers does it?" I said.

Mr. O shook his head and smiled. "Nothing but Broncos stickers around here," he said. "It's a rule."

"Well, I guess it's OK then."

Officer Mike turned to me. "I think Holly was really enjoying dancing," he said. "How about if you take the last dance with her?"

"I ain't much of a dancer," I said. But Holly had come up next to me and she grabbed my hand.

"Come on," she said. "You'll do fine." She pulled me along until we was right in the middle of all the quiet people crazy dancing to whatever music was in their own headphones.

"Let me see your control box," she said and held out her hand. I gave it to her mostly because she asked. I would of give her a kidney if that's what she wanted.

"OK," she said, looking at the little box. "I think let's do a waltz, OK? That means three-four time instead of four-four." She pushed a button. "I'm on channel six," she said. "So I'll be hearing the Blue Danube Waltz. She touched the number six channel on my box and I started to hear violins in my ears. "But you can hear any station you want and it will play right along. Try it, it's fun."

I hit one of the other channels and an old guy was singing about a Tennessee waltz. Another channel had a piano and saxophone. I said one-two-three, one-two-three and I could count right along no matter what channel was playing.

"That's pretty cool," I said. I punched channel six again so Holly and me would be hearing the same song and violins started playing in my ears again. Holly took my right hand and set it on her waist, and then she held my left hand almost straight out to the side. "Ready?" she said. "One-two-three..."

I didn't remember much about waltz dancing except that you were mostly supposed to move your foot when you said one. I tried to move about the same way as Holly did, which is how I done it with Mom. A couple of times I guessed wrong and we bumped into each other but Holly laughed like that was part of the game.

It felt like I was in a dream, dancing with Holly. Or maybe in one of them old movies with the sound turned down on everybody else. I could see Holly in full color like we was in a big new movie theater and she was on the big screen but everybody else was just gray shadows moving around to music I couldn't hear.

Then I tried a experiment. Officer Mike said he gave me channel 20, so I touched number 20 on the screen. I could still count one-two-three without missing a beat. Only now I wasn't hearing violins. I was hearing a guy with a scratchy voice. He was singing "Daisy, Daisy give me your answer do."

All of a sudden the whole room had bright colors. The people crazy-dancing around me looked happier and I could smell Holly's perfume or maybe her shampoo which was sweet and spicy. She was smiling so big she could of sold cars on TV commercials.

When the song ended, she leaned toward me and whispered in my ear. "Push the button again," she said. "Let's dance one more time."

I could of been in the middle of a Walt Disney cartoon with bright colored butterflies and princesses, with little rabbits bouncing around and singing songs. Mortimer sat on my shoulder and purred.

It's about the happiest I ever been.

"The sleek and solitary wasp may wield a fearsome lance, yet nameless bees— who shake their humble weapons in secret communion— compose more magic nectar." — 17

Chapter Twenty-two

A couple of days later they turned professor Reginald loose from the jail. Officer Mike promised to pick him up at the jail but he picked up me and Holly first so we could ride along. The professor was interested to meet Tonto so we was going to stop at Linda's house on the way to the professor's house. Before we got to the jail I had some questions for Officer Mike.

"Who's gonna clean his house?" I asked. "It's really tore up."

"He's got a lot of friends at the University," Officer Mike said. "Several of them have spent the last few days over there. Once we determined it wasn't a crime scene, things moved fast."

"I hope him and Tonto get along," I said. "But he probably still misses his real dog. Dogs ain't like car parts where if you break one you can just plug a new one in. They're more like a friend. Maybe we should take Tonto someplace and see if he's got a chip implant. We could find his real owner. I just ain't figured out how to do it exactly. Plus, I'll be sad if Tonto has to move to Cleveland or something."

"You didn't actually call the collar company, did you? You didn't check the GPS?"

"Nah. I was sort of bluffing."

"Didn't you think there was a chance the dog you found was the professor's lost dog?"

"At first I did. That would of been cool. Only I asked the professor if his dog was named Tonto and he said no. A detective can't just change the evidence."

Officer Mike nodded his head. "That's true," he said. "At least the professor will get to meet a cute little girl. That should cheer him up."

"Maybe two little girls," I said. "If Fiona's still visiting. She can tell him all about growing garlic."

265

"And he can tell her everything about Hamlet and Macbeth."

Holly laughed. "That sounds like a good conversation," she said. We was both sitting in the back seat since the professor should sit in the front seat so he could talk to Officer Mike. If we thought hard about it, one of us could of sat in front until we picked up the professor but I was kind of glad we didn't think all that hard.

We stopped in front of the jail building. There was a skinny old guy standing on the sidewalk. He was holding a cane in one hand and leaning on it so hard it was like he was trying to push it into the ground.

"That's him!" I said in a loud voice. I jumped out of the car to go help him. "Professor Reginald!" I shouted. "We're over here!"

He squinted his eyes looking at me. "Orderly Number Ten?" he said.

"Yeah," I said. I grabbed his elbow. "Only I ain't in uniform today. I guess I'm a plain clothes orderly. Plus, I mostly retired from the orderly business."

"You've overcome your bedpan proclivities?"

I laughed. "Sometimes it's like you're talking Klingon."

He nodded. "Right," he said. "I'll eschew my lexicon in the interest of clarity."

"Good," I said. "If that means 'beam me up Scotty,' your shuttlecraft is right here." I opened the front door of Officer Mike's SUV. The professor stopped. He put his hand on my arm and looked right in my eyes. "Did you find the hidden... ?"

I knew what he talking about

"Yeah, I think so. It was about a perfect hiding place. It's safe, but I didn't look at it since it wasn't my business."

"Thanks," he said and he got into the SUV.

I introduced him to Holly and Officer Mike. They asked how he was feeling and he said fine, they asked about being in the jail hospital and he said the people was nice to him. We was all curious about the thing he'd hid away, and the murder, and if there was a secret treasure, but you gotta start conversations with easier stuff. Luckily, Holly was good at starting conversations on easy stuff.

"I work at the hospital," she said. "People said you had a secret treasure map."

The professor laughed a little, a quiet old-guy laugh.

"For a while I thought I did. Now it doesn't really matter."

Officer Mike nodded. "You know, we've got a little drive before we get to our first stop. We'd all like to know anything you'd like to share."

The professor nodded several times.

"OK," he said. He waited a little bit longer, like he had to get the whole story gathered together in his brain first. Then he nodded again and started talking.

"I was doing research at a small agrestic library in England, associated with a nearly dormant college in a bucolic setting. I'd been hired to ascertain if there was anything of historic import among the papers of a minor poet who has, thankfully, descended into oblivion. Anything worth digitizing, specifically. I'd done some undergraduate work on this fellow, so I got the call. The poet had only the most oblique and tangential relation to Elizabethan theater."

He shrugged. I was still wondering what his first sentence meant, so I hadn't caught up with the rest of his words.

"I had no illusion that I might find an original copy of *Love's Labor Won*, or *Cardinia*. But they paid for my airline ticket and a week's stay at a modest inn. I didn't complain. I got an invigorating respite from the mundane at only the cost of my meals and a few hours in a library. Which is no dear penance for those of my ilk."

I cleared my throat.

"Sorry," he said. "What I mean is, I didn't mind the gig."

"A bundle of papers was obviously misfiled, a condition more prevalent than one would hope. It was labeled 'Various for William Camden.' I thought it was a joke. Camden was a famous antiquarian in the early 16th century. I could not imagine anything with his name being shoved to the back of a file drawer. I carefully opened it. It was comprised of the most commonplace documents, completely banal. A very old letter fell out. I didn't read it carefully, assuming it but one more shopping list or advert for a mummer's elixir. What caught my attention was the signature. There was no name, only the number 17. And below that, a dark spot that could have easily been a spot of faded blood.

"I immediately thought of my friend Isaac. The letter itself surely had no value except for its antiquity, especially without a signature or provenance. But if Isaac's new technology could extract any interesting forensics from that 400 year old spot, that would be the kind of human interest story that propels stock issues to the front page of a business paper.

"So I purloined the letter."

"You cooked an old paper?"

"No. I stole it. It was only much later, after reading it more carefully, that I realized it was a cautiously worded plot to contrive a counterfeit murder. From four hundred years ago. Alas, Isaac was killed before I could give it to him. And now it doesn't really matter."

"Them limitation statues has probably all run away," I said.

"True. Plus I don't think any serious laws were broken."

Holly was leaning forward and listening hard.

"Whose murder?" she said. "Who sent the letter? Why did they want to fake a murder?"

"The prospective victim was Christopher Marlowe."

"The writer?" Officer Mike sounded surprised.

"Indeed. Some people conjecture he wrote the plays we now attribute to Shakespeare. Those people call themselves 'Marlovians.' Four of the bard's plays are more masterful revisions of Marlowe's plays. But Marlowe was murdered weeks before the first Shakespearean play was published."

"Well, if he was already dead, I bet he didn't write any of the episodes."

"Many scholars agree."

"So who was 17?" Holly said.

"Of course we can't know. And I confess the controversy never interested me, so I'm no expert. I've always believed specific authorship was less salient than the words themselves. But I think it was Edward de Vere, the 17th Earl of Oxford."

"Seventeen is a good nickname. Even better than Earl," I said. I'd already heard this story, but a good detective likes to get testimony from a bunch of witnesses, so I pretended it was brand new. Plus it would be mean to tell a guy you already heard something he wanted to tell even if it was a joke you heard a hundred times.

"I still don't get it," Holly said.

"Marlowe was a fine writer, younger than de Vere, a man who de Vere had mentored. But he made political blunders and was deeply in debt. Powerful people wanted him dead. If he continued to produce provocative scenes laced with controversial politics and sarcastic humor, it was only a matter of time before it caught up with him. The authorities found a note

269

they deemed heretical; his former roommate said it belonged to Marlowe. When the authorities issued a warrant for his arrest, Marlowe knew his time was up. His only real escape was to stop writing what he wanted to write and flee the country."

"That don't explain Mr. Seventeen."

"Many scholars are convinced de Vere was secretly the bard. They call themselves 'Oxfordians.' Writing plays was considered undignified, beneath an earl. Plus he, too, had enemies. Having a character on stage say the wrong thing could have been fatal for him as well."

Holly smiled and I could see she put some puzzle pieces together. "So, if everyone thought Marlowe was dead, and de Vere wrote under a phony name, they could keep writing whatever they wanted."

"Exactly. I believe they bought or stole a corpse that looked a bit like Marlowe. Some people think it was a fellow who had been hung the day before. They dressed the corpse in clothes identical to what Marlow had worn all day while drinking and playing cards. When the innkeeper was out of the room, they posed the dead imposter and started yelling, as if in an argument over the reckoning. That is, the bill. When the innkeeper returned he saw the bloody body in Marlowe's clothes and assumed it was Marlowe. He'd heard the argument so he wasn't surprised. The others in the room pretended it was Marlowe."

"Couldn't he tell by looking at the face?"

Professor Reginald smiled. "Probably, if he'd looked closely. But they had stabbed the corpse in the eye with a dagger. No one wanted to examine that face too closely."

"What was in it for de Vere?"

"A writing partner and a friend. He had a big house and was financially comfortable. I think Marlowe moved in with him and they collaborated. A magical synergy can spring from the creative intercourse between similarly gifted writer. Think of Lennon and McCartney. Their collaboration produced art elevated above any of their individual works. Even their solo compositions seemed enhanced by the association. Marlowe could let his hair grow longer, wear different kinds of clothing, and adopt a pseudonym. Perhaps he became Christopher Marlowe's long-lost cousin from Ireland in the event someone remarked on the resemblance. The letter also mentions "Verulamium" which was where Francis Bacon was born. Mark Twain was convinced that the "real" Shakespeare was Bacon. Bacon grew up in the same house as de Vere, they were friends. He was a lawyer, even more educated than the others, but also more ambitious. He obtained important positions in the government; being seen as a mere playwright would damage his career. He could easily have joined de Vere and Marlowe for long weekends of concentrated writing."

"Wasn't there already a guy named Shakespeare? Ain't I seen pictures of him?"

"Yes. He was a relatively uneducated actor who became the front-man. Ultimately, he managed the Globe Theater and made a tidy sum producing the plays. But he had no political role, no power. He wasn't threatening so the authorities ignored him. One contemporary called him an 'upstart crow.'"

"And the letter you found proves all this?"

"No, that would be too strong. The letter lays out the plot in a cautious, oblique way, maintaining plausible deniability. Simply speaking, I think de Vere helped fake Marlowe's death and Marlowe came to live with him. I think Bacon, as a powerful lawyer and politician, made the murder case disappear, then joined them to write plays. Each of them had different strengths and experiences. The unique light that shone from each of their minds was amplified and reflected by the others. If someone agrees with my theory, the letter would provide strong corroboration, but not proof. People set in their beliefs would remain unmoved. They would assert that I'm delusional. Which I might be."

"Them guys have been dead a lot of years. Nobody alive today knew them. It's sort of like they're imaginary friends. Why would somebody get mad about somebody else's imaginary friends?"

The professor nodded. Then he said, "More wars have been fought over imaginary friends than anything else. The first step toward world peace is realizing that my imaginary friend loves your imaginary friend."

"Maybe if you explained it real slow and used little words so they understood?"

"Baconians would scoff, Stratfordians would sneer in the snottiest of ways, Marlovians would simply laugh. Of course, if we could prove that de Vere wrote the letter..."

"The spot of blood!" Holly said.

"Exactly. De Vere has descendants. We could have compared DNA."

"Why didn't anybody say nothing at the time?" I said. "I bet the neighbors seen them guys sneaking in out of Seventeen's house."

"Their close friends probably understood the whole scheme. They wouldn't inform on their friends and coincidentally risk arrest as an accomplice. The perspicacious strategy back then was silence."

"As it is today," Officer Mike said.

"Yes," the professor said. "Illusions become beliefs and beliefs become reality. The truth may not be as important as the story. As Hamlet said, 'the play's the thing.' There was a purpose to my investigation when it could help Isaac. Now, the various factions take such delight in the conflict itself, I hate to spoil their glee with something as boring as facts and truth."

"Like being friends with a Raiders fan."

"Just like that. Such a thing might create a rift in reality."

"By the way, you're about to meet a couple of cute kids that is strong Broncos fans. Plus a Golden Retriever dog named Tonto who's really smart, so he probably likes the Broncos too."

We knocked on Linda's door and her mom opened it.

"This is Professor Reginald," I said. "He's the guy who lost his own Golden Retriever dog and I thought he might like to meet Tonto."

"Pleased to meet you," she said, and they shook hands.

"You already know Holly and Officer Mike," I said.

"Good to see you both," she said and shook their hands too. "Linda and Fiona are in the back yard. Why don't you spring chickens walk around there? I'll bring the professor through the house. I heard you were in the hospital and carpet might be easier to navigate than paving stones."

"Thank you," the professor said. He followed Linda's mom into the house.

"I ain't been called a spring chicken before," I said as we was walking.

Officer Mike smiled. "It's not a bad thing. She just means you're young."

When we opened the gate to the back yard, Linda and Fiona seen us right away. They was playing catch with Tonto. All of them came running. Even if I seen them all a week or two ago, I could of swore both them little girls had grown about a foot.

"Hey, Tonto," I said when he jumped up to say hello. "I ain't sure you met these other people. This big one is Officer Mike and the pretty one is Holly." They both petted his head.

Holly said, "And you must be Fiona." She reached out and shook hands. "And this is Mike."

"I would of remembered to introduce you guys in about a minute," I said and my face felt hot. I maybe should of done the human introductions first, but I ain't ever had so many introductions and handshakes to keep track of before so it was confusing.

"It's OK," Holly said. "We're all friends now."

Then Linda's mom led the professor out onto the back porch. He looked a little confused, which is how old guys look most of the time. He stood there looking out at the back yard. I waved at him and was about to tell him to come on over, when his eyes got big.

"Touchstone!" he said. He said it like it was a magic word, or maybe a prayer. Then he said it again, only louder.

Tonto looked up when he said that and give a little bark. Then he started waving his tail back and forth faster than I ever seen him before. He ran toward the professor about as excited as if the old guy was a squirrel.

"Careful, boy!" I shouted. "Don't knock him down!"

But there wasn't much chances of that. The professor had kneeled down on one knee and when Tonto got there the professor grabbed him with both arms. The dog was going too fast to stop, so they both rolled over onto the floor of the porch like they was wrestling. The professor was laughing, which I didn't think he knew how to do. The rest of us went over to watch.

"Boy, some people have a way with dogs!" I said.

Tonto was licking the professor's face like it was an ice cream cone that was melting and if you didn't lick it fast it was going to drip on clothes you was supposed to be careful with. After a minute, the professor pushed Tonto's face away.

"Touchstone! Desist!" he said. As quick as a Jedi mind trick, Tonto backed off and sat down wagging his tail and grinning. The professor sat up. He took a clean handkerchief out of his back pocket and dried off his face.

"What does desist mean?" I said.

Both Holly and Officer Mike said "stop" at the same time.

"Why?" I said. "I wasn't doing nothing."

"Desist means stop."

"How come a dog knows more words than me?"

"He probably paid attention in class," Officer Mike said.

The professor stood up and walked down the porch steps onto the grass. "Touchstone, accompany!"

Tonto followed along about two feet behind him. "Well done," the professor said. "Shall we test your retention?"

Tonto wagged his tail. "Would you care to elaborate?" the professor said. Tonto barked three times.

"Recline," the professor said and Tonto laid down like he was about to take a nap. The professor looked over at Linda.

"Did I hear that you had a frisbee?" he said. Linda got it and handed it to him.

"Touchstone, hold!" he said and he threw the frisbee. He threw it good for an old guy. It went sailing above the lawn almost level. The dog sat real still except for his tail wagging. You could see he wanted to go chase that frisbee.

"OK, now," the professor said. "Retrieve!"

That dog could not have started faster if a firecracker went off behind him. I didn't think he'd catch up with the frisbee in a million years but he ran his fastest and caught it in the air. When he come back, he dropped it right on the professor's shoes and sat down to wait for the next game.

"It's weird that Tonto knows the same words as your dog did," I said.

Holly looked at me like I said something dumb.

"Jumper, Tonto is the professor's dog. His name is Touchstone which sounds enough like Tonto he responded to it."

"That ain't a bad theory," I said. "I gotta admit, it explains some loose ends."

"I'm glad you found the professor," Linda said. "But I'm going to miss Tonto. I mean Touchstone."

The professor smiled. "I'm glad he made such good new friends. I hope you'll come and visit him often. Both of you." He looked at Fiona.

"Are you the horticulturalist?" he said.

"I like to grow garlic," she said.

"Ah, yes!" he said. "The allium family has played a significant role in history and literature. Of course, the literary filigree some refer to as garlic is close to my own heart. But the totemic aspect of garlic itself to ward off malevolence transcends folklore and literature..." He stopped and cleared his throat. "Plus, it tastes good," he said.

The rest of us stared at him, since there wasn't much else to say about garlic in literature. Or in spaghetti for that matter. I don't think Fiona understood a word of it either, but it didn't scare her off. She punched back.

"It's the allicin, allin, and ajoenes," Fiona said. "They're the thiosulfinates in garlic that give it the taste and make it healthy." We stared at her. "You know, thiamine," she said, but that didn't mean more to me than some Vulcan word. "Vitamin B1," she said. "You've heard of vitamins haven't you?" and the rest of us nodded. Even I've heard of vitamins. Nobody asked her much more questions. I ain't got a lot of stories about thiamine and maybe neither did the professor, or Officer Mike, or Holly. But the professor ain't a guy you can scare off easy with big words that don't mean nothing.

"Hamlet talked about garlic in a soliloquy," the professor said.

I ain't sure what a soliloquy is, but I bet I can't afford one.

He went on. "Hamlet said, 'I had rather live with cheese and garlic in a windmill far than feed on cates and have him talk to me in any summerhouse in Christendom'."

"What's cates?" I asked.

"Sorry," the professor said. 'Cates' are delicacies. A guy named Hotspur..." he stopped. "Hamlet thought the other guy was boring," he said. "So he's saying, 'I'd rather live all alone in an isolated place and eat simple food like cheese and garlic than be rich in a grand home and eat fancy food if that means I have to listen to the boring guy.'"

We looked at him for a minute but didn't say nothing. He looked back at us.

"I'm sure you can all sympathize with that," he said.

Officer Mike and Holly smiled.

"Cheese and garlic sounds good," I said.

The professor turned to Linda. "I understand you have a new dartboard?"

"No sir. Mr. Jumper said it was yours but I could babysit it for a while. Until you were all better. Would you like me to get it?"

"Yes, thank you. I hid a paper in its frame. It means something to me but it would be boring to you. And probably everyone else in the world. It's a letter from someone you don't know. If I can retrieve it... I mean, if I can get it, then you can keep the dartboard. Is that fair?"

"Yes, sir!" she said with a big grin and ran off to her bedroom.

When she come back, she handed the dartboard to the professor. He pulled a pocket knife out of his pocket. There were little staples around the frame in the back bent over to hold the cardboard on tight. One by one he used his knife to straighten them out. The little girls leaned in to watch him, like he was opening a Christmas present. When all the staples were straight, the cardboard fell off the back of the dartboard. Behind it was a big sturdy envelope like the government might use to mail out important stuff, like letters saying it was time to send them money. The professor held it about his head and talked to it.

"Alas, poor Yorick," he said.

"Ain't you going to open it?" I said.

"Not right now," he said. "I've read it a hundred times. It begins, 'Dearest Kit.'" He looked straight at me. "Yorick's skull was the truth, but it wasn't the whole truth. The whole truth was hidden in the story. Not in the name of a shadow behind a curtain whispering lines for an actor to shout at the audience. No, like Hamlet said, the play's the thing."

We was all quiet, since we never knew Mr. Yorick or Mr. Hamlet. We stood there looking at the grass like it was a big green TV. I didn't think any of us would ever say something again. After a while Linda said something that didn't have much to do with garlic, or dogs, or vitamins, or Hamlet.

"I like the rookie cornerback the Broncos drafted," she said.

Fiona looked up. "I do too! He's really fast. Did you see his combine workout?" They both sat down on the grass.

The professor nodded. "Yes, he'll be great in coverage. But if you watch his college highlights, he can also tackle." He leaned on his cane with both hands to help him sit down. Holly and Officer Mike and me all sat down too, so we was in a circle on the grass. Tonto laid his head down on the professor's lap, only his name might really be Touchstone, which I ain't sure is even a real name. Mortimer went over and sniffed the dog's nose. Tonto (or maybe Touchstone) didn't complain, he just wagged his tail. Then Mortimer come over and curled up in my lap for a nap.

"I like corners that can tackle," I said. "Maybe we can use him to blitz the quarterback."

Then Holly said, "That's all fine. But can he keep up with that wide receiver the Raiders drafted?"

Officer Mike nodded. "I think so. That kid is fast too, but he runs sloppy routes."

The professor shook his head. "We were having such a pleasant afternoon and you had to bring up the Raiders."

Everybody laughed at that.

Once we was all talking about football, it was like we suddenly recognized each other, like we was all old friends who ain't seen each other in a long time. Officer Mike and Holly argued about which of our receivers could run a slant route. Linda and Fiona was mostly interested in kickers, since field goals is like kicking a soccer ball, which they did every day.

Me and the professor talked about the coaches and which plans they had that was good and which ones was stupid. We both said that the play you call needs some luck since the other team has plans too. Calling the right play is tricky and sometimes you gotta change the one you called.

"If your fastest receiver is running a post pattern," he said. "And they're trying to cover him man to man, your quarterback's got to see he's got an easy touchdown. And he's got to see it fast."

"Yeah," I said "Even if the tight end is his primary on that play the coaches got to teach him about quick choices."

"And the coach has to call plays that take advantage of his strengths. Play calling is the most important thing. Communication, that's the key."

"Yeah," I said. "Like your buddy Mr. Hamlet said, the play's the thing."

THE END

POEM-WORD SOURCES

page 43 Polonius, Iago and Brutus are characters in Shakespearian plays

Page 49 "A Midsummer Night's Dream" is a play by Shakespeare. In it, one character's head is magically transformed into a donkey head. Puck is a trickster in the play

page 50 "spots"— a reference to Lady MacBeth's line "out, out damned spots." The bloody spots on her hands in a dream symbolize her guilt. "Signifying nothing" is also from MacBeth

Page 51 "Lord what fools..." from Midsummer Night's Dream. Puck says "Lord what fools these mortals be."

page 52 "Something in his origin story is an albatross in the ancient mariner sense." is a reference to a poem by Coleridge, "The Rime of the Ancient Mariner"

page 56 "Such a one is a natural philosopher. Wast ever in court, shepherd?" from "As You Like It" by Shakespeare, spoken by Touchstone

page 56 "one drop of wine is enough to redden a whole glass of water." from "The Hunchback of Notre Dame" by Victor Hugo

"One moment a maniac at another a queen." from "The Hunchback of Notre Dame" by Victor Hugo

"Just stoic silence, speechless... ruin stared straight back … …." from "Dream Song" by John Berryman

"eyes are nothing like the sun" Shakespeare sonnet #130

"One who does not weep does not see," from "Les Miserables" by Victor Hugo

"I reach in my pocket and find only reality."" from "The Hunchback of Notre Dame" by Victor Hugo

page 57 "They are fools. And a fool doth think himself wise but a wise man knows... No, I am here with thee and thy goats " Shakespeare, spoken by Touchstone

"May the saints be your friends, and bless you. May the monsters be your friends and watch over you" from "The Hunchback of Notre Dame" by Victor Hugo

page 77 "I reached for my pocket and found only reality." and "Drink, poured out of a cup into a..." Victor Hugo

"I bear the dungeon within me. Within me is winter, ice and despair..." from "The Hunchback of Notre Dame" by Victor Hugo

page 114-115 "The Ogre" by W.H. Auden

page 115 "how do you like your blue eyed boy" from "Buffalo Bill" by ee cummings

page 115 "not eve the rain has such small hands" from the poem "somewhere i have never traveled, gladly beyond" by ee cummings

page 119 "All the black same I dance my blue head off" from "King David Dances" by John Berryman

page 119 "Cloudy, cloudy is the stuff of stones," from "Epistemology" by Richard Wilbur

page 123 "Which in the world is upside down, the fish hook or the question mark?" from "Casting" by Howard Nemerov

page 124 "the feelings you say you have, you don't have." from "To Women as Far as I'm Concerned" by D.H. Lawrence

page 125 "Where peat hags gape too black." from "In Teesdale" by Andrew Young

page 126 "Where the toad lives on starlight," from "Water" by Ted Hughes

page 128 "A graceful error may correct the cave" from "Mind" by Richard Wilbur

page138 "More geese than swans now live, more fools than wise." from "The Swan Song" Anonymous

page139 "in the dust, in the cool tombs." from "Cool Tombs" by Carl Sandburg

page 141 "Made of nothing except loneliness" from "no time ago or else a life" by ee cummings

page 141 "small strategy" from "The Compassionate Fool" by Norman Cameron

page 142 "Like Daddy loves his dollar" from "American Primitive" by William Jay Smith

"The winter of love is a cellar of empty bins...in an orchard soft with rot" from "Never May the Fruit Be Plucked" by Edna St. Vincent Millay'

page 150 "permit you to get the mange," from "The Glass of Beer" by James Stephens

page 231 "In me she has drowned a young girl, and in me an old woman rises toward her day after day ...like a terrible fish." from "The Mirror" by Sylvia Plath

page 269 "Love's Labor Won" and "Cardinia." Two plays credited to Shakespeare that have been lost.